A Case of Peaches

*From the Case Files of
Adoption Worker, June Hunter*

Kathleen D Tresemer

DEDICATION

For my husband Dennis, who taught me to drive a team of horses, bale and stack hay, fix fence, and deliver a foal because "curly girls" can do anything!

ACKNOWLEDGEMENTS

From all the foster kids and families, I gained knowledge, inspiration, gratification, and appreciation for the many ways people make a family. Without you, this book would not be possible.

Many case managers, supervisors, investigators, adoption workers, licensing agents and others from IL DCFS and Rockford Catholic Charities taught me so much about working with kids and families. I could not have done it without their continued support and fabulous training. Eneree Sockwell, Virginia Steele, Greg Fliehler, Louise Cook, Anne Politic, Mary Anne Rotello, and Char Ramsey are just a few of my former colleagues and each contributed in some way to this novel.

Winnebago County Family Court judges (Hon. Janet R. Holmgren in particular) and attorneys (especially Gary Golian and "Little" Al Altamore) really do care about the plight of kids in the system; they work way too many hours for way too little pay. Likewise, the police detectives and officers who investigate abuse/neglect of minors are dedicated in their pursuit of safety for children; Detectives 'Trez' and Mary Denton-Ponds, I'm talking about you. All of these professionals demonstrated authentic concern, respect, consideration, and kindness to the children and their families.

I am fortunate to have the best writing companions in the world: Catherine Conroy, Debbie Winnekins Deutsch, and Mary Lamphere, thank you for always supporting me and remaining a champion of June and Flora. You three are my friends and sisters; I love you!

AUTHOR'S NOTE

Imagine someone you do not know shows up at your door unannounced, gives you a few minutes to gather some belongings, then without explanation, takes you away? You aren't sure why you have to leave. You aren't sure where they are taking you. And they don't tell you anything except, "it's for your protection."

Next, you're standing with strangers in their home with a bag of your personal belongings. You don't know these people; they don't know you. You have so many questions: How should you act? Can you call someone? What if you forgot something?

Maybe you're 'lucky' and are placed in a relative's home. Even then, it's abrupt and complicated. What if these relatives resent keeping you? What if they can't afford to? You know your presence is an inconvenience; you feel unwanted, untethered.

Then, in a couple of days, a different person tells you this was only temporary and moves you to yet another place. And then another. How do you feel? Are you scared? Can you focus at work? Can you sleep? Are you trying to figure out how to get back to the life you knew?

My Dear Readers, this would be a challenge for any adult. Lots of children, even very young children, are made to do this every day. Adults wonder why these kids act out, withdraw, get sick, underperform, become depressed or angry.

As a former Child Welfare professional, I did what June Hunter does: help kids in this situation. No, it ain't easy. But yes, I loved it.

PROLOGUE

"Happy endings aren't always all that happy," June Hunter mutters through clenched teeth.

The caseworker is beating herself up for this adoption. Her primary goal – Always keep kids together! – didn't work out this time. The adoptive father of the oldest kids, three boys, doesn't want the youngest, a little girl. After all, she does not carry his DNA.

The four children cluster together awkwardly, patting and hugging each other.

"Am I still your sister?" the little girl asks. She's clearly confused at the adoption of her brothers.

The girl's foster parents are great, supporting her through this whole mess, never giving up. But they are not in a position to adopt her.

While the adults celebrate and plan to get the children together some time soon, the older kids murmur platitudes:

We'll always be family.
We're still your brothers.
We'll never forget you.

Over the past two years, they had each asked June why they couldn't be together. Every time, the caseworker said basically the same thing, "I wish you could stay together too, but it doesn't always work out that way."

Feeling like a failure, June huddles in the corner.

"You did the best you could, June, under the circumstances. Stop beating yourself up."

Judge Conroy stands by her side and speaks with a big fake smile, hand on her shoulder as if she were congratulating the caseworker. She is more than familiar with the situation, the whys and wherefores of the case.

"Yeah," June answers through a plastic smile, "but this

1

time my 'best' fell way too short."

She'll send the little girl's file back to the Adoption Unit and the child will be assigned to another caseworker. June's case load consists of difficult-to-place kids (i.e., teens, sexual abuse victims, or sibling groups). This kid is young and cute and engaging. Another caseworker with an easier work load will find her a good home.

Leaving the Judge's Chambers, June walks the few blocks back to her office in a meditative state. In spite of the sunshine, the early springtime weather chills her even further. She pulls her requisite trench coat tight around her neck and shoulders.

No celebration today.

"On to the next case, saving another kid," she thinks, trying to bolster herself as she approaches her office building.

A quiet voice in her head answers morosely, "Sure. Maybe."

I. CASE HISTORY

1.

Flora gazes around her bedroom. *My own little island, where I can be myself and no one can see me.*

Safe.

Peaceful.

Private.

An amazing room, decorated like one of those TV re-do shows: pale peach and white, with luxurious fabrics and super-thick carpet. Flora thought it was too girly at first, like nothing she had ever seen before, but the place grew on her pretty fast. Like in ten minutes. For the first time in her life, she felt like a princess.

In the hallway, mounted next to the doorjamb, is a gold plaque engraved in fancy script, *Flora's Room - Private*. Step inside and close the door. It's like pressing a giant pillow over your head with everything soft, sweet-smelling, and muffled.

Now she's ruined everything. Her island is about to sink into the ocean.

2.

June Hunter drags herself up two flights of stairs to her office, breathless as she pushes through the door marked Department of Child Welfare.

"I'm getting too old for this," she says, pulling her silk shirt away from damp skin. "Twenty years ago, I could have double-timed up those stairs. But, in the 21st century, is it too much to ask for a working elevator?"

Government offices for low level employees are mostly the same: cheaply furnished, dingy, with a view of a vacant lot or dirty alley. June's department occupies two dusty floors in the former Illinois IRS building. Old, old building. Full of character. A history of neglect. Perfect for those social work types who say things like "can't judge a book by its cover" and "money isn't everything."

Even so, June feels lucky. Of the desks scattered across the third floor, she'd managed to secure a prized spot tucked in a corner next to an east-facing window with a low deep sill. This placement offers sunshine in the early hours and moonlight depending on the hours she spends on a given case. She loves the ancient carved wood desk, too heavy for the former tenants to haul away. The antique leather chair's silky seat still provides moderate back support, her reward for twenty years of sacrifice and saving the world. These simple things give her moments of great joy.

Lesser girls would have chosen a more lucrative profession, or perhaps a mate with a lucrative profession. However, June and her kind were heavily influenced by the social revolution begun in the 60's and continued until the start of the new millennium. All they needed was love, they thought.

None of June's crowd worried about a future with job shortages, racial or gender inequality, and economic instability. They knew love had the power to change all that, love and action.

After all, they thought, changing the world is each of our responsibilities. No excuses. June found herself following that dream of saving the world by dedicating her life after college to social service.

3.

Flora sits frozen at her desk, book open, pen in hand, homework forgotten. Trapped.

Who knew the ring of a doorbell and presence of two strangers could change everything so fast? Muffled voices of a man and a woman start out polite, friendly really, but become very tense, very fast.

"How dare you even suggest such a thing?" Her foster mother screeches, out of control. "My Brendan is an honor student and an athlete, one of the most popular boys in school! He would never touch that piece of trash."

The woman's fury, her hysteria, is terrifying. It snakes through the house as if it's alive, slithering through the family room, moving down the hall into Flora's lovely quiet island, striking like a deadly cobra.

Bile rises in her throat. She wishes for a bottle of water to wash it back down, but there is none. She swallows hard. Now there's the man's voice, deep and commanding.

"Mr. and Mrs. Jacobie, I understand you're upset but we take these reports seriously. We'll need to speak to both of them privately."

Flora doodles on her pad, but the hand holding her pen shakes and it turns into scribbles.

He said 'both of them'. That means they're coming for me.

Frantic for any escape, she plugs her ears with her fingers like she did when she was little, shutting out all sound. What a contrast. Nothing but peach and white, peaceful and safe again.

A vision swims up behind her eyes, a memory from four years ago. A floaty, feminine dress made of the finest fabric, spread out on her pale bedspread. With matching shoes and hair ribbon, the dress was a surprise from her new foster mother. It was the color of green apples and made her hazel eyes look a shade darker than the fabric. The ribbon held her thick hair away from her face, allowing it to wave darkly over her shoulders in brilliant contrast to the pale bodice of the dress. Like a fairytale princess.

Even at eleven years old, Flora understood what that dress meant. It was a disguise, camouflage, to help her transition into this family of quiet strangers. They looked so perfect, seemed so perfectly happy.

She wore that dress to church every Sunday for more than a year, in spite of the woman's objections: "You have lots of nice things to wear now, Flora." In that dress, though, she knew she would fit in with the other perfect children and their oh-so-perfect families. No one would see her for who she really was.

Reject.

Throwaway kid.

Less than.

Releasing the fingers from her ears brings back the noise and anger and fear. Trapped in this pastel prison, Flora listens to the hysterical woman—the one who thoughtfully gave her that beautiful fairytale dress on her first day with the family—call her a "lying, filthy whore."

Sweat trickles down her side, under her shirt. Instead of only her hands shaking, now her entire body quivers out of control. It's hard to breathe, too, like a bear hug gone too far.

Then Flora's foster father speaks up, challenging the strangers whose knock at their door brought this terrible storm. "You may speak to the girl, but my son will not be interrogated without our attorney present!"

It hurt, Dad calling her the girl. Not Flora. She can almost see Brendan's dad, roaring like an angry bull before these people. Protecting his golden son.

Still frozen in her chair, she struggles with conflicting images of these people she sometimes calls Mom and Dad. An abrupt knock on the door makes her jump. One of the strangers, the woman, says, "Flora? I need to come in, honey."

Eyes frantically dart around the room. Nowhere to go. Resigned, Flora stands to face the fury.

Another knock. Then a thin woman with brown frizzy hair and glasses opens the door. She carries a leather tote slung over her shoulder and her trench coat is flopped open, unbuckled belt hanging down on each side. Like she got dressed in a hurry or a long time ago.

Frizzy Hair walks right in without an invitation. She introduces herself in a quiet voice saying, "Hello Flora, I'm Ms. Denton. We need to pack up a few things, honey. You probably won't be coming back, so show me what's most important to you."

Not coming back.

Barely listening to her hoarse explanations, Flora stuffs her prized possessions into her backpack while Frizzy Hair grabs clothes from the dresser. The bag is plum-colored Kate Spade, a gift from her foster mom when she started high school. "You'll fit in with the other girls carrying this," she told her. She meant it to be reassuring but it made Flora feel small.

What happens when I put the backpack under my seat or in my locker? Must I carry it everywhere so they never see the real me? That in mind, she never let the bag get far from her. "Oh, Kate Spade!" The other girls would say, sometimes touching it reverently. "Nice!"

Mom Jacobie was right. It worked...at first, anyway. The trick was not to let them get close enough for a real look at her.

She notices Frizzy Hair sort of talking to herself, which is weird. "Let's see, we need jeans for school tomorrow, underwear, this top should work." She hands flora a fluffy green hoody. "Put this on, it's chilly. We'll try and get the rest later, honey, don't worry."

Then Frizzy Hair takes Flora by the arm, rushing her away from the peach and white room and out through the front door, flying past the continued rage her foster mom and dad spew at the deep-voiced man. She propels her down the driveway and into the back of a dirty white car, one that smells like cigarettes and is littered with fast food containers.

Shutting the door and shutting out the world, Frizzy Hair locks eyes on her. "Flora, I need to ask you some questions now."

They hunch together in the back seat while she pulls the facts from the girl: how Brendan touched her, when, where, why, what did she see, smell, taste, and what happened next.

So gross!

Gazing down at her lap, totally embarrassed, Flora's surprised to see her trembling fingers still clutching the purple pen, her favorite for doing homework. She stares at it, remembering how things happened with Brendan in unbearable detail. Mumbling answers to the questions, it feels like stones clog her throat. Every word hurts.

Suddenly sick, the gorge rises no matter how hard she swallows. "I'm… I'm gonna be…" At that moment she catches sight of what's happening outside of the car.

"Oh, no!"

Mr. and Mrs. Jacobie, Flora's parents for the last four years, stagger out of the house. Carrying several black garbage bags, heavy looking, they pitch them onto the driveway. Hard, as hard as they can. Mrs. Jacobie is crying, ugly.

"Get her out of here, that ungrateful monster. And keep her away from my son! Take all her stuff with you!"

She kicks at one of the bags, almost falling. Totally stunned by what happens next, Flora watches as this very proper woman actually spits on the bags before running back into her home.

Mr. Jacobie grabs the papers from Deep-Voiced Man, shaking his head and pointing at the car, at Flora. She can't hear his words but they churn around him like a dangerous wind. Then he turns his back and walks quickly into the house. To be with his real family.

Deep-Voiced Man walks back toward the car in a hurry, opening the trunk. He grabs the bags, tosses them in, and gets behind the wheel. Turning the key, he looks over his shoulder and says, "Hello, Flora. I'm Mr. George. Sorry about all this."

As the car speeds away, Frizzy Hair says, "It's ok,

Flora. You don't need to be afraid now. We're taking you someplace safe."

Swallowing hard against the bile, almost frantic, she whispers, "Help me, please? I…I think…I'm gonna be sick…"

"Ed!" the woman screams. "Pull over!"

Screeech!

The car slams to a stop and Flora jumps out, retching violently against the curb. In complete embarrassment, she bursts into tears.

Frizzy Hair hops out of the car cheerfully, singing, "No problem! You're fine now."

The woman hands her a bottle of water and a wad of fast-food napkins, cooing platitudes as Flora frantically attempts to wipe the sour splatter off her jeans.

4.

Buried in paperwork, time passes without notice for June. The sun is too close to setting for any warmth. In fact, the light is slipping away and the afternoon cooling makes her shiver.

She reaches for her coffee and raises it to her lips. It's skimmed over from hours of neglect. She sighs and sets it back down, sloshing cold coffee and cream on the wood surface. In this business, rings on a desk are like diamonds on Marilyn, plentiful and expected. Still, she tenderly wipes away the dampness with the palm of her hand and sets a pink message pad underneath, smearing the name and number scribbled there. June has always loved handcrafted things and this desk was a beauty in her eyes.

No matter how old and scuffed, craftsmanship like this should be respected.

"Hunter, what've you got goin' tonight?" Sarge hollers from his office. The one negative of her primo location is that it's within spitting distance of the boss's office.

She looks up. He's standing in his doorway, sleeves rolled up, tie wadded and stuffed in his pants pocket. Generally rumpled. He doesn't make eye contact. He's paging through a thick file with an unlit cigarette clamped between his teeth.

He's got something big for me. Otherwise, he wouldn't inquire about her evening plans. He'd just charge over and drop it on her desk with a mumbled "new case for you." Nope. This is serious.

"Tonight?" She shakes her head. "The usual, Sarge, nothing much. What's up?"

He summons her with a wave. June hustles after him into his office and perches on a chair, the only one free of procedural manuals, manila files, and thick binders. And she waits.

Still standing, Sarge slaps the file closed, grabs the cig out of his mouth, and holds the folder in the space between them. Finally, eye contact.

"This one's got your name all over it, Hunter. Tricky. You up for some delicate maneuvering?"

Delicate. That's code for managing people who are social uppity-ups, or heavily connected, or both. Whatever it is, June needs to handle these people delicately or their rich lawyers will crush her like a Japanese beetle.

"Up for it? You know I am."

They grin at each other.

"Then little miss Flora and her wicked foster family is all yours. This one has everything: rich family, community connections, orphan teen, sexual abuse, and a very tight window for adoption. Have fun but double-time this one. Tick-tock, Hunter!"

Back in her chair, June's desk phone is silent. Has been for a while. Could it be broken again? She glances at the duct tape where she'd fixed the frayed cord last month. Still intact. Lifting the receiver, she catches a dial tone. Phone confirmed working, no one needs her at the moment. Unusual. Lucky!

"Sarge," she hollers. "How about I take off?"

Sarge, his face in another file, waves good-bye from behind his desk.

It's the time average working Americans are packing it up and going home, but Child Welfare workers almost never escape so early. Snickering like a kid playing hooky, she stuffs the new case file into her messenger bag, slings it over her head, and hightails it.

A rare event, going home when the sun's still over the horizon. A good feeling, sure, but she's distracted by the knowledge that her day isn't over yet.

Her plan? Spend the evening tearing apart this file, learning everything she can about a teenage girl named Flora and what makes her life so damned special that Sarge earmarked this case for her. Tossing the messenger bag onto the passenger seat, she slides behind the wheel.

June winces as the old, beat-up Mustang screeches upon ignition, then settles into a moderate purr.

"I gotta get Quinn to replace the belt in this baby."

Putting it in gear, she speeds out of the parking garage. Slipping in and around traffic gives her the usual kick and her spirits rise. Happiness has always led June to lean a little heavy on the accelerator. She scans the road ahead for cops.

"I don't need another ticket!"

Driving defensively, however, is not the same thing as slowing down. She hits the clutch and shifts, taking it up to an exhilarating speed.

Satellite radio was the first thing she added when she bought her retro ride, and she'd never regretted it. Punching the buttons, she settles on old school rock, singing along to Janis Joplin's *Piece of My Heart*.

"Oh, yeah! It doesn't get much better than this!"

Traffic turns wispy as she darts away from the city. By the time Clapton is crying over Layla, she's really flying. Corn and soybean fields border the highway, with a smattering of woodlands in between. Signs for The

Orchards slow her down and she cranks the wheel to the left into a gravel drive. Parking at the far end of the lot is a habit, forcing herself to walk and wind down.

Entering the pristine red and white building, June inhales deeply. *Ahhh*! Fragrant, like a spring meadow. She waves to the woman behind the counter. "Hey, Karen!"

"Hello, June," the woman calls out, glancing at the apple-shaped clock. "You're here kind of early. Is today a government holiday or something?"

Karen's a third-generation owner of the farm. Her dedication to offering city people what she calls "The Modern Ag Experience" has led to the family's incredible success. June's been a regular customer since the days they operated out of a dinky little shack, selling nothing but apples. Their organic apples are fantastic, always have been, but now they sell a number of delicious treats and orchard-style entertainment year-round, such as hayrides and cider-pressing parties. They also carry a huge inventory of touristy stuff in the gift shop, from apple Christmas ornaments to thematic quilts and clothing.

June grins at the woman. "You got me, Karen. Once in a while, I manage to sneak out on the boss. Besides, I've got paperwork to do tonight."

She claps her hand to her forehead. "Paperwork! Now that's the June I know and love. What's your pleasure today? Cider? Caramel apple?"

"It's perfect apple pie weather, don't you think?"

"Indeed, my friend," Karen says. "Any weather is perfect pie weather, if you ask me."

She proceeds to fill her in on the local gossip: who's raising new crops, which sheep ranch is selling the nicest lambs, and what farmer's son took out the new tractor on a drunk drive and ran it into the river.

The whole time she's talking, June watches her remove a beautiful pie from the cooler, wrap it in tissue, and slip it into a pie box. Then she puts it in the bottom of a craft paper bag with ribbon handles, setting a smaller bag lightly beside it. *I bet that's full of cider donuts, a particular favorite at my house.*

"Now this is for Quinn," she says. "You give that handsome man of yours a big kiss for me and remind him to stop in once in a while. Maybe to announce your engagement, hmmm?"

"Engagement!" June laughs. "I've heard he's a confirmed bachelor and you know I'm a regular hermit, right?" And they laugh together.

As she hands June the package, Karen drops a handful of her homemade dog treats inside. "For my big ol' Tully!"

"Aww, thanks," June says, handing her enough cash to cover it and then some. She loves that the woman always remembers her man and her dog. Good people do exist.

I should hang out with regular people more often.

Since her job mostly takes her to the underbelly of contemporary society, June's been making an effort to choose people in her private life carefully – less drama, more joy.

Trying to salvage society's worst-of-the-worst in order to save a kid... well, that can get tiring. Soul-sucking. Not a great emotional state for a caseworker. She wonders for a moment how far gone she is, if her soul is completely lost.

Probably time for a change, she thinks, away from the Saving the World business. But June knows she's weak. A really challenging case always sucks her back in.

Flora's case might be a bit more challenging than I want, the final straw. After this one, who knows?

She pulls out of The Orchards with her treats and hits the road again. Turning on the music, Jethro Tull sings about what wise men don't know.

"Maybe this is the sign I've been looking for!"

Laughing out loud, she cranks up the tune and downshifts, shooting toward home.

5.

Pulling up to the curb, Flora sees a sign in the yard, near the steps up to the wide porch: Crossette Shelter for Girls. At first glance, the place reminds her of the dilapidated mansion in the Addams Family movie. Trees and shrubs still naked, brown grass, no flowers. She shivers.

You're not in foster care anymore, Flora.

Flora watches Big Investigator Man pull the garbage bags of her stuff out of the trunk. She slips out of the car with her backpack and follows Frizzy Hair, who seems eager to get rid of her now. They both rush to help carry the bags inside the big old three-story house.

A sloppy woman in a sweat suit and flip-flops stands in the doorway. She wrestles her fingers through tangled hair as she talks to Big Investigator Man. "You can put her things right there." She points toward a corner.

They told her this messy woman was the House Parent. But what was her name? Arlene? Irene? Flora's head felt hazy after all that had happened this evening.

Investigator Man and Frizzy Hair are in a big hurry to leave, trotting out the door and down the steps saying, "Good luck, Flora, you'll be safe now."

Safe…really?

She's a little rusty after staying in one placement for so long but she knows the drill. She won't be seeing those two for a while. They said they'd probably touch base before the court hearing. For now, Big Investigator Man and Frizzy Hair are no longer her worry.

House Parent Whatsername introduces Flora to a tall, thin redhead named Deidre.

"Flora, huh? Cool," the girl says, looking her up and down. "You can call me Dee. Everybody does."

Flora figures Dee's about her age. Everything about the girl says she's tough. She wears a ton of make-up including black liner circling greenish eyes, pale skin, and red-red lips. Silver hoops and strands dangle from her lobes. She counts five piercings in the left ear. Her eyebrow has some sort of silver cross stuck through it and there's a teeny crystal imbedded high on her right nostril. With a stretchy green tank and low-cut black jeans, the girl shows lots of skin. She tries not to stare at the rhinestone spider poking from Dee's belly button, but it screams, "Look at me!"

It's funny, how the way you look kinda tells people how to treat you. This tough-girl guise can help when dealing with some people and get in the way with others. She wonders if Dee is using this look to her advantage.

When she was little, Flora discovered how a wide-eyed frightened look could make you appear vulnerable and bring out the kindness in certain types of grown-ups. Her blank look freaks out almost all the adults. With other kids, though, it can be tricky.

Until I learn the rules of this place, especially the unwritten ones, it's best to try and blend in.

"Come on." Dee cocks her head and leads the way to their room, dragging the bags along the floor. At the doorway, she points to a worn-out dresser and naked mattress with sheets and stuff piled on it. "You'll be over there." She looks tough, but her voice is soft.

Almost friendly.

"Have you been here very long, Dee?"

Flora starts the process of collecting those bits of information that might later turn out to be significant. Scanning the room, she makes mental notes. Faded purple comforter. Dirty clothes littering the floor. A tangle of crappy jewelry on the nightstand. Dee's stuff.

"Oh, this is my second time," she says casually, fluffing her wild red hair in the dresser mirror. "I've been here about two weeks."

"What happened to your roommate?"

Flora wonders if Dee's pissed at having to share her space.

"She went back home once her mom's boyfriend moved out." Dee seems happy to spit out all the intimate details. "She was only twelve, and the kid cried her eyes out the whole time she was here. She was all worried that her mom would leave her in here so she could stay with that asshole. Why would any mom want to be with a guy who tried to screw her own daughter?" Dee tosses out the question but doesn't wait for an answer. "Some women are morons, I guess. Anyway, that kid only stayed a few days."

She seems ok about sharing her space, maybe even likes it.

Dee shrugs, bored with her story, and reaches for one of the bags. "Let's get you unpacked." Her words are matter-of-fact but her eyes have a greedy look to them. Pawing through Flora's stuff, it's like she's hunting for treasure.

Not wanting this girl touching her things, or even looking at them, she tries to distract her. "Hey, um, first could you show me around?"

"Oh. Yeah, come on…"

Dee sighs, drops the bag and waves her into the hall. "The office and dayroom are down there by the kitchen. These three bedrooms are the only ones on the main floor, except for hers." She points at the House Parent. "And the upstairs floors have five bedrooms each and a dayroom and bathrooms, of course. The second floor is full right now, but I think two kids moved out of the third floor today. This is the kitchen…"

Scratched wooden trim.

Chipped, stained countertop.

Finger-printed cabinets.

Grimy floorboards.

A dramatic contrast to the immaculate household where Flora lived for the past few years. Thinking of the Jacobie's friendly housekeeper, she wonders if the girls at Crossette are required to clean the house themselves.

Damn! Her stomach knots up. Not wanting to puke again, she takes a deep breath and follows Dee through the halls. Keeping up and pretending to listen.

Are all group homes in old, used-up houses? Do they all have burned-out light bulbs and scuffed up furniture and smell like overcooked garlic bread? Do they all feel like nobody cares?

By the time the tour is over, Dee is busy gossiping with some girl from the second floor. Moving quickly, Flora stuffs the contents of her garbage bags into the dresser drawers, trying not to look. She doesn't want to pick through the broken trinkets or look for missing pieces of her life.

Here's the plan: Make the bed. Get in it. Act like I'm asleep. Hope it keeps these girls away from me and my stuff until morning.

Grabbing the sheets, she works fast, ticking off bits of information like a checklist.

Dee wants to be the boss: OK.

House Parent Whatsername wants to do as little as possible: Whatever.

Everybody else wants to get their hands on my stuff: Not gonna happen.

The bed's made, sort of. Good enough. She closes the door, rips off her splattered jeans, and slides into a pair of pajama pants. Pulling out her backpack, she sorts the possessions and chooses what to keep with her:

Stuff I absolutely need.

Stuff I totally want.

Stuff other kids might want to steal.

These are the essentials that go into the backpack. The rest of the things can stay in the dresser. Those things are now expendable, the decoy stuff. Sometime tomorrow, she will act upset over something supposedly missing, like, "Who the hell ripped off my leather belt with the silver buckle?!" That puts attention on her room and belongings, so snoops will stay away.

According to Dee, 'lights out' is early on school nights. The house is quieting down from chattering, laughing, and running the stairs, to murmuring conversations and doors gently closing. Flora turns off the light and slides into bed, tucking the backpack between her body and the wall.

This baby stays with me, no matter what.

Trying to control her breathing, Flora pretends to sleep. *It was pretty nice at Jacobie's house; I loved my room.* Now she needs to recall those skills from before, when life was different.

How hard can it be?

She pulls the covers up around her ears, trying not to miss her peaches and cream life.

I survived before, when Mom died, and after...

A sense of calm rolls over her. *This time is different. This time I'm older, practically an adult. This time I know things are completely messed up and no one can be trusted. Just gotta watch my back.*

Flora understands the Jacobies might even be dangerous. They hate her now, which is totally unfair. They'll probably want to get even. When somebody gossiped about the family or pissed off her foster dad, he would always say, "Nobody in this community messes with me or my family. Nobody!" Like he's a cowboy in the Old West or something. Crazy.

She knows how crappy they treat teenagers in the system, especially the ones that cause trouble, so she'll lay low. Be as invisible as possible while she pushes toward her eighteenth birthday and freedom.

If I was legal, I'd never have to depend on anyone else ever again. I could take care of myself.

But she's not legal yet, not quite sixteen. On alert, feeling vulnerable with her back to the door, Flora wonders what comes next.

6.

INTAKE FORM

Child Name: Flora ███████   **DOB:** ███████
Current Age: 15 years
Age at Initial Custody: 11 years

Initial Reason for Custody (i.e., Abuse / Neglect / Abandoned / Orphaned / Juvenile incarceration / Medical / Failed Adoption):
Both parents deceased; guardianship with paternal grandmother until GM's death; Orphan.

Brief Description of Report: Hononegah HS social worker initiated Report; both parents deceased, Paternal Grandmother served as child guardian until her death; no known relatives; entered system via foster care, brief stay at temporary group home and in emergency foster care until placement in Jacobie FH; Music Teacher & School Social Worker reported child's complaint that 17-year-old foster brother Brandon Jacobie sexually molested her.

Primary Language: English
Other Languages: limited Spanish

Mother's Name: Jane Doe
Primary Language: English
Mother's Status/Occupation: deceased; welfare system
Address/City/State: Rockford IL at time of death; Death Certificate on file from Winnebago County.

Father's Name: John Smith
Primary Language: English & Spanish
Father's Status/Occupation: deceased; reported drug dealer

Address/City/State: Mexico at time of death; no Death Certificate.

Guardian: Maria Smith, Paternal Grandmother
Guardian Occupation: deceased; retired office worker - Woodward Governor Corp.
Address/City/State: South Beloit IL at time of death; death cert. Beloit Memorial Hospital

Siblings: no known sibs

Medical Status: born to drug-dependent mother; currently healthy; no known physical disabilities or diseases; medical & dental records intact.

Educational Status: Flora was placed from So. Beloit school district to Rockton district; currently at Hononegah HS, Rockton; Special Ed/Learning Disability services for all classes – reading at 5th grade level; all academics – limited progress since entering into foster care; prior school records (So. Beloit) show steady progress & average student; IEP in place & current; extra-curricular – Music; participation in Music indicated by pre-placement school records; since placement, academics stagnated but interest in Music increased dramatically; can read Music but "memorizes the words" since reading-impaired; singing voice described as "remarkable" by current Music teacher.

Child Social Skills: Flora has always been quiet, pleasant, and cooperative but increasingly withdrawn; remains more engaged with adults than peers; no identifiable friends since entering Hononegah HS.

Placement Information: At the time of initial report, Flora had a 15-day stay at Macktown Home for Babies & Children; then two temporary placements, each less than a week, until placement in Jacobie FH for close to 4 years;

placement stable throughout, but Jacobie family never willing to adopt.

Placement Status: free for Adoption.
Placement Goal: Adoption.

Completed by: <u>M. M. Denton, DCW Child Investigator</u>
Completed by: <u>E. D. George, DCW Child Investigator</u>

7.

From her kitchen window, June can see down the gravel lane that serves as her driveway. She's not fond of early spring, but a green tinge to the trees means buds and leaves are on their way. It feels hopeful.

Where the lane meets the main road, Quinn's work truck turns in. The truck is splattered with mud from his latest worksite. Deep, excited barking announces his arrival.

"Ok Tully, out you go," she says, opening the door for him. The Irish Wolfhound rips around the yard a few times, then ambushes Quinn as he climbs out of the truck. With his giant grey paws on the man's shoulders, the two of them are about the same height.

"Good to see you, boy," he says, rubbing the dog and wrestling a bit. Tully barks his pleasure.

Like a school girl, June's heart always jumps when she sees him. Today's no exception, especially when he grabs her at the door and plants a big kiss on her mouth.

A giant next to her, Quinn stands over six feet tall with eyes like the sky and dark shaggy hair going a bit gray. A thick mustache frames a wide smile and, in the winter, he usually dons a salt-and-pepper beard for warmth. He moves easily with a quiet strength, muscles visible through his open jacket, t-shirt, and jeans. Watching him split wood is a special treat for June.

She thinks, *Quinn Harimann, you are the love of my life.*

She says, "Hey, how'd you know I was home?"

He grins. "I didn't know. I planned to get the grill going and then text you a picture of *this* to get you out of the office." He holds up a package wrapped in white butcher paper.

"Steak? You're the devil, Mr. Harimann! It would have worked, too, if I hadn't escaped on my own."

Quinn brings in wood and sets a small fire in the stove, while he waits for the coals in the grill to heat up. June prepares a salad and cuts some crusty bread. While setting the table together, she apologizes for the work she needs to do tonight.

"No problem," he says. "I've got a bid to put together for a new project and some supplies to load for the morning. Gonna head out pretty quickly after we eat."

A building contractor, his work demands are as unpredictable as hers. That's a plus. None of this "how come I never see you?" stuff their colleagues complain about with their significant others.

Loving but not needy. Strong. Kind.

An independent woman can only tolerate so much neediness in a guy. June gets plenty of that from her clients, managing the cases with a combination of steel and grace. But a seriously romantic gesture by this big tough man just about causes her to swoon.

After eating dinner, they make a huge dent in the apple pie. Then Quinn takes off for his bungalow on the outskirts of town, in an area with easy access to many of his building projects but far enough away to offer peace. Like the cabin June calls home.

She puts on a pot of dark roast coffee and opens the messenger bag. There it is, the bulging case file labeled FLORA. The new kid beckons. She had only really glanced at the Intake Form in the office. "Let's find out what is so special about Flora."

The big dog drops to the floor with a sigh, eyes fixed on the folder, tail thumping.

Settling into her chair by the woodstove, she opens the file to Child History and scans the story of this troubled new kid on her caseload. Soon, Tully rests his head on her feet and closes his eyes.

Flora. Pretty name. It'd be really cool if the kid was named after the Roman Goddess of Flowers. In a not-so-charming twist, however, the child was named after her mother's favorite brand of reefer. The pot was called 'Frisco Flora' for its West Coast origins and excessive production of flower buds.

It seems Mommy Dearest died when Flora was five years old, in a one-car crash, DUI. A fiery altercation with a tree. There wasn't much left to bury. No proof, but the cops figured she chose this way, instead of a more difficult hanging or slitting of wrists.

The girl lived with her paternal grandmother until the woman died of emphysema.

Flora's Daddy had been a U.S. citizen hiding from American authorities somewhere in Mexico, the land of his great grandparents. He was eventually shot and killed in a drug deal gone bad. Cousins from Mexico finally brought the cremains back to his mother, who didn't get to gaze at her boy's face one last time. His only child, Flora, never even met him. So sad!

Grandma buried his ashes only a few weeks before she suffocated from her disease. Thankfully, the woman died in the hospital while Flora was at school. The child was eleven years old by then, her Mommy a vague memory and her Daddy a total stranger.

Her last look at her grandmother, the only mother she ever really knew, was at the hospital in a quiet room, a staff social worker holding her hand. There was no funeral since there was no family that anyone knew about. A policewoman brought the girl some personal items from the house in a lidded cardboard box, marked with Grandma's name on the lid and sides. Flora never returned to her home or neighborhood and never asked to visit. So as not to stir up emotions in the girl, nobody ever offered.

After a brief go-round in an area shelter and the homes of temporary caregivers, the girl was placed in the Jacobie foster home where she lived until yesterday. Since her placement, Flora remained academically arrested at the 5th grade level and her report cards repeatedly declared, little to no progress. She's frozen in time. June sighs.

No surprise. Traumatized kids often remain stunted, stuck emotionally and mentally at the age of the incident.

Trauma does that to people. Even with Special Ed help, the girl still reads and writes like an eleven-year-old, exhibits only rudimentary math skills, and struggles in every area except music.

Here's something interesting. Her teachers say she can sing like a pro.

"Wow." June leans over and rubs Tully's head. "This kid's life pretty much sucks from the beginning to now."
She flips the file to the *Abuse Report*. Pretty thin but the investigation just got started. Flora says her foster brother was touching her inappropriately. Not much to go on, and it looks like one of those her-word-against-his situations.
The smell of coffee distracts her. Pouring a refill, she notices Quinn left her one of Karen's donuts for a late-night snack. *What a guy!*

Coffee in one hand and a donut in the other, she settles in again and opens the file to the section marked *Foster Parent Profile*.

The Jacobie family has social standing in this community. Mr. J is a VP at one of the area's largest corporations and sits on numerous boards, most notably the city Board of Police Commissioners. Mrs. J is Junior League all the way, volunteering and such. Well-connected. Accusing their Golden Boy of sexually abusing his foster sister isn't gonna sit well.

Regarding their relationship with Flora, the records show little personal involvement by Mr. and Mrs. Jacobie, only minimal contact with school personnel or at court. They left that stuff to her caseworkers.

June recognizes this type of foster placement, offering the basic 'cot and three hots', to meet some presumed social obligation and boost their public image. An extension of Mrs. J's volunteerism, maybe.

All of their prior placements were young, lasted less than 6 months, and female. Mrs. J told the licensing agent that she would rather have girls because she never had one of her own. The bedroom they reserved for placements was decorated in a very feminine style. The woman explained, "so the poor little things can enjoy the princess experience, if only for a short while."

Flora has been their longest placement by far. She's facing her sixteenth birthday this summer.

"Hey, Tully, wanna see what she looks like? We've got a picture in here somewhere..."

Sliding out the photo, June checks the label: age 15, height 5'10", weight 165 lbs., hair black, eyes hazel. The girl has sort of an exotic look to her, not surprising with a Caucasian mother and Hispanic father. Large wide-set eyes peer out at the photographer, with thick brows and full lips. Her hair is parted on the side and a bit wavy, long enough to brush past her shoulders. Staring into the camera, Flora isn't smiling—she has a faraway look like someone listening intently to a distant melody.

"And now you're my responsibility," she says to the photo. "Happy Birthday, Homeless Princess."

Closing the file with a flourish causes Tully to sit up. He nestles his head in her lap, looking mournfully into her eyes.

"Yeah," she agrees with Tully. "It doesn't look good, but I've seen worse."

8.

"She's been pretty quiet since she got here last night, June."

In her office with the door closed, House Parent Irene confides like a BFF. "You know she got sick on the way here, right? Barely made it out of the investigator's car. Insisted on a bottle of water to rinse out her mouth and napkins to clean off her jeans...like anyone here cares about that."

June's not sure if Irene is gossiping, sympathetic, or just being bitchy, but she puts on her 'We're on the Same Side' face. "OK, thanks." She shakes her head and sighs, universal body language for 'That Sucks', and asks, "Where's Flora now?"

"She's in her room, down there." Irene gestures in the direction of the hallway. "Holding onto that backpack like it contains the crown jewels. I guess that's all the poor girl has to call her own."

"Seems about par for the course. She's had it rough... lots of losses." Thanks to her late night with Flora's file, June's pretty much up to speed this morning.

While the House Parent shoves paperwork at June, she tries to imagine what it must have been like for the kid. Flora lived with the Jacobie family for four years before she spilled the beans to the school nurse. She tearfully revealed that seventeen-year-old Brendan had been sexually molesting her after his parents left for work in the mornings.

So, when that allegation hit the fan, the foster parents accused her of jealousy, seduction, and anything else they could think of, bagged up all of the kid's stuff and tossed it into the manicured driveway of their lovely suburban home.

Sympathetic, Irene says in a stage whisper, "How could those people throw her out like that, after she lived there for so long? Unbelievable!"

"Well, they sure don't want their darling boy to get into any legal trouble," June says, quietly. "He could go to prison for something like this, you know. Forced to register as a child sex offender."

"I guess so," she grouses, moving in closer. "I hope they get the bastard!"

Giving her the Team Social Work nod, June moves away, unwilling to share too much. The kid deserves some privacy, after all.

"Why is it so freakin' dark in here?" June mumbles, hurrying down the hall. Stopping in the open doorway, she figures she'd have recognized Flora even if she hadn't seen her photo. The girl's dressed neatly for school, sitting quietly on her freshly made bed, backpack between her feet. Waiting. Oozing alone-ness.

"Hello, Flora, I'm June Hunter, your new caseworker."

The girl gives sort of a nod, but no sound comes out just yet. She appears stunned, even after so many hours have passed. Not surprising, it's a lot to process. And, as if things aren't crappy enough, the shelter can only keep her for a limited time. It's the law.

June steps into the room and pulls back the curtains to let in some light. "OK, Flora, let's talk about what happened…"

June slips into her routine, explaining how the abuse complaint came in, that the investigators picked her up for her own safety, blah, blah, blah. She knows she's talking *at* the kid, but it's the fastest way to get the basics out of the way.

"I see Nora was your old caseworker. When was the last time you met with her, do you remember?"

Shrug.

Hmmm. "Were you close with Nora?"

Shrug and head shake.

"Not really, huh? Well, since your situation has changed, I'll be taking over. I'm gonna help you find a new home. That's my specialty." Kindly smile.

Nothing from Flora. Blank stare. Vulnerable demeanor.

June pauses to assess the kid. Looks really fragile. She's lost another home and family, an orphan for the second time. It totally sucks, however self-serving the Jacobies turned out to be. For her, this should really cement the notion that no one can be trusted. Ever.

And now, as her adoption worker, it's June's responsibility to find the girl a permanent home. Sometimes the job feels like a bad game show:

Let's welcome our first contestant, ladies and gentlemen: June Hunter! Here's her challenge – this seriously messed up foster kid named Flora has been languishing in the system without much attention. If our contestant can't find this child an adoptive placement soon, she'll never have a permanent home and family.

The clock is running out for young Flora and, if it does, here's what she wins, Monty:

Behind Door #1 - A $30.00 suitcase;

Behind Door #2 - $2000.00 in social security money;

Behind Door #3 - A shitty apartment in the Projects;

And Behind the Curtain - A referral to her local community college financial aid office.

Thank you for playing Let's Make a Crappy Deal!

Over the years, June knew a few kids who got dropped into "transitional living" by the State. Without a strong support system, some got arrested for theft, or selling drugs, or prostitution, if they didn't get pregnant or die of an overdose. Not all, but enough of them to cause June's fight response to kick in.

Even beginning caseworkers know the solution from Social Work 101: find someone to adopt them and parent them into adulthood, someone to support them through good times and bad, a real family so they don't become a statistic. Simple, right?

"Sounds like you've had a rough time lately, Flora. And, um…this place is…well, it isn't the greatest, I know. Do you need anything right away?"

She gets a slight shrug and that blank stare in response. Flora hasn't uttered a single word.

That's fine, I'm patient. I've dealt with kids like this before.

"I have contacted the school and you'll be completing your schoolwork here for now. A Resource Teacher will come over this morning to review your current classes and see how we can keep you up to speed until we get you placed in another home. Does that sound good?"

Flora stares at her shoes.

Yeah, kid, everything has changed. I'm pretty sure nothing sounds good right now.

"This is for your protection, Flora. You didn't do anything wrong...you understand?"

She nods.

June wonders what her voice is like, remembering she likes to sing. Then a thought slips in and burns. *Will this kid ever feel like singing again?*

"Here's my card with my office and cell numbers. Leave a message if I don't answer." June smiles. "And if the staff here hassles you, call me. I'll whip 'em into shape!"

No reaction to a lame attempt at humor. Too early for that. The kid's staring at her, assessing her, deciding if she's worthy of attention. Trying too hard at this point will either turn her off or scare her away, so June picks up her bag to show Flora she's done tormenting her for now.

"I'll swing by here most days to see you and I'll call you as soon as I know our court date, Flora. I'm itching to get started on the next steps. I'm heading back to my office now – see you tomorrow."

Flora's mouth turns up the tiniest bit at the corners. "Thank you, June."

She spoke!

June's happy for the sound of her voice, the almost-smile, reassurance that she's made the slightest connection.

"No problem, kiddo. I like a challenge. All you have to do for the next few days is do your schoolwork and stay out of trouble. I think you're pretty good at that, right?"

Another almost-smile.

At the door, turning to say good-bye, she sees Flora gazing at her reflection in the mirror. That 'deer-in-the-headlights' look bounces back at her.

June gets a violent shiver, like the Ghost of Flora's Past just slithered over her shoulder and out the door ahead of her.

When it comes to this particular race against time, I fear I'm already way behind.

9.

"Come on or we'll miss the bus," Dee yells, rushing for the door.

Flora hears another girl running down the stairs calling, "I'm coming, hold on!"

She watches out the window as a handful of girls tromp out the door and across the battered lawn toward the corner, where a school bus is squealing to a halt. Once it pulls away, the quiet is almost delicious.

Flora had been astounded at the clatter of the girls getting ready for school. She dressed and brushed her teeth but it seemed smart to wait until they were all out of the way to eat.

With everyone gone, I don't even need to drag my backpack where ever I go.

She toasts one piece of generic white bread in the kitchen and pours a glass of juice. Someone left a big jar of peanut butter open on the counter, so she sticks a knife in it and smears a blob on her toast. She's careful to put the cap back on the jar and sweep up her crumbs with a paper towel before heading for the kitchen table. Dee told her they are supposed to clean up after themselves.

She lets loose a big sigh as she sits down with her breakfast, saying out loud to no one, "Peace and quiet!"

Shortly thereafter, her moment of solitude is disturbed mid-chew.

"Hi." A skinny girl with dark hair slips into the kitchen. "I'm just gonna get something..."

"Hi," Flora says, surprised. Assuming she was the only one getting school at the home, she asks, "Did you miss the bus?"

"No, I take my classes here until they figure something else out. There are three or four of us who do distance classes. Welcome to the group."

The doorbell interrupts them.

Grabbing a granola bar and stuffing it into her hoodie

pocket, the girl says, "There's the teachers – gotta go." Then she slips out.

Flora wolfs down the last of her toast, finishes off her juice, and heads toward the office to see what's going on. She hears people talking and clattering up the stairs to the second floor.

"Oh Flora, there you are," Irene calls out to her, waving. "Your Resources Teacher is here!"

A woman who looks to be about ninety-years-old smiles at her from the front hall. "Hello, Flora. I'm Mrs. Dewey. I've brought your Chromebook and assignments."

She follows the woman to the first-floor dayroom and watches her plug in the laptop.

"Do you know how to use one of these, Flora?" the woman asks.

She nods, "Sort of…"

Mrs. Dewey sits herself down at the game table, moving the deck of cards and Scrabble game box to the shelf behind her. She opens the laptop and it chimes.

"Ready!" Mrs. Dewey says. "I'll show you how to access all the course information and how to submit your work. Have a seat."

For the first 45 minutes, Mrs. Dewey teaches her how to use this kind of laptop, find her schedule of assignments, where to access her coursework, and how to submit it. She'd had a MacBook at the Jacobie's but this computer's different. It appears less complicated but Flora's having a hard time remembering the steps.

At some point, Mrs. Dewey stops her. "Have you ever been tested for a learning disability, dear?"

OMG! So embarrassing!

Flora flushes red with humiliation and hangs her head. "Yes."

The woman waits for her to go on.

"I took some tests when I first went to the Jacobie's house. I know my foster mom talked with the school psychologist about it but she told me she didn't want my school work 'tinted by the results'. After that, I met with a tutor during free period."

Mrs. Dewey stares at her.

I wish I would die right now!

Mrs. Dewey finally says, "I think she meant she didn't want your performance *tainted*, meaning she didn't want you to feel different. Does that sound right to you?"

Flora shrugs. "I guess. Or maybe she was embarrassed because I *am* different."

Mrs. Dewey looks pissed. "To be fair to you, I'm going to look into this. People learn in different ways, Flora. Just because you learn differently from the way I learn, doesn't make it wrong. You shouldn't have to struggle if there are easier ways for you to learn."

Flora watches in silence as the woman writes furiously in her notebook. *I totally want to disappear.*

After a couple of hours of basic stuff, trying to figure out what work Flora has been doing at school, they close down the laptop. Mrs. Dewey puts the Chromebook in a slender computer bag and stuffs her own notebook into a tote. She hands Flora the computer bag and says, "It's all yours."

She walks with the woman to the door. "Flora, I'm going to email you some assignments later this afternoon. They'll have verbal instructions so you will need to use headphones. Do you have any?"

Flora shakes her head.

"Use these for now, then," she says, handing Flora a package of new earbuds, "and I'll bring you headphones tomorrow. I like them better than buds – those make my ears itch!" She laughs and winks. "The headphones have the added advantage of stopping others from bothering you. Can't hear them with headphones on, right? You decide which works best for you. Sound good?"

"Uh, huh," she says. "Um, thank you, Mrs. Dewey."

The woman startles Flora by cupping a hand to her cheek. "Thank *you*, Flora! You are such a lovely child. I'm honored by this opportunity to work with you."

The tenderness of her touch and gentle, loving words bring tears to Flora's eyes. She watches the woman walk carefully down the front steps, climb into her battered old car, and drive away.

She closes the door, taking her new laptop back to her room and sets it next to her backpack. Then she climbs onto her bed and falls into a deep, dreamless sleep.

10.

Slumped in the boss' office chair, June fills him in on her first face-to-face with Flora.

"A lovable teenager's chance of getting adopted is almost zero. Flora's not loveable. She's pretty, in an exotic way, but not engaging. Distant. Not a lot going for her."

Sarge doesn't flinch at the harsh assessment. "Adoptive parents won't find the daughter-they-never-had in Flora, that's for sure. They'll be parenting her without reward. Then again, if you think about it, isn't that like most parents of teens?"

"But they'll have no loving memories of sticky childhood kisses to get them through the tough times." These brainstorming sessions help June work through the negative thoughts so she can be productive.

Sarge nods. "Yeah, let me take a look."

She hands him Flora's photo. "She isn't exactly a delicate flower. She has thick, black hair to her shoulders, large eyes, gorgeous really. But she's big boned, sturdy, and out of shape like any inactive kid that eats junk food. The real problem is, she hardly ever smiles and she's as detached as a piece of furniture."

"All right, let's get it on paper." Sarge hands her a legal pad and a pen. "Make the columns."

Two columns, for Pros and Cons. Third column, Notes.

June works out loud, while jotting notes. "Pro: Quiet, compliant. Con: Distant, hard to engage. Note: Parents cannot be the needy type."

Sarge adds his thoughts. "Pro: no trouble at school or with cops. Con: Minimally social. Note: Suggest few or no other kids at home."

"Good point," June says. "Pro: Sings beautifully. Con: Poor performance in school. Note: Look for creative types with a history/knowledge of child development and educational difficulties."

As they brainstorm, the perfect couple takes shape. They fall into the category June calls Collectors. That type of foster parent believes every kid needs someone who gives a damn about them. This imaginary couple won't be put off by her distance. Rather, they'll be enchanted by her skills and potential, excited to help her blossom into a fully-functioning adult. Instead of crying when she doesn't declare her love for them, they'll celebrate every success and declare undying confidence in her. They are a rare pair.

I swear I'm gonna find them.

Introductions need to be handled with care. June knows they can't have a repeat of her first encounter with an adoptive prospect four years ago. The eager couple just *knew* they could make this little girl love them by the end of a twenty-minute visit at the DCW offices. The case file detailed that poorly-managed visit:

Scene 1: Enter the well-meaning potential adoptive parents.

"Hello, Flora, what a lovely name! Doesn't that mean 'flowers' or something?"

Scene 2: Flora takes a moment or three to focus on their faces …big pause… Then, when they really start to fidget, she nods and almost whispers, "Yes. Yes, it does."

Scene 3: Gazing down at her hands for a few seconds, Flora finally gets up and walks to the window to stare out at the rain. They call her name but she is unresponsive. The uncomfortable couple is left to their own devices for 20 more minutes, while the kid contemplates the meaning of life in a raindrop or some such shit.

"Flora can be sorta spooky," June mumbles. "I wonder if she did it on purpose?"

That meeting ended with the would-be adoptive couple practically running from the room, wondering why we didn't tell them she was some kind of freak. Shortly after that, she was placed with the Jacobie family until a suitable adoptive home could be found.

Apparently, there was no *suitable adoptive couple*. June wonders if her worker even tried. After all, that was the only documented parent meeting in her file. Some caseworkers figure it's too much work with not much potential and go straight to preparing the kid for independent living.

Sadly, Flora's demeanor will not allow for a typical family to play the 'getting to know you' game with her. She already believes most people, even those who might be willing, are full of shit. Those big, glassy eyes seem to burrow into your soul. Needy folks will not be able to tolerate that, too challenging.

"Nice defense, actually," June says. "Good way to weed out the losers."

"Kind of an elegant look to her," Sarge says, gazing at her photo. "Classic, like Jane Russell or Lauren Bacall."

He hands back her picture and looks at the chart they've made. "A singer, huh?" He says, "I read in one report that the kid's rendition of *Over the Rainbow* made her music teacher cry."

"Partially from heartbreak, I'm guessing, with a healthy dose of frustration on the side." June puts down her pen and stretches.

"Looks like you've got plenty to go on," Sarge says, dismissing her with a gesture. "Like I said, Hunter, this case is right up your alley."

I wish I had his confidence.

11.

Once the bus drops off the other girls from school, the first-floor dayroom is quieter than the rest of the house. Flora notices it now smells like lemon furniture polish. The kind Mom Jacobie used on their furniture, or rather the housekeeper did. It calms Flora and she breathes deep with her eyes closed.

I wonder who uses that stuff here at Crossette?

Dee comes flouncing in with some books and drops into the chair across from her at the table. "Smell that? The weekly cleaning crew was here today. Did you see 'em?"

Flora shakes her head.

"So, you got your school work," she says, gazing at Flora's laptop. "Life sucks and then you die."

Real cheery. Flora gives her a weak smile.

Dee snickers. "What's up with your case today?"

"Not much, I guess," Flora murmurs. She doesn't love the idea of one more caseworker nosing around in her life, but she doesn't really have a choice.

Dee says, "Ya know, if you don't get placed in an actual home, they send you to County."

I'll have to find out what 'County' is. It doesn't sound good.

"Hi, ladies!" Irene comes in carrying a stack of books. "We just got a donation of new books. You two can be first to look 'em over."

As the lady fusses by the bookshelves, Flora gathers she's checking to make sure they're doing their homework instead of goofing around.

The buzzing from her butt makes her jump. When you go to Crossette, or any of the shelters, they issue you a prepaid phone loaded with 60 minutes. It's supposed to be for talking to your caseworker, parents if you got 'em, the House Parent, school, your lawyer, and other important calls. The told her to "use it sparingly" unless she's got a hidden stash of money somewhere and can buy additional minutes. Flora has exactly $2.73 in her backpack. The phone has gone unused.

Buzzzzzz, bzzzzzz.

Sneaking a look, Flora sees Dee texting from behind a schoolbook with a picture of an elephant on the cover.

I have no idea how she got the number. She's a slick one!

Dee: Any homework?

Flora: Y, worksheets. U?

Dee: Y, 2 much.

Flora: Talk later?

Dee: k.

Flora figures it's good she doesn't ride the bus to school or Dee would be bossing her all over the place. But she doesn't want to alienate her either.

I don't want to be besties. I can't trust her at all. She'll be going home soon, I hope.

She refocuses on her laptop and looks up the parts of a flower for biology class: petal, stamen, pistil, and a few more.

Can't really concentrate. The only one I remember is petal. So stupid.

Flora hates Dummy Bio Class, all the Dummy Classes actually, but at least Mrs. Dewey is nice.

For some reason, I really want to do well for her.

"Make sure you fill in the worksheet as you find each one," Mrs. Dewey had said earlier. "There's a quiz on Friday."

She had paused for a second, then told Flora, "Don't worry, the worksheet is identical to your quiz. Learn this and you'll ace the test."

Good to know.

She moves her backpack to the floor next to her and it falls sideways, a pen rolling out onto the floor. The pen

38

she brought from home…er, from Jacobie's house.

Staring at the pen, it all comes rushing back to her. The shouting, the smelly car, Frizzy Hair and her sloppy trench coat. Brendan and his parents. Looking up at the haunted house that is the Crossette Shelter and wishing she could slow it all down.

It feels like the Earth is spinning faster and faster. She presses her chest and fights panic. No home, no family, no friends.

It's my own fault. I started it. I told.

She stuffs the pen back in the pack and shakes it off. Or at least she tries. *Breathe in and count to five, breathe out and count… focus on the laptop, focus on the worksheet, don't think, just breathe…*

After a while, her heart slows down and the panic recedes. She gazes down at the worksheet and frowns. It looks all mixed up, letters quivering on the screen. She can't remember anything to fill in the blanks.

She puts in her earbuds and turns on the voice.

"Section 12. Flowers. The parts of flowers."

All I remember is petal. Dewey's gonna think I'm an idiot.

She doesn't want that. She wants her to be pleased when she comes back, so she listens to the voice tell her the parts and repeats softly after each one. Typing the names into the worksheet, she hopes she's getting the spelling right.

The panic is gone. For now.

12.

The day after brainstorming with Sarge, June goes to the shelter armed with her best weapon, the truth.

"Flora, we need to find you a family. A real family. Not a foster home, a family that will adopt you and be there for you, for the rest of your life."

The girl peers at her through the waning sunlight in the

dayroom, her backpack on the floor by her side. "How? Who?"

Perfectly good questions. No answers...yet. But she's talking to me, at least.

"Well, for example, we want someone who thinks you deserve a chance to graduate from high school, maybe go to college, and get a great job someday."

She stares at me like I just turned purple. "I'm in the Dummy Classes at school, June. All Dummy Classes, except music. I'll never be able to go to college."

Crap! That was a stupid thing to say to her.

"I know, but you've had a hard time. At some point, you'll be able to do better." This is not where I meant to go, so I switch gears. "I want you to know there are people out there who really want to give kids a chance. We just need to find the right family for you."

"They tried before..." she starts to explain, decides against it. "How will *you* find one that wants me?" she asks, completely serious and businesslike.

Damn, I'd take you home myself if you didn't deserve so much better.

"Look, Flora, I think you need to tell your own story, in your own words. You know, like a scrapbook. We call that a Life Book because it tells the story of your life up until now, as well as your dreams for the future. We could take pictures, too, and put in things that would help people get to know you. Then I could find a few families who seem right for you and we'd show it to them. What do you think?"

Flora almost smiles. "I think that would be ok. Do I get to see their Life Books, too? You know, before I decide if I want to meet them? That would be fair, right?"

Bold!

June laughs. "You certainly should get to see their books and, if they want to meet you, I'm going to insist on it. Have you ever thought of a career in business, Flora? I think you have a knack for negotiating!"

Her serious face returns. "Do you think I could, really? Wouldn't I have to go to college?"

This kid is a constant reminder to engage my filter before speaking.

"Well, I think you could do a lot of things if you had a family to help you." June searches her memory, hitting on something she thinks Flora can relate to. "Remember the Wizard of Oz?"

She nods.

"Glinda the Good Witch said Dorothy and the others had everything they needed inside of them all along. They just had to figure it out for themselves. Who helped Dorothy figure it out, do you remember?"

"Her friends?"

"Yeah, her friends. But weren't they kinda like her family? Real families help each other when times are hard and celebrate together when things are fun and exciting."

June sees she's willing to buy this, for the time being. The good thing about her never having had a 'real' family, at least not a functioning one, is that she doesn't know what to expect. She just knows it would feel nice.

"Spend some time thinking about what should be in your book," June tells her. "Photos, mementos, anything that would be special enough to share with someone who might become your Mom or Dad."

During the next couple of weeks, they work on her book almost daily.

June gets her a cheap digital camera and they drive around, taking pictures of places Flora likes and things that were important to her in the past. Anything they can't get a real shot of, like a childhood pet or a swing set in a backyard, a reasonable facsimile from magazines or old greeting cards will work. June keeps things at her office for just such projects, in a cute wooden treasure chest. She and Quinn found the chest at a junk shop and he was happy to paint it for her, a pale blue with shiny gold hinges and hasp, and vivid purple letters that spell TREASURE –

KEEP OUT!

The chest holds magazines, cards, markers, stickers, and other supplies used to make Life Books. Inside, is a stock of various toys, games, treats, and little take-home gifts, distractions for the sad and troubled kids that find themselves in her company.

It's funny, but I never met a kid of any age who didn't smile at the possibility of taking a secret treasure out of that chest.

"Let's start with the hospital where you were born."

"Yes, the front door to your Grandma's house is a nice touch!"

"Pictures of a horse and a kitten could be cut from a magazine, Flora, if they're things you've always dreamed of having."

"I could try to find pictures of your Mom and Dad for you…"

June doesn't tell her she has, in her files, a mug shot of Dad and an obituary column with a grainy, black and white photo of Mom. She'll get an artistic colleague at the office to help crop and enlarge them so they look passable. She knows Flora won't care how they look she'll be thrilled to have such treasures.

Flora's Story is the title of her Life Book.

There isn't a ton of writing in it, because writing is so hard for her, but the book really tells the tale of this enigmatic young lady. The first page is a photo taken from the parking lot of the hospital where Flora was born, along with a copy of her hospital birth certificate. You know, the kind of certificate with the little footprints. June gazes at the tiny baby feet with slender, elegant toes. She can tell that Flora has a grace about her, grace that has been there from the beginning and just needs someone to help cultivate it.

On the page next to the birth certificate and hospital photo, Flora writes:

This is the place I was born. I think my Mom was happy, but my Dad was never around to see me grow up. My Gramma told me that I didn't eat hardly anything for 3 days after I was born, but then I ate and ate and ate. She said when I got bigger my favorite food was those little jars of peaches.

Under this is a label from a baby food jar, PEACHES. Flora says she took it off of a jar at the Food Mart. She hopes that's ok, since it wasn't like she stole anything. "I left the jar there, I swear, so another mother could see it was peaches inside and buy it for her little baby."

Coughing at the lump in her throat, June reassures her, "That was a nice thing to do, Flora. I wouldn't worry about it."

The evening after that conversation, June can't unwind. She lights a fire and sits by the woodstove, wrapped in a quilt. With brandy for support, she thinks about her own Mom who died when she was nineteen.

I still remember how she used to tell me the story of my birth. I must have asked to hear it a thousand times.

Missing Mom, even still.

"At least I had a mother," she says into the fire. That woman was busy and trapped by the convention of 1950's womanhood, but she tried to give her daughter a normal life. Whatever that was.

I hate being an orphan, even if I didn't become one until I was an adult.

That's always driven her to go the extra mile for kids on her caseload. She knows first-hand that nobody loves being an orphan.

How would I feel about a mother like Flora's, a mother who named me after her favorite drug and killed herself by getting stoned and driving into a tree the year I entered kindergarten?

She already knows the answer.

I'd wish she was still here.

We all want those special memories, like the way our

mom fed us peaches. Even a teenager can make great memories!

June's desperation keeps her from sleep until sunrise. Driving to her office in the watery morning light, she asks the Universe to help her find another Mom for Flora, one that picked her from all the other kids and loves her forever. Like a Hallmark movie.

Man, this job sucks!

13.

Flora hurries around the dayroom, cleaning up the papers and scraps from her biggest project ever, The Life Book. June just left with the finished product, telling her, "This is amazing, Flora! I can't wait to show it around."

Since then, she's had time to think. Now her stomach is fluttering and the voice in her head's shouting at her:

What if I told too much about myself?

What if no one wants to meet me?

What if they laugh at my stupid Life Book?

June'll be back tomorrow with a few folders to look at, profiles of families looking to adopt an older kid. She says it's Flora's job to decide.

I don't really want to do this! Do I?

"Are you done cuddling with your new caseworker yet?" Dee charges into the dayroom. "You two are sure getting cozy."

"She's pretty nice," Flora says, trying to avoid conversation with Dee. Her roommate's gotten more obnoxious since she found out her return-home date. Obviously, she's got mixed feelings about that.

"So, what were you guys making here?" She's shuffling through my magazine cutouts. "Art project?"

"June's trying to find me an adoptive family." That doesn't exactly explain it but it's all she could come up with.

Dee drops onto the couch. "Oh yeah? That's not gonna be easy."

She drops the scraps in the wastebasket and looks hard at her roommate. "What's that supposed to mean?"

"Oh, come on, Flora. Most teenagers can't even get into a foster home, let alone getting adopted. Nobody wants us!"

Tipping her head forward so the hair hides her face, Flora picks up her favorite pen and wonders if Dee's right.

Is this just a way for June to keep me busy until I get shipped off to County?

"Look, no offense, but you aren't exactly adoption material," Dee says. "You were kicked out of your last home, 'got busy' with your foster brother, and then turned him in. How do you think that's gonna look to a nice young couple?"

Fighting tears, Flora grits her teeth. "What a bitch," she says and runs back to her room, muffling a sob with her hand.

"Come on! Don't be a baby," Dee yells.

Flora slams the door to her laughter. The last thing she hears is Dee bragging to the other girls, "I was just being straight with her and she got all weepy. Some people can't handle the truth."

Pushing her face into the pillow, she finally lets it out.

I hate her!
I hate this place!
I hate June!
I hate Brendan!
I hate the Jacobies!
Why is this happening to me?

There's a shuffling noise outside the door, like someone's listening. Flora jumps up, ready to fight, and yanks the door open. That skinny dark-haired girl from the second floor falls backward on her ass, wide eyed and breathless.

"I was just..." She holds out her hand and pushes a

card at Flora. There's a picture of a kitten clinging to a rope. Inside, it says *Hang in there!*

"I'm…what? Is this for me?"

Still on the floor, the girl says, "I wanted you to know it's gonna be ok.

Flora reaches a hand down and pulls the girl to her feet. "Why do you care?"

Her eyes dart around like she's afraid and she practically whispers, "Dee gets mean sometimes. She's so jealous you have a caseworker that does stuff for you."

"Why? Where's her caseworker anyway?" Flora reaches out her hand and helps the girl to her feet.

The girl moves close and speaks low. "That's the thing. Her caseworker's never even been here. She only calls and tells Dee about court and stuff. It's like nobody really cares about her. Her mom is totally messed up. Heroin."

"Oh wow, that's bad," Flora says. "But why is she so mad at me?"

The girl gives her a look like she's beyond stupid. "Come on, you have June! She always tears it up for her kids. When she's assigned to one of us, we see her almost every day. She works the staff so they take care of you, treat you right, that kinda thing. She calls her girls all the time, making sure they know she's on the job for them. That lady's gonna get you a home, you wait and see! Dee just keeps going back, to her mom and all that mess."

She doesn't know how to answer that. "Hey, sorry I scared you. I'm Flora."

The girl smiles. "I'm Gina."

"So, how do you know all this, Gina?"

"June was caseworker for another girl from here. We all know about her. She's like a fairy godmother or something, totally kicks ass. Even the staff adores her. You're lucky."

Flora wonders if Gina's a little jealous too. "But don't you have a caseworker?"

The girl shrugs her knobby shoulders. "Yeah, I got

Alexis. She's ok, I guess. She's nice enough, but that doesn't help when your time runs out, you know?"

"Time runs out?"

She looks around, like she's scared again. "You know you can't stay here, right? Pretty soon we all get sent to County unless they find us a home. I'm going there soon unless a miracle happens. Foster parents are scared of a girl who cuts."

Cuts. Flora steals a quick look but can't see any evidence of wounds on her. It'd be hard to, since she's pretty much covered neck to feet. That should have been a clue.

"They aren't where you can see 'em," she says. "But my last family freaked out when one of their real kids saw me doing it. I guess they thought I'd rub off on her or something."

"How old are you, Gina?"

"Sixteen," she says. "Too old to get adopted, too young to leave me alone."

They talk some more. All the other girls know DCW basically stops looking for a permanent home when you hit sixteen. It takes months and months to get an adoption finalized and most parents want younger kids anyway. At sixteen, they figure you've missed your chance for a new family.

Gina says that's when they teach you how to live on your own instead. Prep you for the real world. They enroll you in a class called Life Skills, to learn about paying rent and budgeting and stuff.

"I only know two girls who went on to Independent Living," Gina says. "They gave 'em apartments of their own, helped 'em get jobs, the works. It sounded so cool, you know? At least it did at first. One girl OD'ed about two weeks after she moved in, and the other girl is on welfare with a new baby and no man. She's so pissed off and depressed, no one can stand being around her. It's scary, girl."

They both get quiet after that. Independent Living does sound cool. Flora's pretty sure she could handle it better than those girls, but she's starting to worry about Gina.

Can a girl cut herself to death?

14.

June's work on locating an adoptive home for Flora has been progressing slowly. She hears Sarge's voice in her head, "Tick-tock, Hunter; tick-tock!"

When June first met her boss years ago, she thought: *Drill Sergeant.* His manner of speaking is authoritative and abrupt. He's built like a fireplug, stocky and on the short side.

She had shaken his hand and said, "It'll be great working with you, Sarge." He never flinched, acted like he didn't notice. Some people kinda like nicknames. He must be one of them.

Outside of his generally curt demeanor, he's a guy who has your back. Trustworthy. Dedicated. Tough. Like a poster for the Marines, with a heart for protecting kids.

He clearly respects her too, because he always asks if she'll take the tough cases, the ones he can't risk giving to a slacker. She's never refused him, never could.

Secretly, she's thrilled at his trust in her. Plus, she gets first crack at the really challenging cases. Win-win.

Sarge turns the corner and heads toward her desk. He looks kinda rumpled for so early in the day: a not-so-white dress shirt, no tie, shirt sleeves rolled up onto his forearms.

Sarge and me. What a team! I can't believe we've worked together for twelve years already. It always feels fresh and new.

"What the hell are you doing to me, Hunter?"

"What's up, Sarge?"

He oozes tar and nicotine. Breathing deeply, June sucks in the fragrance with a combination of greed and remorse. He must have come directly from the smoker's alcove, her old hang-out.

The State cheerfully provides a not-so-cozy place for the overwhelming number of smokers on the payroll. Ironically, they also doubled the employee cost of medical insurance for active smokers. Fortunately, June quit ten years ago but still misses it on days like today.

Lately, she thinks, these kinds of days are becoming more frequent.

"Uh…" Sarge looks around for a place to perch. Aggravation radiates off of him. June jumps to clear a stack of files off the chair facing her desk and waves at him to sit. He drops down hard. Folding his hands together on top of his head, elbows pointing out to the sides like triangular wings, he stares at a point above her head.

"You're killing me. You know that, right?"

She tries to guess what's bugging him. "Are we talking about Flora? Because, if we are, I'm making headway in the 'find her a family' department."

Sarge rolls his eyes upward and reports, "The Chairman of the Board for that shelter, Dr. Grossman, just called and chewed my ass about you."

The reference to the Crossette Shelter causes her to flinch.

"He says you're taking advantage of his staff, manipulating them to feel sorry for that kid so they'll keep her longer."

Obviously. That's the way things get done around here.

Sarge and Grossman both know that. June was rather proud of her efforts too, until now. Now she feels guilty. Sort of.

"Sarge, you know that ninety days is not long enough to find a decent family for this kid. She's almost sixteen, for God's sake, and she's been vilified in the foster community as some sort of Jezebel. Gimme a break!"

Again with the growling. "Your concern is truly enchanting, but it ain't gonna fly with me. Here's how it works, Hunter: the Shelter has a contract with the State for 'temporary placements'. 'Temporary' means 'no more than ninety days.' After that, if you can't find a placement, the kid gets sent to County."

County my ass!

The County Residential Home is a sort of juvenile prison except the guards are called Residence Workers and the kids get to go outside once in a while. The place is a nightmare, a real disgrace to the system, and DCW has tons of kids in there. She cannot bear to put a kid in County, but her options are limited.

"The workers over there love this kid, and they want to blame me for jerking 'em around?" June expected this discussion but thought she had more time before the suits started screaming. "I'm knocking myself out to find the right home for her, Sarge. I just don't want them sending her up the river before I can get the job done. You know I'm no slacker!"

Success in circumventing the ninety-day rule, getting Crossette to keep her kids a bit longer, is a skill carefully tended. Over the years, she's cultivated friends at the Shelter who work with her. In return, there's the occasional favor like getting a job resume to the right person, writing a letter to the Judge when someone wants court action, or assisting with a personal problem. Normally, everybody looks the other way when she's bargaining for time. It isn't a great system, but it's worked so far.

Sarge takes a great big breath, blows it out. "I know you usually work that system without a lot of hoopla, Hunter, but you must have pissed somebody off. Who are you working with over there?"

They go on like that for a while longer, but Sarge is distracted and they don't accomplish much. Finally, he grabs the cig from behind his ear and heads for the stairwell. "You have a deadline, Hunter. I can't help you on this one."

Only a couple of months to find Flora a family... I feel like I'm on The Bachelorette, but the potential bridegrooms are all made of smoke.

Hitting the copy center the minute Flora's Story was completed, June was able to send the book out to a number of waiting families. One couple in particular looks very positive, Michael and Rosemary West. They had taken some temporary placements in the beginning. A few years ago, they were all set to adopt a beautiful, but terminally ill, little girl. They fostered her for almost two years and doctors figured the kid had eight to ten years more on this earth. With decent care, she would have a good, albeit short, life. Sadly, right before the adoption hearing, the kid developed pneumonia and died. She was four years old.

Horrible. The West's took themselves off the adoption rosters then, not because they blamed anybody, but because they wanted to grieve and show respect for the child who had given them so much in her short time on Earth.

The grapevine says they're thinking about adopting again, looking for a child who needs them. They could be a good match, so June sets up a preliminary meeting.

She and Rosemary meet at the coffeehouse near the office, so June can feel her out about being ready to try again. They drink some excellent coffee, chat a little, and she hands over a copy of Flora's Story.

"Food for thought," she says.

The next day, there's a message on the office voicemail: "June Hunter, this is Rosemary West. I want you to come by as soon as possible. I have something for you to give to Flora."

Thirty miles out of town is the dusty gravel lane leading to the eclectic home of the West family. They live in the country on fifteen acres with horses, goats, dogs, and various other creatures. A glow-in-the-dark peacock squawks at her in the driveway, dragging his feathers on the ground before her feet.

June peeks through the screen door. A big, furry face

51

peers back.

"Hi there, big fella!" She coos at the giant dog who woofs back at her, wagging his tail.

"June? Come on in!" Rosemary runs down a flight of stairs to greet her, a large wooden box in her hands. "Thanks for coming so quickly."

She sets the box on the kitchen counter and throws her arms around the caseworker.

Rosemary is a hugger.

June comes from the school of 'don't touch me and I won't touch you' but, in Rosemary's case, she makes an exception. It's like kissing the Pope's ring. How do you get out of it without looking like a world-class jerk?

Rosemary releases her with a big dramatic sigh. "Oh, that Flora. She had me at the peaches, June!" She clasps her hands over her heart and rolls her eyes to heaven.

"I know what you mean." Getting a kick out of her dramatics, June rolls her eyes in return and says, "She has the same effect on me."

"I want to talk honestly with you, though," Rosemary says, more serious now.

Pulling out a stool for her at the counter, she sets June up with coffee and a brownie. "I think this child deserves better than a typical adoption."

Oh, shit. Here we go, letting me down easy.

"What do you mean, Rose?" she asks, heart sputtering with dread.

Rosemary sits carefully, folding her hands on the counter as if to pray. "We think Flora is too old to be 'placed'. She needs to choose her own family. You know, like a marriage. It needs to be mutual, not forced or out of her control. She isn't a little kid who can't make that kind of decision, June. She's almost grown, for heaven's sake."

June's heart resumes beating, but jumpy-like, in tentative excitement. She tells Rosemary, "I want you to know, this girl may take some getting used to. She's got attachment issues like I said. She can be distant at first, or even seem spacey."

Rose waves her hand in dismissal and continues on as if June had not even spoken. "That's my point! She has to decide for herself. Michael and I put together a book about us and a video to go with it, sort of a guided tour of our life. We want Flora to see all of it and talk about it with you. If she's still interested in us after that, we would like her to come out for the day, say this Saturday?"

June toys with the brownie for a moment and then takes a big bite.

Chocolate helps me think.

"Wow. Well, sure, Rose, I can get this stuff to her tonight, or tomorrow at the latest." Trying not to jump up and down with excitement, June reminds her, "But you know she has precious little time. Only a couple of months at Crossette, and then she gets dumped at County."

She stops talking for a moment because her mouth is full of something too glorious to ignore.

"My God, Rose, this is the best brownie I have ever eaten!"

Rosemary takes a deep breath as she ponders this information about Flora, all the while wrapping a couple of brownies in a cloth napkin. She hands them over with a smile. "Here, take these for the road. I guess Flora has some work to do. You too, June."

They both nod their heads in a solemn agreement and sip their coffee.

Michael and Rosemary are brilliant, really caring, and a bit on the crazy side, the kind of parents that might successfully raise this unconventional kid. Plus, they would be *so fun* to work with. It might be hard to get a Judge to be impressed, though: their place tends to be messy due to the constant flow of baby animals and gifts from the garden; their schedule is really wild, packed with traveling, interesting guests, and wonderful activities; and they have a reputation for always trying to bend the rules, in the best interest of the child of course.

High on hope as June drives down their lane, her initial enthusiasm starts to wane on the trip back to reality. She thinks, *it doesn't really matter that I like this family or think they'd make a good home for Flora.* Rosemary and Michael want the consent of a messed-up teenager before they'll agree to placement.

Navigating the curving county roads, June breaks off pieces of brownie and chews. In between bites, she wonders, "What will Flora think?"

15.

Irene, the House Parent, gestures for Flora to follow her from the dayroom doorway. "Right now, please," she says sharply.

The girl reaches down between her feet and grabs her backpack, inching her way out of her chair without disturbing her schoolwork or Mrs. Dewey.

Getting up from in-house class isn't usually acceptable but Flora can tell something is going on and figures it can't be good. She sees a couple of the workers in the hall, whispering frantically to one another.

What did I do?

Irene looks really mad. Her eyes are all squinty and her shoulders are hunched up practically to her ears.

Is she gonna bounce me out of here?

She stops in front of the closed door to her office and brings her face closer to Flora's, close enough to see beads of sweat on the woman's nose.

In a low and raspy voice, she says, "Flora. I won't leave you alone with them. I promise. Don't say anything until the GAL gets here."

Irene then explains that a GAL, or Guardian Ad Litem, is her legal advocate for court.

That court guy? Oh, crap, this is serious!

The door to Irene's little office opens and it looks like a

clown car, with all the people squeezed inside: two guys in suits that take up a lot of room; one giant cop in uniform; and a lady who looks like the witch in Hansel and Gretel. They all stand and look at the two standing in the doorway. No one says anything. A very heavy moment.

"Ahem, you must be Flora." Witch Lady has a mean sort of voice, even though she's trying to be nice. Her eyes are twitchy too.

Irene steps in front of Flora and puts her hand out. "I spoke to you on the phone, I believe. I'm Irene, the House Parent here at Crossette."

Then everyone is nodding, saying their names, and shaking hands. Not a lot of smiling.

One of the Suit Guys says, "Young lady, we need to speak to you about something important. Please sit down." He points to a chair.

When Flora sits down, they all gather around her except Big Cop. He backs up and posts himself next to the closed door.

Does he think I'm gonna run?

The Suit Guy clears his throat and leans forward, his elbows on his knees and his hands clasped. With a voice deep and serious, he says, "Like I said, Flora, this is serious business. Did you speak with the school nurse about Brendan?"

She looks at Irene, not knowing what to say, and shrugs her shoulders. Irene winks.

"Ok, so here's the thing, the Other Suit Guy says. "Brendan has filed charges against you for making a false report against him. We are here to officially charge you..."

They're here to arrest me?

Flora jumps up out of the chair, her eyes wide and darting. Her heart pounds in her chest and she's shivering like it's the dead of winter.

"What?! No, wait. I...I can't breathe," she gasps.

Everyone else jumps up too and starts talking at once. No one is even looking at her.

All Flora can hear are angry voices. The color starts to drain out of the room and everything turns gray. Then white.

Then it all goes dark.

16.

Sarge is waiting for June when she gets back to the office, red-faced and scowling. "Pardon me, Hunter, I hate to interfere with your important social engagements, but where the hell have you been? You didn't answer my texts."

Oh, good: sarcasm. That points to a new adventure in dialog ahead.

"Sorry, Sarge, but Rosemary West wanted me to pick up some stuff for Flora: you know, their life story book, a video of their farm, stuff like that." He shoots her a serious glare.

Fishing for a positive response, she asks, "Umm… that's progress, don't you think?"

Sarge's response is not good. Without a word, he walks ahead of her into his office and stands by the door with his hand on the knob.

"Uh, oh! What did I do this time?" June kids around, trying to make light but no response. It's a losing battle and she can feel the wind leaving her sails. While shuffling after him, she reviews all the dicey things she's done lately that could be catching up to her at this very moment. Nothing comes to mind that would warrant the look on Sarge's face.

I don't want to sit down, she thinks. Like maybe if I don't sit, he won't talk.

She sits anyway.

So does he.

June finds herself babbling.

"Look Sarge, I'm sorry to be gone so long but the West

place is over forty-five minutes away in traffic. I didn't want 'em to wait and maybe change their minds or anything, you know how it is. I should have told the Front Desk where I went, I just… I forgot again. I should have called when I saw your texts but you know I don't use my phone when I'm driving. I was hurrying back anyway so I knew I'd see you soon. I won't…I'm…I can…"

Faced with a heavy silence, she trails off. She tries to read Sarge's expression.

What is that, concern?

"It seems your Flora is in a bit of trouble."

Sarge turns away to look out the window, gazing at the wall of the old factory building across the street like it was a view of the Rockies.

She croaks, "What happened?"

"Flora's been formally charged with a crime, June. The Jacobie family is pressing charges, claiming she filed a false police report against Brendan."

Crap!

"This is ridiculous! She didn't file the complaint, the school nurse did, and the PD dropped the case. No witnesses, one of those 'he said—she said' cases, no physical evidence since it was only touching. Damn it! What do they think they're doing?"

Still looking out the window, he says, "Well, the Jacobie kid is trying to get accepted into a high-rev university. Evidently, this is a speed bump in his road to fame and fortune. Mumsy and Daddy are trying to get his name cleared by making Flora the villain. A little bit of 'tit-for-tat,' you know."

She scowls at the pun but sees it was unintended. When she speaks, her voice is louder than she means it to be, and almost babbling.

"They can't really claim Defamation of Character or anything. I mean, she's a minor…at her age, how can they even demonstrate Intent to Harm? Emotionally, she's barely a teenager and any credible counselor can testify to that."

In spite of what she's spewing, June knows the truth: a teenager can certainly be held responsible for her actions by the court. Faking sexual abuse is serious business. Her ranting is not entirely for Sarge's benefit; it's in preparation for an imaginary judge and jury.

Sarge slumps into the chair and scrubs his face with his hands. He's used to her thinking aloud and uses his commanding voice to stop her.

"I called Hal! We need to be in the Guardian Ad Litem's office to see him in twenty minutes."

He stands up with a grunt.

"Grab your coat and fix your face, Your Highness. Erase that defiant expression. I want you reasonable and logical…it instills trust, you know."

He stomps out, pulling the ever-present cigarette from behind his ear and clamping it between his teeth. Sarge looks old today, worn out. She wonders if he's thinking the same thing about her.

The Guardian Ad Litem, Hal Franklin, is a pretty nice guy but not what you'd call a real powerhouse. June knows he likes things neat and wrapped up, not messy the way most of these cases are. If you talk softly, calm and reasonable, get him on your side with logic, he's likely to support you.

The walk with Sarge has left June quiet, prepping to see Hal and fight the good fight.

Hal greets them with a shout, "Hey, Junie! I haven't seen you in court the past few weeks. You aren't retiring yet, are you?"

Hal smiles, but the joke falls flat. She sees he's taking these charges seriously.

"I will if you will, Hal!" June forces her grin, trying to connect on a 'we're in this together' level. In a way, he's Flora's only hope.

Hal and June go all the way back to the days when they first started in this business. He was a Public Defender then, right out of law school. June was, well, mostly like she is now, only nicer. Their relationship is a bit like sibling rivalry because the Child Welfare business is so like a family. As with any brother and sister, their interactions can go either way.

Now that he's a GAL, June can get frustrated by Hal's authority over her cases. Occasionally June gets rank with him, pushing a few too many personal buttons, and he gets his feelings hurt. Sarge's motivation is to keep the meeting productive, no kid stuff to muck things up.

June sees Sarge is more invested in the life of this kid than he lets on, demonstrating some paternal feelings for their little Flora.

"OK, you kids, no talk of retirement just yet. I need you both." Sarge takes over the meeting smoothly. "What's the bottom line with these folks, Hal?"

"Bottom line? The Jacobies are really pissed off. Seems the boy's application to Uppity-up University is being delayed. The academics have concerns about him being a potential predator on campus, what with that stuff all over the news these days. I don't know how they found out, since we never even took the case. The school counselor might have been a little wishy-washy in his recommendation, or another kid's parents could have ratted him out, in the hopes that their little darling might take his place. Acceptance to the Ivy League is pretty cut-throat. The family wants the kid's reputation back, something we can't give him."

"OK, so they want retaliation," Sarge says. "How do we calm this thing down?"

June knows one thing for sure: if the Jacobie family is pressing charges, they'll spend a fortune on a great lawyer. Summation will go something like this:

"Wonderful family, those Jacobies! They are well-respected in the community and loving enough to give this poor unfortunate girl a home, an opportunity to live a very comfortable life. And how does she pay them back after their years of kindness? By trying to ruin

their reputation and hurt everyone who has helped her! No conscience, no gratitude. Punish the selfish little monster, that'll teach her to mess with such caring, giving folks!"

"We really don't have anything to give them, Sol," Hal says, calling Sarge by his real name. "Unless you want to write a letter to the University, clearing the kid?"

Sarge shoots June a look, knowing she might explode. She knows they'd be secretly selling out Flora to secure her safe passage into adulthood.

"What do I say in a letter like this, Hal? I can't lie."

"Let me talk to the Jacobie's lawyer, see what will satisfy them."

Hal stands up. "They'll be coming in to see me in about half an hour. I'll call as soon as they leave. Still be in your office around four thirty?"

"You bet, Hal, thanks. What happens to Flora in the meantime?"

"Seeing as how she's a minor already in the custody of the State, she stays put." Hal grins. "These people thought they could punish her by humiliation … you know, fingerprinting, mug shot, the whole works just like on TV. I didn't tell them we don't do that shit to kids who are already victims. Let 'em think they got even, eh?"

June prays silently, to any gods that will listen, "Let this case get resolved outside the court room, preferably without Flora. Please?"

Then, out loud, she says, "Thanks, Hal, you're a jewel."

He is sweet, but we all know the minefield ahead.

"Don't thank me yet, Junie," he calls to us down the hallway. "Hey, Sol, if I pull this off, you guys owe me!"

Sarge and June move quickly, wanting to get out of the State's Attorney's Office without running into the Jacobie family. No use throwing gas on the fire or doing anything that would allow them to claim they were impeding justice.

They walk the three blocks back to DCW and June stops in the parking lot.

"Sarge, I'm going over to see Flora, if that's ok. I have all this stuff from Rosemary West to preview with her. I want to give her the chance to think it over tonight."

"Hunter, don't discuss this legal shit with the kid. You can tell her sometimes the family files charges back at the victim, and this is just part of the investigation. Let's not make any more out of it for now. Got it?"

She nods in agreement. It's easy to see Sarge doesn't like this situation. It stinks of politics.

"Call me when you get word from Hal, will ya?"

Sarge gives a half-assed salute and turns away, dismissing her.

Jumping into her car, June takes off. She notices Sarge in her mirror. He doesn't have that worn-out walk now, more serious and determined. She feels a rush of gratitude for the man.

"He's one of the good ones," she tells herself.

In her not-so-younger days, June would be fuming by now, waxing loud and furious at the thought of compromise. Tending to respond with passion, screaming bloody murder if she thinks something unethical is going on, she breathes evenly and deliberately. Wisdom comes with age and she's learning to temper that fury.

Sarge and Hal have both been instrumental in June's education regarding social justice and reality. Engaging in long, angry discussions about fairness and ethics, they have been patient and listened to her arguments. But, in the end, it all comes down to the three big questions:

1. *Which solution gives your client the best opportunity for success or happiness?*
2. *Would you rather be 'right' and lose the case, or 'work it' a little and win?*
3. *What allows you to sleep at night?*

17.

Standing in the doorway, Flora watches June pull up to the curb. She wanted to explain in person about what happened with the charges and all.

"They have everything," Flora cried, "Why would the Jacobies be so mean?"

"It's like a game," June explained. "And I'm really good at playing. Don't worry about any of it, Flora. That's my job."

Sure, like I'd just leave it to you.

Later, she figures, she can see what Gina knows about this stuff. Maybe even ask Irene. She was pretty protective in that meeting. She could go thank her later and see what happens.

June said she was bringing her something from that family she liked, Rosemary and Michael West. Watching her grab stuff from the car doesn't give her enough information to decide if she's excited, bummed, optimistic, pissed off, or whatever.

Hmmm. She's carrying a box.

Flora remembers that girl, Pandora, she read about in class last week. Her box contained all the evils of the world. Maybe this box is full of crap.

Flora smiles and gives a little wave.

"Hi, June."

She smiles back but looks strange, nervous or worried or something.

Not good.

Together, they head to the Shelter's sun room, a little area off the kitchen. June sets her stuff on the coffee table and says, "Oh good you have a TV in here. They made you a video."

Holding her hands on either side of the box, Flora takes a deep breath. The lid has delicate carving on it, a tree with lacy branches. Pretty. The hinges are gold and the latch on the front has a blue glass bead for a handle.

"Here goes."

Once she lifts the lid, the contents swim in front of her eyes. Can't focus.

Choosing a family was my own idea but I'm kinda freaked out about it now.

"What should we do first?"

"Look ... a note," June says, "Let's start here."

She gets things rolling by handing Flora the folded letter off the top. It is addressed to her.

Skimming through it fast, trying not to cry, she finds her hands are shaking. The first part is written in pretty cursive, Rosemary's handwriting. There's a short second part written in block letters, Michael's introduction. She shakes her head and hands it to June, who reads it out loud:

Dear Flora,

Thank you for sharing your story with us. It was very interesting, and really quite moving. I feel like I know you just a little bit already.

I put this box together for you, Flora. Take your time, look it over, see if we might be the Special Someones you could call "family" someday. If you'd like to get to know us more, we are ready and hopeful.

If you do decide to meet, Michael and I would appreciate it if you would write down any questions, ideas, or thoughts that come to you, so we have a place to start at our visit. I hope you don't mind, but when something is as important as deciding who will be your family, I believe taking notes helps.

I look forward to meeting you (actually, I can hardly wait!),
Rosemary West

Dear Flora,

Your story has inspired me and I have made a decision: this year, I am raising peaches on our farm. I don't know how well the trees grow in this climate, but I am the kind of person who believes that home is where you make it.

Maybe the peach tree won't care that this is not where she started out, as long as she is well cared for, and happy, and loved. What do you think?

I hope you choose to meet with us, Flora. You seem like the kind of person who could be happy as a member of our family. Rosemary and I are not afraid to try new things, even if they seem difficult at first. We usually have a lot of fun!

Soon,

Michael West

Rosemary's letter makes Flora's shaking even worse, talking about choosing her own family. She sounds kinda like June. But Michael's letter makes her fight to keep from crying. She swallows hard.

He planted peaches! For me!

June sets the letter on the table. "Well, what do you think? Should we check out the book they made or watch the video next?"

Can't make my mouth work. I feel June's eyes on me.

"Are you ok, kiddo?"

"Yeah." She tries to answer like nothing's up, but it comes out all squeaky. "This is scary."

"What's scary?"

She can't look at June, afraid she'll chicken out. Staring out the window, she says, "When I went to the Jacobie's to live, it was ok, no big thing. I never thought of staying there forever, I just got used to them after a while. This is different. It's a really big deal! What if I screw this up, too?"

"Hold on, Flora. How do you think you screwed up?"

Flora starts to lose it, her voice shaking and tears threatening to fall.

"Brendan is so mad at me. He told me not to tell anyone or he would make me sorry! Now everything is messed up. The detective asked me more about it today, acting like I lied. I wish I never said anything; then I wouldn't have to find a new place to live!"

When June puts her arm around her shoulders, something breaks apart inside.

Now I'm crying like a freakin' baby! I hate this!

June's voice is gentle. "I can't make it go away. I can't even promise things will get better. All I can do is promise to be here for you. We'll do this together, Flora."

"What did I do?" she whispers into June's shoulder. "I should have kept it a secret."

June's reaction startles her. She grabs Flora's shoulders, eyes sparking with anger, and speaks slowly and evenly to the girl.

"Let's get something straight right now: you did the right thing. Nobody should ever touch you without your consent."

She leans back a little and grabs Flora's hands in hers.

"Life changes constantly. You can't stop it. Sometimes it's good and sometimes not, but change keeps coming. Part of growing up is learning how to handle change, even preparing for it. We can do this. YOU can do this!"

Her crying slows to sniffles and gulps. "But if I didn't tell, maybe they would have kept me."

June jumps up and paces back and forth, like a tiger at the zoo. She's pissed.

"The truth is, you weren't going to stay with the Jacobie family much longer anyway. They were *not* going to adopt you, Flora, you know that. This just moved things along a little faster, that's all."

She had heard all the speeches in health class: you control your body and if someone touches you in a way you don't want, it's your job to stop them. People will try to take your power away, but you have to stand up for yourself.

They never talk about what happens *after* you take your stand.

June says, "Let me ask you: if your best friend came to you and told you someone was touching her or threatening her, what would you say?"

Flora doesn't have any friends but she knows the answer June wants to hear.

"I would tell her to get away and tell someone."

"Right! Every time you aren't sure about the right way to go, ask yourself what you would tell your best friend."

Flora surprises herself then, by speaking up.

"Honestly, June? Here's what I would say, 'Brendan is mean and selfish, and doesn't like you. He's getting meaner, too, because he's leaving soon. He will *never* get caught once he's gone. No one will believe you then!' That's what I would say."

The second it's out she's breathless, horrified at revealing such strong emotions.

June only smiles. "You got it, kid! That's how it's done."

Then they both laugh a little. Flora feels better, sort of.

"Now, what?" June looks into the box, like nothing happened. "Do we talk some more or do you want to watch a video?"

"Video!"

The tension is gone. Flora rustles around the contents of the box, pulling out the disc marked "The Royal Kingdom of West."

These people are so funny and interesting. First there's music that's jazzy and upbeat, with a close-up of a peacock fanning his feathers, all shimmering blue and green. Then the camera pans out to two pair of feet, one in work boots the other in cowgirl boots. As the camera moves back and up, we see their clothes: sort of bohemian chic, funny dress-up clothes. Rosemary wears a flowery dress, striped cardigan, and big hat with giant silk roses on it. Michael has on bib overalls, a worn-out tuxedo jacket with tails, and a beat-up fedora.

They're both grinning and shout at the camera, "Welcome to Peacock Palace, Flora, where everyone is treated like royalty!"

The royalty theme is so crazy, with stuff like a tour of the castle, the royal stable, and the imperial property. The butler makes Flora laugh: a big, messy sheepdog they call Jeeves that carries in the newspaper and shakes mud all over. She loves the close-up of Rosemary's face when she sees the mess and yells, "Noooooooooooooooooo!"

Hilarious!

In the last scene, Rosemary and Michael sit on a picnic table, holding hands. Michael speaks directly into the camera, "We know real life is not always so much fun, Flora. Lots of bad stuff happens. We think the best way to get through those bad times is to have as many good times as we can. We have to store them up, like in a treasure chest, and hold them close when times get tough. Sometimes the only comfort is in knowing that somebody else cares about you and will stand by you until those bad things pass. They always pass, by the way. They float away and make room for more laughter and fun. In our family, we like to go for the gusto whenever we can. Maybe you could join us."

Michael and Rosemary wave and laugh. "Hope to see you soon!"

They walk off down the lane as the camera fades back.

Amazing!

"They *are* pretty cool, June."

Hard to believe anybody could be so fun. Digging into the box again, Flora feels like a little kid, excited to see what else they sent her.

18.

At home, in her sweats in front of the woodstove, June drinks herbal tea that claims to encourage relaxation, maybe even sleep. Clearly, the stuff isn't working. She's so jazzed up, she's vibrating.

Leaving a grinning Flora with the box was easy.

Waiting to hear from her is not. The West's clearly know what they're doing with the letters, the video, and all the rest of their stuff. Total mind game. What Michael said about the peach trees…even June almost cried. She can only hope they're using their powers for good, not evil. After reviewing that shit, *anyone* would want to go live with them!

She remembers Flora's outburst about Brendan being mean, his warning her not to tell. Her sobbing. Wishing she never told.

Damn!

All kids think it's their fault when a placement falls apart, but this case is worse than most. Those foster parents want her to take the blame *legally*.

A glance at her watch says it's 5:23. *How could I forget about Sarge and Hal? Why hasn't Sarge called?*

Not a good sign. Calling for an update is out of the question. No one calls Sarge unless they're on fire. He'll call if he has any news. She trusts him. She guesses the Jacobie's are "sleeping on it" and they'll answer when they're good and ready. *Control freaks.*

A big, rugged man stamps his feet at the door and tears off his coat.

"Warm enough in here, Junie?"

Quinn.

Her heart jumps a little at the sound of his voice. June finds it amazing that he thinks she's so terrific but, if that's his biggest flaw, she'll take it.

"C'mon, dude! You know this cold and damp weather bugs me. I need a fire."

"Maybe I can help," he says, wrapping her up in his arms and squeezing 'til she laughs and gasps. He smells of wind and pine.

"Help! I'm warm, I'm warm!"

He plunks her back in the chair and heads for the fridge. When he returns, he's eating a piece of cold pizza.

"I checked, and you have enough wood to get you

through until next week." Quinn talks around a mouthful of pizza like it isn't even there. "I let Tully out when I came in, and he took off after something, maybe a raccoon. In about ten minutes, remind me to whistle for him."

June smiles and sips tea, waiting for him to see through her. He doesn't disappoint.

"What's going on, Junie?"

"Whatever do you mean, sir?"

"Seriously? I can tell how bad it is by how hot you make your fire."

Quinn smiles that I-know-you smile and June begins: "Well, things started out great when I got a call from this couple about Flora ..."

The big guy settles in while she brings him up to date on the case.

If she's lucky, she thinks, talking it out with Quinn might even let her sleep tonight.

19.

"Flora, I'm really sorry they did you like that." Over breakfast, Irene talks about yesterday's episode with the police. "At least they didn't take you into the station."

"They could do that?" she asks. "Has it ever happened to any of the other girls?"

Irene tells her about this girl and that girl getting brought into the station and locked up for stealing or assault, but nothing helpful. She ends with, "I don't know these Jacobie people, but I can tell you this: rich people have all the power in this world. Try not to piss 'em off."

Great. Maybe Gina will know more.

Later that afternoon, Gina stops in Flora's room and she asks about jail.

"I did know a 14-year-old girl who lied about her foster dad, told everybody he made her touch his nasty parts,"

Gina says. "She hated the guy for some reason, I don't know why. They found out she made it all up and put her in juvey until she's 21."

Geez, seven years. "No kidding? How'd they find out?"

"They asked her questions about what she saw, like birthmarks and stuff. I guess the guy had a really big tattoo down there and she didn't know anything about it. She described him as all pale and hairy. Stupid."

"That's just gross." And it doesn't help at all.

"I know, right?" Gina checks over her shoulder and lowers her voice. "I heard Dee talking yesterday, after the detectives left. She was listening to them talk outside when they were coming home from school. They said this guy Hal is really going to bat for you, making sure you don't get a raw deal. Who's Hal anyway?"

Flora searches her brain but doesn't remember a Hal. "I have no idea! What else did she say?"

Gina shakes her head. "I didn't hear anything else about it, other than Dee's smartass comments about you having big-time friends in high places."

Crap! What friends?

"What does she mean by that? I don't know anyone important, other than the Jacobie's. And they sure aren't my friends anymore."

Gina jumps up and says, "I don't know either. Hey, something smells good! Let's go find out what it is."

What the hell, Flora thinks. What's with the change of subject?

"Hey, Dee," Gina says, real friendly-like. "Who's cooking dinner tonight?" Dee walks in and she gets it – Gina was protecting her privacy.

Dee walks past Gina and shoves her with her shoulder. "I don't know and I don't care. Go find out for yourself."

Gina crosses herself behind Dee's back and hustles out of the room.

Dee drops down on her bed. "So, Flora, are you going to jail or what?"

"What? No, I mean I don't know. I didn't do anything wrong, so..."

She doesn't wait for her to finish. "Your new bestie, June, must be telling you something. Sounds like your brother-boyfriend doesn't like that you ratted him out, huh?"

A million nasty answers run through her mind, but Flora doesn't want to piss her off. She gives Dee a confused look and says, "I...I guess not."

The other girl glares at her for an eternity, like she's trying to decide how to play this. Finally, she stands up and heads for the door.

"It's meatloaf tonight," she says. "Let's go eat."

20

Thanks to Quinn and his late-night listening skills, June woke up rested this morning. Her recent dabbling in meditation and breathing techniques seems to help with concentration. Now at her desk, focused, she plows through a ton of paperwork.

Ahh! Progress is good.

But two cups of coffee, a candy bar, and a couple of hours of work later, she's losing her Zen. Sarge isn't in his office and no one seems to know where he is.

What the hell is going on?

"The SA is on line three for you, June," a gravelly voice stops me mid-anxiety attack.

"Thanks, Dora, you're a jewel."

She punches the speaker button. "Hal?"

"Yep, it's me, Junie. How are you this morning?"

"Rested for a change." *I am calm, I am casual, I am Zen.* "Life is good. So, how did things go with my best friends, the Jacobies?"

Hal pauses too long and my Zen flies out the window. "Can you come over, June? Sol is here and we want you in on this."

Shit!

"On my way." Already standing, she slips her arm in a coat sleeve, "Do I need to bring anything?"

"Just your brilliant mind and a couple of glazed donuts for your favorite colleagues," and he hangs up on her. *Cute.*

Heading out the door, she calls to Dora, "I've been summoned! See you later."

Five bucks at the diner gets June a whole variety box of donuts. She figures they might be there awhile so why not be sociable? Quinn's always reminding her to do the social stuff, be the better person. As charming and handsome as he is, he probably never needs to bring anybody donuts. But Quinn sees each act of kindness and respect as an investment in any future relationship. June knows he's right. Still, she wonders, when will these donuts finally pay off?

Entering the State's Attorney's Office is always daunting. Lawyers dressed in expensive suits bustle about with an air of great importance. She struggles to act like she belongs.

"DCW," she says to the security guard, handing over her ID. The briefcase, purse, and box of donuts roll through x-ray. "Fresh donut?"

"Not allowed." He hands back her ID and winks. "You could be bribing me." June places a donut next to his monitor and walks.

The Juvenile State's Attorney depends heavily on a caseworker's documentation. Hal always reminds June that her investigative reports are pivotal to winning his cases. She likes being needed and respected. She doesn't like that anxious feeling in the pit of her stomach, so she hurries to Hal's office.

"Finally...food!" Hal grabs the box out of her hands like a hungry toddler.

"My pleasure, you're welcome," she snips at him and turns to greet her boss. He looks like a train wreck.

"When was your last smoke, Sarge?"

"Seems like a year. Come with me for the vicarious thrill, Hunter, and I'll fill you in. Need a break, Hal?"

Hal shakes his head, mouth full, toasting them with his coffee mug. They split, leaving the SA to his sugar and caffeine.

Outside, Sarge sucks hard and blows smoke blissfully. "Thanks, Hunter, I've been here all morning without a break."

"Really?!" She erupts. "Why I never even noticed you were gone. And I completely forgot you were gonna call me last night. You know, with a case this screwed up, I simply put it out of my mind. Never gave it another thought…"

"I get it! Jesus." Sarge leans back against the brick wall, eyes to the heavens. "Can you listen now?"

The grim tone quiets her. He lays out for her in a singsong, storytelling voice. A bad sign.

"This morning's deposition was a true delight. Our boy Brendan, in an effort to cover his sorry ass, is now crying 'victim'. He describes his year-long struggle with Flora as her 'sad infatuation' with a brilliant and devastatingly good-looking upperclassman. He speculates that, as a neglected child, she probably wanted to feel important by association with a bright, athletic, and handsome fellow such as himself. As he puts it, 'Who wouldn't?' Certainly, all of her freshman and sophomore girlfriends were envious of her close proximity to such a catch."

Sarge lights another cig on the coal of the last and continues: "The Jacobie household had been subject to frequent 'hang-up' phone calls in recent months. Brendan is sure these were Flora's little friends calling him, desperately hoping to hear his voice but too young and socially inept to actually initiate a conversation.

"When Flora was alone with Brendan, he says she begged for attention, wanting rides in his car or to hang out with his friends. It was downright embarrassing to the poor boy, but he knew she was a troubled young thing so he tolerated it gracefully. This was, after all, what he learned in the Foster Family Classes he attended with his folks; these poor kids can be so needy! He never expected this to happen to him. As humble as he is, her attraction was quite a surprise. The boy tried to discourage her...gently, of course. He never said anything before because he felt so sorry for her."

Sarge pauses. Anger radiates from him. He takes a deep drag, rubs his eyes with his free hand, and continues.

"Recently, when Brendan spoke about going away to the East Coast for school and how excited he was, little Flora became clingy and emotional. He tried to be kind and supportive, even told her he'd stay in touch, but he can see now that she was determined to keep him close to home. That's why he figures she made up this story, to keep him from going away. Sad, really. But poor Brendan can't put his life on hold for such a pathetic young girl, especially now that she is delusional or, worse, dangerous. All he really wants from the court is to see that she gets the mental health support she needs, in a place where she can't hurt anyone else."

Sarge coughs and grinds out the butt with his toe, signaling the end of the story. "Mr. Jacobie's attorney has secured a court date in two weeks to request just such action from the Judge."

He's trying to get her locked up in a mental institution. Unbelievable!

"I can see you're speechless, Hunter, so listen up." Sarge lowers his voice and gets in her face. "This is pretty ugly and that boy is as slick as snot. He doesn't have a shred of evidence to back up his story. This legal ploy is just his way of screwing with the girl, keeping her from making any more trouble. We know it. Hal knows it. Now, we need to make sure the Judge knows it. No mistakes, Hunter. We need to get this right."

June's way ahead of him. "OK, Sarge, first we need to

get statements from some credible witnesses: the therapist that's been working with Flora; the School Nurse who reported the abuse; maybe the Music Teacher or somebody to verify that Flora didn't have any close friends who might call... Hey, what about the household's phone records, identifying regular callers? Oh, I just remembered, Brendan had a girlfriend he took to Homecoming last semester; maybe she'll verify..."

"Hold up, Hunter," Sarge says. "What do you think you're doing?"

"What? My job, Sarge." June feels herself choking up.

Is he kicking me off the case?!

"That's Hal's job, not yours. Come on, let's go." Sarge starts walking but she's frozen in place. "Now!"

Swallowing hard, June follows him back upstairs into Hal's office. He closes the door, sticks a donut in her hand, pours her a cup of coffee, and points to the chair. "Sit."

She sits.

"Now eat, drink, and listen to Hal."

They both know June's like a tiger with cubs when it comes to the kids, and she doesn't trust anyone else to protect them. She takes a bite of the donut, chocolate with glaze, and a big swallow of coffee.

Breathe, June, breathe!

When she looks up, Hal is sitting on his desktop with one foot on the floor, looking like a high school principal chatting up a student. He is smiling at her.

"What?"

"You actually did better than I thought, Junie. Sol, our little girl is growing up."

Sarge shakes his head. "Not over yet, Hal. Tread lightly."

Hal moves around to his desk chair and sits, folding his hands on top of the papers. "June, this boy's story has a million holes in it. I've assigned a paralegal to do some digging for me. This is what we've already got: the School

Nurse gave us her notes, documenting Flora's increasing fear of her foster brother and her expressed desire to avoid him; the Nurse collaborated with the Music Teacher, whose written statement outlines her efforts to keep Flora at school early mornings, late afternoons, and evenings; the School Social Worker had been meeting with Flora 'unofficially' but she kept notes of her observations; and we're waiting on the phone company for home phone records."

He leans back in his chair, folding his hands behind his head. "We also have the girl Brendan was dating. It seems he broke up with her right after Thanksgiving. Pam is interviewing her right now, down the hall, to see if we can get some dirt on the kid. The Football Team Mascot is also reported to have been a victim of this asshole and his evil ways, so we have him coming in for an interview in about an hour, escorted by the Team Manager. The Coach thinks Brendan walks on water, but the little prince seems to have treated everyone else like shit."

Sarge reaches out for the donuts and turns to her. "Hunter, pay attention now. Here's what we need from you…"

21.

June's finally here!

All weekend, Flora's been thinking about what to say and how to say it, reading their letters, and imagining the whole scene.

Flora's ready. Nervous, but ready. Ready to be what they want her to be. Ready to woo them, make them like her, make them want her to be their child.

"Could I call Rosemary now? Would she be home, do you think?"

Do it quick, before you lose your nerve.

June says, "Sure, we could call her now. Let me pull up

her number. She told me she might be working but we're supposed to leave a message. Here."

June thrusts the phone at her with the number already pulled up.

Instinctively, Flora pulls back. "Wait, what should I say?"

They hash out what to say, how she wants to visit them and get to know them better. Ready to leave a message, she's stunned when someone picks up.

"Um, Rosemary?" *OMG, how stupid. Bad start!*

"Flora, is that you?"

How did she know it was me? "Yes. It's me."

"Oh, fantastic! Your voice is exactly like I thought it would be. How are you feeling about all this?"

Feeling? "I'm... excited. Nervous, well, a little nervous. How about you?"

Rosemary laughs. "I'm nervous too. I was worried you'd think we were too goofy, like we weren't fun or anything. Hey, this is a big deal, right?"

"Totally a big deal," Flora says.

"Huge," Rosemary says.

"Gigantic," Flora says.

They both laugh.

"Want to come over?"

"I do," Flora tells her. "Is that ok?"

"It's really the only way," Rosemary says.

Flora gets that.

After the call, she's vibrating. "Rosemary said I should come on Friday and stay the weekend. That's ok, isn't it, June?"

"Sure, a weekend visit sounds like fun. I know they'll have a bunch of stuff planned for you, too. What time is she expecting us?"

"After I'm done with my school..." Flora's a little nauseous, embarrassed too. She's not comfortable with this feeling, whatever it is, like falling from the sky. To distract herself, she starts planning out loud. "Let's see,

Mrs. Dewey leaves about 11:30, eat lunch, sign in after 1:00 to get my assignments, then I need to shower and change, maybe I'll just pack the night before...could you drive me over there about 2:30?"

June rolls her eyes. "Are you sure that'll give you enough time to get ready? I think the other day you took longer than that to tie your shoes."

She's pretty funny. It's crazy but she makes this feel like it's no big deal.

Together, they review Flora's list of questions for the Wests and the things she wants them to know about her. After she makes her list, she realizes something. "You have a lot of secrets, don't you, June?"

"Of course I do, Flora. My work's all about keeping confidences. That's the same thing as secrets."

"Is it hard?"

For some reason, talking with June is different now, less social work-y, more real. She remembers Gina's assessment, "She totally kicks ass for her kids."

"My work? Yeah, it's hard sometimes. But it's exciting and rewarding, too. I guess I like a challenge."

"So, if I tell you something, do you *have* to keep it a secret?"

She puts her hand on Flora's shoulder. "That depends. If you tell me about something that's harmful to you or someone else, I can't keep it a secret. Let's say you told me you get sick every time you eat. In that case, I would have to take you to a doctor. I would ask you to tell the doctor yourself about what's going on, but if you wouldn't or couldn't, I would have to do it. That's fair, right?"

"Sure," she says. "Does every kid you work with have secrets?"

"I think every *person* has secrets, kids and adults. If the secret doesn't hurt anyone, then it's not a problem. But if someone's getting hurt, my job is to tell the right people."

That makes sense. "But people don't always understand when you tell. Or why."

"I know," she says, "and that's the challenge. Flora, do you think I'm keeping important secrets from you or sharing your secrets with other people? Are you keeping secrets from me?"

Flora shrugs. "I wonder if I should have told the nurse about Brendan or if it would've been better to keep it a secret."

June shrugs too. "Well, you can always apply the test."

"There's a test? What is it?"

June is completely serious. "I ask myself how the secret makes me feel."

I'm disappointed. That sounds ridiculous.

Even though Flora doesn't say it, June seems to know what she's thinking.

"No, really!" she says. "Let's say you have a secret…um, you're buying me something fantastic for my birthday. How does that make you feel?"

Flora plays along. "Well, I'd feel good if I could afford to get a really cool present."

"So, that secret feels good, you say?"

"Right."

"What if the secret is that your foster brother's touching you?"

Seriously. "You already know *that* doesn't feel good at all."

"I do. Bad feeling, bad secret. So, what do you think? Does the test work?"

This test is a little too simple. Nothing is that simple. "I guess I need to think about it some more, June."

She laughs. "Good. You get back to me on that."

22.

Before Flora's visit on Friday, June needs to complete her home study interviews. First comes Rosemary, a morning person by her own description.

Rosemary pours two mugs of dark coffee as they get settled out on her deck. It's only 6:30 in the morning and the spring sunrise has set the stage for a balmy day. However, to ward off the early dampness and chill, the women are draped in quilt throws.

"Michael has already gone to work," she explains, "and this is my special time."

Jeeves, the sheepdog, lays on top of her bare feet. "He must think it's too early to be out without shoes," she says, patting his huge head. She chats a little about planting the gardens, birthing the lambs, and putting in the screens as the weather warms up.

"I wonder if this year will be different," she says. "Our life is rich and full, to be sure. We could go on forever without kids, if it turns out that way. But I can't shake the belief that Michael and I have been waiting for a higher purpose."

Does she think Flora is their higher purpose?

Ten years ago, Rosemary learned she would never bear a child. The doctor was straight with her, never gave her false hope. She worried that Michael would resent her later, or even leave her someday for a younger, more fertile partner. As it turned out, he kind of enjoyed the adoption idea.

"But he thought differently than I did, June. He told me, 'Kids are like anything else you raise: your responsibility until the end and your joy and wonder throughout. And every kid deserves a family, especially if they've already lost one.' He gave me a completely different perspective."

She tells June how Michael was raised in a blended home, learning early on that 'blood does not a family make'. He joked that they had more choices than other Yuppies.

"We choose our kids and they get to choose us," he would boast to their friends, but not recently. Not since Amanda died.

Amanda had been so sick. Death was truly a relief, for her and everyone who knew her. Still, it seemed so unfair! She was supposed to have at least another decade of life. Rosemary learned just how powerless she was in the face of a four-year-old and her disease. She believed, back then, that love was enough. So naïve.

Rosemary grew up an only child of two educators but had never been without childhood companions. Her parents ran a private boarding school out East, providing elementary and secondary education. The school was set in the bucolic countryside of Western Pennsylvania, southeast of Pittsburgh. In the academic turmoil of the late 1960's, the percentage of kids enrolled in area public schools was low, leaving about a fourth of the region's finest youth to attend private institutions. The quality of education at Great Laurel Academy was of the highest in the country, and its graduates attended the finest universities. Rosemary was among them.

She was raised in a period of great social change believing strongly, thanks to her very liberal parents, that women were the best thing to happen to this country.

"I was conceived by flower children and educated alongside the rich and famous. I got to see both sides of the rainbow!" Happily pursuing both the fine arts and the sciences, she attended the prestigious Northwestern University on a full scholarship. She proudly graduated cum laude with dual degrees: Bachelor of Fine Arts *and* Bachelor of Environmental Science, a relatively new course of study at that time.

During her years in Chicago, Rosemary met Michael West, the promising young sculptor. Michael was also attending school on a scholarship, coming from a blue-collar Midwestern family. His family thought it strange that he would actually 'study' what came so naturally to him, especially something like art. The University paid most of his way. The rest, Michael earned working for a cabinet maker in Evanston, creating lovely homes for the well-heeled of Chicago's North Shore.

Both Rosemary and Michael spent a couple of extra years in undergraduate study. Rosemary needed the time to gain her dual degrees and Michael had to work, so graduation was delayed. They were a little older and wiser than typical graduates when they left Chicago. Married in their mid-twenties, they moved to a rural community in Northern Illinois a couple of hours away from the city. There, they both found gratifying work. The couple saved and planned until they could purchase these fifteen acres of land and build their home.

Gazing over her coffee cup at their beautiful property, reminiscing about those days, she sighs, "We're so lucky!"

They've since earned their Master Degrees. Rosemary works as an occasional consultant to the State Environmental Protection Agency and teaches an art class at the local community college. For the most part, she makes her own schedule.

Michael is a Master Sculptor at a nearby private University. He maintains a wood shop on their farm, contracting custom woodwork for high-end home builders and selling his beautiful carved sculptures to art lovers and collectors from all over the country. The shop also serves as an internship classroom for a select few, partially subsidized by the University. There's a separate lane leading to the shop, about a half-mile down the road from the farm entrance. The lane is marked with a beautiful wooden sign: *Westwoods*.

Rosemary tells June her old friend Keely Bruce, the famous jazz vocalist, is in town this weekend. "I saw in the notes that Flora loves singing. I thought this might be fun for her." *Holy crap! Keely Bruce?!*

They'd been comped tickets for the concert and, of course, dinner with the performer afterward. "You should come, June!"

June grits her teeth and explains why she must decline the offer, so she can't be accused of taking a bribe. She thanks her, fighting a wave of disappointment. Keely Bruce is one of her favorites.

Next is Michael's interview, so June travels the half-mile to Westwoods. Pulling up in front of the shop, she sees Michael coming out to greet her with a big smile. "You must be June. Come on in!"

They shake hands and get situated, as a young man trots through the door and drops his backpack on a table.

"Hey Pete, how's it goin' this morning?" Michael is enormously cheerful in the mornings, he tells me, a trait his students sometimes find repellent. He counters his merry morning assault by keeping a fresh pot of fantastic coffee available at all times during work hours.

Peeling off his jacket and hat, Pete pours himself a cup and pulls sketches out of his backpack. He has not yet spoken, but hands me a cup with a sleepy grin. "Welcome."

"Thanks." *Wow, that is great coffee!*

The phone interrupts with an earsplitting jangle. Michael says the ringer is set on 'loud' so they can hear it above the drills and saws in the shop. "Westwoods, good morning!"

Michael hangs up and says, "Tera and Ray, are calling from outside in the car. They want us to come on out and look at the sky. They say it's amazing!"

The three of them scurry outside to see brilliant pink, red, and gold streaks backed against pale blue as the sun moves through clouds. "The great thing about artists," Michael says, "is they tend to share beauty wherever they find it."

Michael introduces me to Pete, Tera, and Ray, his independent study students. The come to Westwoods twice a week during the semester and work from 8:00 in the morning until 3:30 in the afternoon. These students are carefully chosen by Michael. Only the most serious artists make the cut into this elite group.

"As hard as I push them," Michael says, "they need to

be self-motivated and very skilled. In return, they can expect to exhibit and sell their work long before graduation, enjoying both professional recognition and financial gain."

June wonders how a delayed student like Flora might fit in here.

He points to a poster tacked to a tree trunk, swirled lime green background with purple letters.

Question: What do you tell a student who wants a career as an artist?

Answer: Go West, young man, go West!

"This one hangs in our University Financial Aid Office." These kids have to be completely trustworthy, Michael says, because he leaves them in charge of Westwoods when other duties demand his attention. For the service of managing the shop, he pays $20.00 an hour. Most interns are unpaid, so this is an unbelievably sweet assignment. However, Michael's students are required to produce. No exceptions.

"OK, guys, let's talk about why the sky is so spectacular this morning." Michael sits on a tree stump chair in the yard and starts class in the open air. He waves at June to join them.

Tera spreads her arms wide. "It must be the dimension of the light."

"Yeah, but what does that mean?"

Ray comes out of the shop carrying two cups of coffee. "It seems to reflect itself." He hands Tera a cup. "It bounces off multiple surfaces and only happens when the moisture in the clouds is just right. Like having a bunch of mirrored plates and crystals, then running the light through them."

Michael perks up. "Good. Now, how can you get a similar effect with wood?"

They are off and running for the day, the kids alert now and thinking like artists. After a bit, Michael leaves them to continue our interview.

Michael West grew up in a house with one sibling, two step-siblings, and two cousins, six kids in all. It was never quiet and the only rule was: "Respect yourself and others, always!" The genders were equal, three girls and three boys, ages spanning a decade. It was a great place to grow up.

His parents had only high school educations but they made out alright. Dad was a contractor and Mom worked in a bookstore. They always managed to feed and clothe everyone, even after Mom's sister died and her kids joined the family. The whole gang worked in the three-acre garden, manning a farm stand where they sold their crops. Everyone earned a share of the profits, but the biggest percentage went to the household. They learned working hard paid off and contributing to their community was a responsibility, not an option. These lessons Michael carried with him, to pass on to his students.

"Got a minute, Michael?" Ray sticks his head through the door. Michael signals June to follow.

"What have you got?"

The kids are fired up, rough sketches in hand. Each has an idea for a special piece, designed to use light as a way to enhance the wood.

Ray shows us his plans for an outdoor patio table with stained glass inlay on top and a solar panel below. As it grows dark, the table will glow underneath the diners.

"Take that, *Tavern on the Green*!"

Pete describes an intricately carved lamp, shaped like a rectangular shadowbox that hangs on the wall. A series of mirrors set into bevels in the wood will reflect light throughout the piece, illuminating a room with warmth and subtlety.

Tera is sketching plans for a carved wood and hammered metal room screen, inlaid with glass tiles and polished stones. Breathtaking, this type of piece could place her in a high-ranking art exhibition.

Inside, we sit and he pours more coffee.

"How do you feel about working with a kid like Flora, Michael? She is the polar opposite of these kids, learning issues that manifest in low motivation and poor follow-through."

He shakes his head. "Most kids have areas of struggle. School might not be her thing. Finding something that inspires her is exciting to me. Then cultivating it so she can grow... Wow! Who wouldn't love that?"

Driving home, June can't stop the turmoil in her head:

How can two people be so perfect?

Where would Flora fit here?

What am I missing?

23.

Talking to Rosemary on the phone's one thing, but going there for a whole weekend? Flora's plan seems to be moving right along but she feels like she's on slippery ground.

What if the video was a scam and they aren't so nice? What if they don't like me?

Dee watches from her bed as Flora packs the little suitcase June gave her. "Leaving tomorrow afternoon, eh?"

"Yeah, coming back Sunday," she says, trying to sound casual. "Are you gonna see your mom this weekend?"

"Yeah," she says. "I'm supposed to go for a long weekend, Friday through Monday, then return home for good on Wednesday if the visit goes ok."

Flora stops and stares at her. "Oh, wow. Home!" She can see the girl is not excited. *This sucks.*

Dee pushes herself up to a sitting position. "Mom finished her rehab last week and the loser boyfriend is in jail so..."

What do you say in this situation: that's great, sounds awesome, good luck? She has this defiant look on her face, like whatever, but Flora knows she doesn't want to go back there.

She must hate me right now, going to this great home with these great people.

Flora quits packing and sits on the bed facing her. "You ok?"

"Sure. No big thing. Mom was all about the love last night, slobbering into the phone. I hate that." She flops back on her pillow. "But maybe this time she'll stay clean and get a job. We'll see."

"That'd be cool," I say.

So lame, but I can't think of anything else to say that won't make it worse.

She jumps to her feet. "Cool? How would you know? Spoiled bitch." She storms out of the room.

She hates me. I get it.

Flora knows what it looks like to someone like Dee. She's had years at a nice home, even if it ended in a sucky way. Now she might get adopted by these really cool people. All Dee has is an addict mom with her sleazy boyfriends, dealers, and pimps. They won't even put her in a foster home because her mom is supposedly still trying. Besides, it's too late. She'll go to County next, then to the Indie program.

That could be me. Shaking all over, Flora can hardly keep from crying. *What if this doesn't work out, if they think I'm too stupid or something? What if nobody ever wants me?*

Irene pops her head in and says, "June left you a message. She says she'll be here at 2:00 tomorrow, so you should finish up your school and chores early."

"I will." Big smile. Start packing again. "I'm almost all packed."

"You must be so excited. I hear thesepeople are really great."

Flora clasps her hands together and gives the House Mother a nervous smile. "Fingers crossed!"

Irene holds up both hands, fingers crossed on each. Then she slips out of the room.

Sitting back down on the bed, Flora closes her eyes and hugs her backpack to her chest, trying to remember what her mom was like, then what her gramma was like. Everything's blank. No songs, no smells, no silly jokes.

No memories.

Nothing.

After a couple of minutes without being able to recall anything from her past, Flora opens her eyes and gets up, stashing her backpack in place between her pillow and the wall. She zips her suitcase closed, and sets it on the floor at the end of the bed next to her computer bag.

Tomorrow, I'll be ready.

24.

Driving home on Thursday, June's mind is racing and her brain is on overdrive. She's still processing all the data she obtained in the interviews with Michael and Rosemary and has almost completed the Home Study.

Speed dating didn't exist when June was a young woman but that's what this process must be like for a kid: meet, sell yourself, scope out the others, and make a commitment to try. Everything is *right now*. She cannot imagine picking a life partner by reviewing their social history, having two or three dates, and then making a decision.

If identifying a foster home is like speed dating, adoption is more like a betrothal: the adults do most of the picking, but the principle is the same. Choices are mostly based on intellectual data, not love. All you can hope for is that everyone learns to care for each other over time, through various emotional trials and the process of growing up.

Definitely not natural, but at least most of my adoptions stick.

Pulling into the lane that leads to her house, June breathes in the fragrance of the woods and the flowers and her brain begins to slow down.

"Hey, Tully, how's my good boy?"

Releasing a wildly barking Tully out of his kennel is like unleashing the Kraken: he runs in circles, creating a whirl of noise and fur, then a thousand legs and tails are upon me. Pretty good medicine.

They trot back down the lane together to pick up the mail. June could stop at the mail box on her way in but this is their special tradition, equivalent to walking your kid home from the bus stop.

"Get it, Tully!"

She sticks the rolled-up newspaper in his mouth. This is their latest trick. Someday, June sees herself sending Tully out to meet the paper carrier or mailman and bring in the bundle himself, like a movie dog. However, this time, he drags the paper for about fifty feet and drops it, running back to her wagging his tail.

"Well," she says, with a rub to his head, "it's a start."

They head toward the house together. "Hey, once you learn to carry stuff, you won't mind hauling in the kindling, will you?"

Tully barks with great enthusiasm, nudging her in the shoulder and nearly knocking her down.

She laughs. "I'll hold you to that!"

Next stop, the wood pile. June gets great satisfaction from building a beautiful fire: hauling in logs from the wood box, stacking the kindling in the woodstove, building a roaring fire. She compares it to sculpting ice: you know it can't last, so you relish it all the more and respect it for its ephemeral nature.

Relationships are like that too, she realizes, requiring deliberate appreciation and a healthy attitude of opportunism. Carpe diem and all that.

Admiring her fire, June checks her phone and smiles at Quinn's message that he's on his way over.

Great, I'm starving!

She heads for the kitchen to season the steaks and

chop vegetables. Not exactly Martha Stewart, but the process quiets her mind.

Tenderly, she lays out sparkling Waterford crystal glasses, plates and salad bowls of blue and white Polish pottery, and heavy stainless tableware. Life in the woods is rustic but there is always room for beautiful things. They soothe the spirit.

Women like her are often viewed as tough or hard, because her job is tough and hard to take sometimes. Not a bad reputation to cultivate – keeps the riff-raff away. Friends see the other layers of her, the few she lets in.

"Hey, hey, what smells like heaven?"

Quinn stomps the dirt off at the door and traps June in a bear hug. "Let me wash up and you can fill me in on the next episode of Adventures in Adoption."

Over steak and salad and hot buttered rolls, she brings him up to speed.

"Man," he says through a mouthful of meat. "One minute the kid is under legal assault; the next minute, Cool Family is falling in love with her. You and your extremes."

"You think I plan it this way? I'd love a case where things go smoothly."

Quinn stops mid-chew. He reaches across the table and cups her face in his hand. "Socrates said it, Gandhi said it, even Ben Franklin said it. Now, I say it to you…know thyself, Girlie. You find this roller coaster exciting."

Immediately defensive. "What are you getting at?"

"Easy there, Tiger." He leans back in his chair and puts up his hands. "If I didn't love that about you, I wouldn't have said it with such fondness. You're a rock star when all seems to be lost. Then you pull a rabbit out of your hat and save the world. It's amazing!"

She melts a little.

"Oh, before I forget," he changes course, "did I tell you I know your buddy, Michael West?"

"Yeah?"

Quinn seems to know everybody.

"Yeah, I recognized the name but didn't quite put it together when you mentioned him before. He's a local saint." He carefully butters another roll. "The guy's a master craftsman and artist, in big demand by the high-rollers. Michael West is to wood what Lew French is to stone, or Frank Lloyd Wright is to architecture."

Huh?

"You know that spa and resort on the river? His stuff is all over that place. The Bailey Estate, too. They wanted all locally grown, handcrafted woodwork in their house and he's their man. He's a genius with 'green' projects. Oh, and his wife being an environmentalist certainly helps."

"Really?" Floored with his expansive knowledge and connections, she asks, "Have you worked with him?"

Quinn is a contractor, so it's possible they would run into each other professionally.

"No, but I'd give my right arm for the chance. 'Green' is the new direction in this industry, mostly on the coasts and down in the gulf. I'd like to promote it around here, Junie, and get a reputation for working with artists like Michael West."

On the phone with Rosemary earlier, June agreed to attend their cookout on Sunday to process things before Flora returns to the group home. The first visit is always a crap shoot: it can be really great or just horrible. Either way, it's her job to ease the transition back. Sometimes that's the toughest part.

Even Cinderella was bummed out after the Ball, date with the Prince notwithstanding.

Dishing up dessert, she says, "It so happens I'm going to a cookout at the West homestead on Sunday. Care to be my date?"

"Hell, yeah." He jumps on it, then stops. "No conflict of interest there?"

"I don't think so, but I'll ask Sarge. It's not like I'm negotiating a deal for you. In my work there's bound to be some crossover, six degrees and all." She makes a mental note to ask Sarge about bringing Quinn as her date.

"Let's watch the sunset."

Quinn tosses me my jacket and heads out the door with Tully. Bowls of ice cream in hand, she follows them outside.

25.

She's here!

Shaking all over with equal parts nervousness and excitement, Flora flies down the front steps of the group home like the building's on fire, backpack on a shoulder, computer in one hand and overnight bag in the other. She throws the bags in the back seat of the car, slamming it with gusto.

Let's go, let's go, LET'S GO!

"Got everything?" June asks.

"I'm ready, June," she says, jumping into the passenger's seat and buckling up, already living the weekend in her head.

Should I shake hands, hug her, what do I do when I meet Rosemary? And what about Michael – say hello, wave hi, curtsy, what?

They drive out to the West's and June leaves the car running in front of the house.

She's not even coming in?

"Flora, I want you to remember something. This is just one visit. We'll talk some more next week, after you get a chance to think and relax. Then we'll decide what happens next, ok? This is only the first step."

Right, right, I get it.

"Rosemary said I should bring my homework so she can help me. She sounds pretty smart."

"Smart enough to tell you to bring your homework… you won't be able to get away with much around those two!" Big smile, ha, ha, ha.

June's tone is off, a little too cheerful but guarded; something's not right.

They step out of the car as Rosemary rushes toward them. "Stay out of trouble!" she says, winking.

Waaay too forced for June. Not good.

June and Rosemary hug, she says, "See you on Sunday," and takes off. Flora's stomach does a flip when she pulls away.

But then Rosemary says something silly and Flora says something silly back. They laugh and Rosemary takes her hand like it's totally normal.

"Let's go inside and have a snack. Michael will be here soon, so we have to get our girl time while we can."

Brownies, apple slices, and herbal tea.

Fancy, sort of. Not too different than Mom Jacobie, just more relaxed. Not totally health food but not Cheetos either.

They talk about school, what the group home is like, her life before foster care. Rosemary tells her funny stories about Jeeves and Michael and her cooking.

Phew! This isn't bad at all.

But then, Rosemary freaks her out by saying, "This picnic on Sunday has gotten a little out of hand, Flora. So many of our friends want to come because the weather is nice, it's springtime, and they love attending a cookout in the country. Besides, everyone wants to meet you. Are you ok with that?"

Who wants to meet me and why would they? Who is 'everyone' anyway?

"Do these people know I'm a... foster kid?"

"No, no! You decide how much you want to share about yourself with everyone, Flora. I've told our guests that one of my favorite young friends will be here visiting, that's all. The only person I've told about you is my best friend, Keely. She was already coming for a visit this weekend, from California. I hope you don't mind. I just told her we were getting to know each other and to see if you might want to join our family."

I can breathe again. She's pretty slick, knows how to handle people. I like that... sort of. As long as she's on my side.

"That sounds ok, I guess. But what if I don't know how to act or say the wrong thing to your friends?"

She laughs, and it sounds like windchimes. "Oh, Flora, you can't mess up with these people! But, since you're concerned, I'll share of few of my tips for how to get along at one of these parties. First, we have to go shopping for a couple of great outfits, one for tonight and one for Sunday. I know just the place..."

Rosemary keeps talking as they move out to her car and off on their shopping spree.

So comfortable, like I've been with her forever. That's unexpected.

26.

Overriding her tendency to ask forgiveness later, June finishes explaining the West's party situation to Sarge then sits quietly in his office and waits for his response. Staying out of trouble is not really her strong suit, so she's proud of herself for being proactive on this one.

"Come on, Hunter, we live in this community, for Pete's sake." He dismisses her concern about a conflict of interest. "The West family invited you and your sweetheart to a gathering, to make it nice and natural for Flora. The guys happen to be in businesses that may or may not cross over. It happens. Don't worry about it."

Crossing that problem off my list. Now, to finish this investigation.

She heads back to her desk and calls her friend who heads up the Foster Parent Training Program. "Can I come by to pick your brain about one of your families, Donna?"

At the office over on the college campus, June's struck by how cheerful it is, how inviting. Donna's brewing a pot of some fragrant tea and waves her in, pouring a cup. She hands her the tea and points to a comfy chair. "Sit. Relax."

"You know just what I need, Donna. Thanks." She breathes in the lemongrass and chamomile, sinking into the chair with a great sigh.

"When are you going to transfer over here, June?" she asks. "You're one of the best trainers I ever had. We could have tons of fun together."

"I know it, Donna," she says, putting her feet up on the magazine table. "This is where I plan to retire, when I'm washed up in the Adoptions Unit."

"Yeah, they need you and all that, but I can't wait!" She takes a deep breath and lowers her voice, "I have an opening next month, June, when my lead trainer moves to Seattle. I'm getting you an application for that position, ready or not."

Even her prodding me does not kill my happy vibe.

Donna puts her feet up too, and smiles big. "Hey, what do you want so much that you'd come all the way over here on a Friday afternoon?"

The tension floods right back. "I need to review one of your training files, for court next week. And that means you'll probably have to testify."

Donna sits upright in her chair and drops her feet to the floor, "Uh, oh... what happened?"

"The Jacobie family is pursuing court action against a foster kid, because she reported their son for sexual molestation." No beating around the bush in this business. Nobody has the time or patience for it. "This is an unofficial heads-up, though. You'll be getting the notice from Sarge next week."

"Oh, shit." Donna jumps up and heads to the file cabinet. "I remember those people! The parents were cool customers, but they were all about needing gratitude from the kids. That's why I recommended older kids, so they couldn't bully 'em too much."

She hands her the file, looking grim.

"Look, it isn't like we can screen 'em all out," June

consoles her, flipping through the record. "Sometimes creeps slip through our radar. You know, if we had placed a boy in their home maybe Brendan would have bullied him or treated him like shit, but with a girl he used sex."

June steps over to the copy machine and starts duplicating the pages she needs. "Anyway, it was the only long-term placement they ever had. It lasted four years before this came out. Wanna know the shittiest part? The SA couldn't make it stick against Brendan, not enough evidence. The family's filing the charges."

"Oh, come on," she says. "How could they?"

Hearing the whole story, Donna's eyes well up with tears. "I'm so sorry. That poor girl!"

"No, this is really a good thing. She would've stayed with the Jacobies until her time ran out and then she'd be alone. She deserves better and I might have found it. Do you remember Rosemary and Michael West?"

Donna lights up like the sunrise. "Do I? They're my heroes! How did you know they were getting back into fostering?"

"They put in the paperwork a couple of weeks ago and I snatched 'em up. They sure seem perfect, Donna, which kind of scares me." Perfection is a big red flag in this business.

"Right," she agrees. "But these two are pretty special. Even I trust them."

"Fatal flaw, please," June asks. Everybody has a fatal flaw, it's just that some are less tolerable than others.

Donna gazes off at the ceiling in contemplation. "They're a couple of flower children from the old days: save the planet, love the world, the whole bit. But they really make it work. Too optimistic for this business, if anything, but not fragile. When Amanda died … remember her? They took it pretty hard. Rosemary believed that love could conquer all and Michael had fallen for the kid like a ton of bricks. I guess they blamed themselves at first, but the autopsy showed them the truth.

The disease had spread much more than the doctors thought. It was a miracle she lived as long, and as well, as she did. I credit Rosemary and Michael for that."

These people are starting to freak me out.

"You're telling me their fatal flaw is: they're too optimistic? No skeletons?"

"Uh, uh, Sunshine, this couple is the genuine article. If anything, they're better than good. These flower children grew up to be quite well-to-do and heavily connected – so that could be the hang-up. They could give *us* a run for our money, in court and out." She gushes, freaking June out even more. "I kinda wish they could adopt ME!"

27.

I think I know how Cinderella must have felt about her fairy godmother – can this be real?

Flora's decked out in new clothes and boots and jewelry. Rosemary did her makeup and hair, too.

And, unlike the dress from Mrs. Jacobie, this is more about me being comfortable, not just looking the part. I got to choose all of it!

Michael walks between them into the concert, arms linked with Flora and Rosemary on either side.

"Keely always gets us great seats," Rosemary tells Flora. "We follow the hall over there to the elevator and insert the key card." The elevator opens onto a private platform with padded chairs, tables, and a dinner buffet. Only about five or six other people are here, besides the waiters and bartender.

"You go ahead and check in," Michael tells Rosemary. "I'll escort my lovely date to her seat." He takes Flora over to a round table with four leather chairs, pushed up by the railing. She gazes out over the auditorium below and sees they are right in front of the stage. Off to the left and right of their box are two giant screens, providing a close-up view of the performer. Last night she had googled Keely and found out she's a legit star. *This is unbelievable!*

"Hey, how are you doing?" Michael watches Flora closely but doesn't talk a lot. "This is crazy, right?"

"Crazy, yeah!"

"We don't always live like this, you know. Keely and Rosemary grew up together and they are closer than most sisters. Whenever Keely comes to town, she spoils us like this."

A voice from behind makes Flora jump.

"But you wouldn't love me if I didn't treat your bride like a queen, would you Mikey?" Keely Bruce puts both hands on Michael's shoulders and kisses the top of his head. Then she slides into a seat at the table and sticks out her hand.

"Flora, I presume. I'm Keely."

I am shaking her hand but can't make words come out. OMG! Keely Bruce!

"I'm so happy to meet you Flora. Rosemary was telling me how special you are. If you and Rosemary and Michael decide to become a family, I'll be like your second mother. Would that be ok?"

"Oh, well… sure."

Stupid! Say something, anything.

"I like to sing too."

OMG, not THAT!

"Great!" she says. "Then we have something in common!" She leans over and whispers, "Besides the fact that we're both foster kids. We'll talk later."

OMG! Still can't talk.

Keely stands up and says, "I have to run, Mikey, gotta show to do. Ro is helping me get ready. See you all backstage!" She disappears through a secret door that looks like a piece of the wall.

Michael watches Flora watching Keely leave.

"I know. She's something, right? Now, let's go get some of that prime rib." And he steers her over to the buffet as if they just got seated at Golden Corral or something. A smiling man in a white jacket and chef hat holds his knife over a giant piece of meat.

"Prime rib all around, sir," Michael declares in a booming voice. "We can't have the young lady walk away hungry!"

Flora can't help but laugh as they pile their plates with food. She forgets to be on guard with Michael, almost like he's another kid.

He's right, this is totally crazy. And so fun!

28.

In her office, June prepares documents to deliver to Hal and makes notes for the Report to the Court. That Report absolutely *must* be delivered by Tuesday noon, to meet the court deadline for evidence submission. The documentation has to be perfect if their plan is going to work.

Happily, Donna is a mighty good witness, cool and articulate on the stand. She knows the file backwards and forwards. Hal should be pleased.

June's tendency to be a little snippy on the stand caused Sarge to insist on being present in court. That happens about as often as glaciers roll by the office, so a little tension is swirling around, no big deal.

Perfect, perfect, everything has to be perfect.

When it's almost dark, she stops. She is empty inside and the nagging voice in her head has stopped screaming details at her.

It's a pretty good initial draft. I'll polish it up Monday morning, so Sarge can review it before we submit it to the Court.

The phone buzzes. Quinn's text says, *Chucks?*

She answers, *See you in 20,* and starts shutting down her computer and filing away her notes.

That guy does make me smile.

Quinn Harimann and June Hunter met quite by

accident, a rare connection with someone who was not a member of her profession.

Three years ago, Quinn entered a charity event for the local Literacy Council. The town was planning to build their own library and this affair was to help fund it. It was a three-day Motorcycle Olympics with races, obstacle courses, games, and the like. The event drew bikers from all over the Midwest, and Quinn's crowd participated with great enthusiasm.

Quinn and most of his buddies had big road bikes and they would go on long rides together a couple of times a year, usually in the Spring and Fall. He really enjoyed customizing his Harley, making the bike uniquely his and reflecting his personal tastes. He chose a Harley-Davidson because he liked the idea of riding something American with a modern cowboy appeal.

On Friday night, while parking his bike for the pig roast, Quinn stopped to admire a newer Indian Spirit: it was sort of a retro-model bike resembling a 1940's military Chief, dressed in red and cream. Sweet.

"What do you think?" June was standing off to his right and a little behind him, hands in her pockets: fortyish-looking, a little more than five feet tall, wavy salt and pepper hair to her shoulders, wearing jeans, a denim shirt, and cowboy boots.

"She's beautiful, but a bit out of my league," Quinn said of the bike. He was making conversation but was obviously studying her. "What do you think of her?"

"Very cool." She stepped forward and put possessive hands on the seat. "I just love her."

Quinn stared. "Wait... she's yours?"

"I'm June," she grinned and put out her hand. "What kind of bike do you have?"

They talked for a while, ate and drank at the pig roast, then wandered over to the concert together. They spent the rest of Friday night and all-day Saturday getting to know each other. By Sunday, the last day of the event,

June was firmly established as a member of his crowd, interacting with his buddies as if she'd known them forever.

His best friend, Ozzie, spilled the beans to June about a year later, about how things went down that day.

Ozzie asked Quinn, "Where the hell did she come from? Why haven't we seen her around?"

"She's pretty driven, I think, married to her work." They both studied June as she laughed and talked easily with both men and women in the group. "She's one of those save the world types, working with messed up kids. Doesn't leave her much time to hang out."

Ozzie pondered that for a minute.

"You know my cousin, Shelley, reddish hair, short, kind of serious? We sat with her at Pete's wedding last year."

"Oh, yeah, yeah," Quinn wasn't paying much attention, still studying June.

"Shelley works for DCW, same kind of stuff June talks about." Ozzie grinned at Quinn. "I just might do a little checking on our new friend here."

Immediately alert, Quinn asked, "Oh, yeah, she works there too? Think they know each other?"

"I don't know," Ozzie said, "but I'll find out. Interested in her, are ya?"

Ozzie and Quinn had known each other forever. There was no point bullshitting him. "Yeah, I'm interested. Why not?"

By the next Monday, Ozzie had the scoop on June, and then some. "She's one of the most respected workers at DCW, pretty much legendary. She makes miracles happen when everyone else thinks a kid doesn't have a chance. Shelley calls her brilliant and really tough."

Not many friends, either, she told Ozzie, mostly keeps to herself. Had a rocky marriage way back, divorced with a little kid. She went to work at DCW to support herself and her young son Leo, never looking back. That was around twenty years ago, Shelley thought, because Leo was grown and out of the house now.

June didn't date a lot as far as she knew, worked all the time, and at work they either liked her or hated her. Shelley liked her. Admired her.

"So, what's the downside," Quinn asked.

Ozzie had already gotten the details.

"You're either in or you're out with June Hunter. Anybody betrays her, she cuts 'em out right now, no next time. Lying, cheating, disrespectful shit is all unacceptable. Nothing a straight shooter like you would ever do."

"Hmm, trust issues," Quinn said, either ignoring or missing that last part. "Somebody must've screwed her over pretty good."

"I guess." Ozzie shrugged. "I didn't get into that. Maybe you want to consider getting to know this one, bro. Seems like you two really clicked together."

Truthfully, though, Quinn had already crashed-and-burned. He was hooked.

"What do you think… is this stupid?"

Ozzie grinned as his friend took out a tiny red velvet bag.

Quinn undid the tie and tipped out the contents into his palm, a silver guardian bell with an angel stamped on it. He picked it out for June, a token meant to protect bikers from harmful spirits.

"No, man, that's real nice!"

Quinn put the bell back in the bag and tucked it into his pocket.

"I figure that woman can handle herself with human threats. It's the invisible evils that might give her some trouble."

29.

Keely and Flora review sheet music and practice singing together for a good part of the morning. Completely infatuated, Flora's willing to practice with her until the sun falls out of the sky. At some point she gathers her courage and asks Keely, "What's it like, being adopted?"

"Being adopted was the easy part," Keely tells her. "Thinking about what to do with the rest of my life was not so easy."

After lunch, Rosemary, Keely, and Flora go window shopping in town. It's a little embarrassing at first, since Flora has never been on an actual shopping spree. Trying on clothes with Rosemary was a lot different than killing an afternoon with these two women.

She carefully watches the two adult friends interacting with each other – talking, laughing, pointing out things the other might like. Sometimes they pick out bizarre items and they laugh their heads off. Other times it's a gorgeous outfit or a beautiful fabric or a striking color.

Soon, Flora joins in the laughter and silliness with the two women, as they trot from one window to another. The girl had never shopped with such a carefree attitude, let alone picked out anything for herself. Her former foster mother always did the choosing for her. Always.

Wait until I get back to the group home and tell Gina about this!

Later, Michael takes Flora down to Westwoods to show her what he does for a living. She finds his work beautiful and delicate, astonishing really.

"Oh, Michael, I can't believe a human can make something like that."

"I'll show you how to work with wood, if you want," he tells her.

He acts like it's nothing, like he could actually do that for me. I don't know how I would even begin.

Michael shocks her by telling her she inspired him. After reading her Life Book, he ordered fruit trees for an orchard.

Walking together through the soon-to-be orchard almost makes Flora cry. He ordered peach trees for her, a few different kinds, as well as plum, apple, and cherry trees. He tells her it's easier to learn about caring and raising plants these days because of the internet.

"When I was your age, we had to find an expert to learn from or hire someone to do it for you. Now, we just look it up. Easy, and way more fun!"

But Michael says he does have some experts who are analyzing his soil and helping him with organic farming techniques.

The dude gets excited about something and he just jumps in. It's like he can do anything!

Sitting in her room, chilling before bedtime, Flora tries to put the pieces together. This place is different from the Jacobie's, for sure. It's different from anyplace she's ever been. It seems like all of their friends are super talented, really smart people. Rosemary helped her with her homework and they were done in a snap. And it was fun! She is so smart, Michael too, and when they talk to Flora she feels like she's smart and interesting.

Michael said everyone has talent and nobody should waste their gifts. Flora said, "I still don't know what my talent is."

He said that's their job, to help me figure it out. How cool is that?

30.

June spends Saturday morning doing laundry and pondering last night. The crowd at Chuck's was definitely June's style. More so, of course, because Quinn was there.

Chuck's is a noisy place, but not overly stimulating. Those chain 'bar & grill' places with their memorabilia on the walls, knickknacks hanging from every fixture, and TV's blaring are too much input for June's over-taxed brain. She has enough to process.

People who don't know June very well assume she's

extraverted, social. She stopped trying to change their minds long ago but her private credo is this: "Most people suck; stay away from them."

While she can often be entertaining, and even charming, June's usually described as 'delightfully irreverent'. Unfortunately, when tired or pissed off, she'll skip the humor and go right for the jugular. Over the years, she's learned a little temperance in this area.

The assumption is that I am the way I am because I do what I do. That may be right, but I suspect it's backwards: 'I do what I do' because 'I am what I am'.

She sits at the table with her coffee and reflects on her evening:

When she entered Chuck's, Ozzie spotted her and yelled, "It's a miracle!" and the whole table pantomimed checking their watches.

"It is an honor just to be nominated," she yelled back and everybody cheered.

Shelley was there with her sweetheart and she raised her coffee cup in an exaggerated toast to June. On-call workers can never drink on duty, but they can hang out with people who drink as long as they have their own transportation. June asked her, "Quiet tonight?"

She smiles widely. "Every minute's a blessing, eh?"

June noticed she was eating her cheeseburger out of a to-go container. Superstitious, but smart.

She stepped around the crowd to Quinn's shoulder and wrapped her arms around him.

"Awwwww!" Their voices rang out and she smiled at them.

I don't have to do anything for their acceptance, they just like me.

Then that little voice in her head hissed, "Maybe it's really Quinn they like." Exit warm moment, enter tiny pang of anxiety, small enough to brush into a corner of her psyche.

"This seat for me?" she asked.

Quinn always finds the right spot. He knows she isn't

comfortable with her back to the door or the crowd, an old habit adopted by cops, gangsters, and social workers. Maybe even more so for social workers because they are unarmed. June hates feeling vulnerable.

"What's new, you guys?" she asked. The stories start to roll.

After about an hour and a half, that overwhelmed feeling started creeping up on her. She found herself straining to participate. Shelley got called out to find some kids a foster home, and June began to worry about the crapshoot of Flora's weekend. The court hearing reared up in her mind, then, and her ability to focus on the outside world became impaired.

Quinn put his arm around her and whispered, "Losing it, are you?"

She gave him 'the look'. He drained his beer, stood up, and put out his hand to help her up. Ozzie noticed and waved. They made their exit easily, and she was immediately soothed by the quiet of the parking lot.

"It's not too late. Are you up for company?"

"I am," she says. "I was just done socializing."

Quinn gets her. She smiles into her empty coffee cup and rises to finish her chores while contemplating their relationship.

I keep waiting for the other shoe to drop. My tendency toward the negative can't be good for us. On the other hand, Quinn seems to think that little trait of mine is amusing. What a sweetie!

31.

Sunday afternoon rolls around and the West party is imminent. The couple climbs into June's car but Quinn takes the wheel. June kicks back to enjoy the leisurely drive in the country. Once they arrive, her weekend is over. This is, after all, work for her.

"You seem pretty relaxed, all things considered." Quinn drives with the easy confidence of a man not threatened by a bunch of strangers. "Feeling good about court?"

"Yeah, I am. Very Zen." She strikes a meditative pose, eyes closed and palms up, chanting, "All things are right with the Universe; everything happens for a reason."

"I've noticed," he says. "I see a changein you lately."

She sits up straight, immediately serious. "Really? Like what?"

"Well, you're more relaxed in spite of the bullshit at work, and more able to wind down afterwards."

She ponders this. "I don't feel so helpless these days, but the sleepless nights are still bugging me... I'm tired."

"It seems like a normal reaction to the responsibilities of your job, Junie."

"I agree, but it doesn't make it easy when I'm perpetually exhausted. Aside from the insomnia, I *am* feeling like a wise old crone these days."

"Hah! Is that a good thing?" Quinn laughs.

"Well, it is if you like prunes!"

He slides into a smooth mood. "June, what do you think about our prospects for the future?"

HUH?!

"Uh, you mean, like, will we stay together, or..."

He says, "This Flora case has gotten me thinking about your Permanence Theory, how everybody is searching for someone to share their life with them."

"I do believe humans are affiliating beings and that most of us function better when we have a community, of sorts," she says. "That could be a family or a close connection, say kids in a fraternity or sorority. I really think we need to feel connected to someone, or some group, to be happy. Otherwise, kids would be flourishing in orphanages and adoption would never be an issue."

"Right! Do you think that's why we're so happy these days? Because we have a good connection?"

"It's possible." She treads lightly. "We support each other pretty well."

"You could say we've created our own community, just you and me, right?"

"Uh, huh."

"We are actually good at it, the connecting part, wouldn't you say so?" He turns the car into the lane leading to Rosemary and Michael's place.

She smiles at him. "I would say we are excellent at connecting."

Quinn parks the car, turns it off and says, "Do you think we'll always be good at it?"

Divorce in her past, excruciatingly nasty, leads her to shrug. "Scary question. If we had a way to test for it, nobody would ever break up."

He steps out and their eyes connect over the top of the car. He says, "I'd say we're in a great place."

"I agree! Hey, thanks for coming with me today."

He moves to her side and grabs her hand. "Wouldn't miss it for the world."

They walk slowly toward the lights of the party, feeling warm and relaxed.

32.

"She should be here soon," Keely says. "Are you ready?"

Flora runs her fingers through her hair and checks in the mirror. *Looking good.*

"Yes, I'm ready." They start downstairs. "Wait, Keely?"

She turns to look at her, eyebrows lifted.

"What if I forget the words or something? I want it to be perfect."

Keely laughs. "No performer is ever perfect. I've got your back, Flora, but you won't need it. You'll knock their socks off. Now, let's go mingle."

Flora already believes Keely is on her side. Besides, she

would do anything for Rosemary. And she understands how important it is for Flora to fit in.

"Look, I know acting is easy for you," Keely says. "It's second nature for kids like us. Today, let people see the Flora that wants everyone here to feel special and cherished. Be their host. Look into their eyes and smile. They really want to like you so make it easy for them. Then, excuse yourself when you need a break."

I can do that.

Outside, the party is in full swing and she slips into her host role, the way Rosemary taught her. *It's like being in a movie only I get to be the star!*

It sounds dorky but she feels different here, grown up. People talk to her like she's an adult and listen to everything she says. So crazy. It's like being a regular person.

While mingling with Rosemary and Michael's friends, she sees June standing across the yard.

Thank God she's finally here! She's gonna love my surprise.

33.

Expecting a small gathering, June's stunned by the number of people at the West Family Picnic. Her first view is akin to one of those movie shots: a gathering of the well to do, all dressed in their casual best, smiling and chatting flawlessly. She suddenly feels out of her league and she's not even sure why.

"June! June, over here." Rosemary moves rapidly, handing off a tray of food stuff to a smiling young man. She greets June with open arms. "Finally, you made it!"

After one of those trademark hugs, June can't help but gush. "Wow, Rosemary, this reminds me of a soirée at the White House Rose Garden. What happened to my favorite country girl?"

"Oh, this is nothing, a trick of the senses is all." She

waves her hand in the air to dismiss the awe. "Nice weather, a few flowers, and some twinkle-y lights will make any yard look fabulous. We got lucky in the weather department."

Not missing a beat, Rosemary plants herself directly in front of Quinn. "And speaking of fabulous, are you ready to introduce us?"

"Of course. Rosemary West, may I present my charming escort, Mr. Quinn Harimann."

Quinn extends his hand, which Rosemary grasps in both of hers. "Welcome, Quinn Harimann. 'Any friend of June's…', and all that."

"Rosemary West, it is an honor." Quinn's so relaxed and comfortable in these situations, it's enviable. "June has elevated you to sainthood and that doesn't happen often. You have a fantastic place here…" and they are off, chatting away like old friends.

While they connect, she steals a moment to scan the yard for Flora. People are dressed in light flowing clothes because it's a warm spring, lending a floaty watercolor effect to the scene. Every age group is represented here, from distinguished elders to babies on the hip. Her eyes move back and forth like a sonar screen, watch for the blip… there!

Flora appears in a long-sleeved, sheer floral dress that just skims her ankles, and her hair is loose and wind-blown. She wears tooled leather cowgirl boots that June immediately lusts after, and a fabulous stone necklace hung low around her neck. She almost doesn't recognize her, not because of her bohemian-chic attire but because of her poised demeanor. The girl seems born to this lifestyle.

June takes a moment to watch the girl. She's deep in conversation with a silver-haired gentleman, who's very intent on her responses. A middle-aged woman carries a tray into their space and speaks directly to Flora, obviously describing the food selection. The girl listens to every word then chooses something carefully. The woman waits while she tastes, clearly expecting a response. Flora's eyes almost shut as she takes a moment to savor, then she touches a hand to her heart and says a few words. The woman beams and starts to walk on. As she moves past her, Flora lightly brushes the woman's arm and her lips form the words, "Thank you."

Even from this distance, June can *feel* the girl's gratitude. In that brief pause, the woman blooms. Then, Flora returns her attention to the gentleman.

Holy crap.

Not having seen Flora in a social situation, especially at this level of sophistication, June expected to witness 'awkward'.

Hell, I feel awkward!

What she saw was the gracious charm natural to those raised in high culture and old money.

Where in the world did she pick this up?

As if she hears the woman's thoughts, Flora stops speaking and turns... her eyes light up and her face animates. She says something to the gentleman, who smiles and waves her away. She almost skips over.

"Oh, June," she breathes with excitement. "This has been the most amazing weekend! I can't wait to tell you everything!"

In that moment, she returns to the childlike bearing June knows so well, clasping her hands in front of her, "Can you believe this beautiful outfit? Rosemary took me shopping. Her friend is an artist and made this necklace. This turquoise rock came from a Native American Reservation in New Mexico."

June fingers the gem, easily worth a fortune, and does her best to hide any concern. "Gorgeous! You look lovely, Flora, really lovely."

Flora chatters a mile a minute. "You have to meet Keely Bruce, she's here at the party. We went to see her concert, oh my god, she was unbelievable, June! Then we got to go back to her dressing room, it was so tiny. She had food in there, like grapes and strawberries and cheese, fancy stuff, and we talked, just like regular people! Rosemary is her friend from when they were in school together, can you believe it? She came over to our house and GAVE ME A SINGING LESSON!"

Our house? Hmmm, that was fast.

Of course, June doesn't say it out loud, but the kid senses something. She stops cold. Wide-eyed, Flora puts her hands over her mouth, literally preventing any more words from pouring out.

Taking her by her shoulders, June looks her right in the eyes and says, "Easy, kid, take a breath."

Grasping her around her shoulders, she steers Flora toward a quieter area. "What a fantastic weekend you're having, so fun." The girl quiets, settling down. "Flora, you have beautiful manners. Have you taken some etiquette classes or something?"

She brightens immediately. "Oh, we learned manners and stuff like that last year at school in ballroom dancing class. Rosemary and Keely coached me too."

Manners? I have a new respect for the curriculum at the local public schools.

"Well, you certainly learned your lessons well. I'm very impressed."

"Thanks, June, I'm trying." She blushes and gives that almost-smile. "Rosemary says 'people are more important than things' so we should treat everybody with respect. She says rich or poor doesn't matter, it's who you are inside that counts. She's like you, that way."

June laughs. "Yep, I told you Rosemary was cool. Now, show me where the food is, before I faint from all this excitement."

34.

Flora and Quinn had not yet been introduced but, by the

look on his face, he recognizes her immediately. He smiles. She smiles back.

Flora thinks, "For a newcomer, he seems totally at home among all these strangers." Quinn escorts Rosemary. Flora follows June. Their paths intersect at the food tables.

"Who is this lovely young lady, June?" Quinn, still smiling, extends his hand.

She reaches out her own hand. "I'm Flora."

"I've heard a lot of nice things about you, Flora," Quinn says, bowing. "I'm Quinn and I'm driving your carriage this evening."

She looks at June for guidance – laugh, be gracious, what?

June reassures her, "Yep, Quinn is our chauffeur this evening, Flora. After such a fancy party we deserve to ride home in style."

"Aren't you the lucky ones," Rosemary says. "Now let me give you all a tour of our food fest." She smoothly moves to make everyone comfortable and the group cooperates, turning their attention to the food table while she describes each of the edible treats.

35.

This food is amazing!

June's duties set aside, she tries to choose between desserts: mini cheesecakes or tiny turtle brownies, delicate fruit tarts or chocolate-dipped strawberries? Noticing Quinn and Michael West chatting in a corner of the yard, she smiles. She sees they're eating chocolate sundaes with what looks like spoon-shaped cookies and heads in their direction.

"Excuse me, fellas, but is this ice cream only for special guests?"

Michael swallows a mouthful and confronts her. "Why, ice cream is served only to the deserving around here.

Have you crafted any magnificent buildings lately?"

"Well, no sir." She hangs her head and shuffles her feet in the dust. "But I did alter the life of a teenage girl recently."

"You win," Michael concedes and moves aside, exposing a sundae table behind him. "Feast, dear woman, with our gratitude!"

Attempting to make a ladylike sundae, June scoops pecans and drizzles caramel as they chat. "I see you two have met."

"June, I have to thank you for bringing Quinn." Michael extends his arms dramatically and scans the party. "Who else would listen to me but a fellow 'wood guy'?"

"Right!" Quinn rolls his eyes. "This guy is an artist. I'm thrilled to pick his brain. We snuck over to Westwoods for a quick tour and he has some cabinets you have to see. The carving is fantastic and the detailing… phenomenal!"

Michael explains that the pieces are an exclusive design created for a local corporate executive building a "green" home. He consults on the project and provides such fine points as hand-carved stair railings, kitchen and bathroom cabinets, and a fireplace with built-in bookshelves on either side of the mantelpiece. Not only is the woodwork carved with botanicals such as Jack in the Pulpit and Maidenhair Fern, but his students are creating stained glass doors for the cabinets and bookshelves in the same theme. Rosemary designed the stained-glass creations, coordinating the Prairie-style architecture with the flavor of this home. When completed, this residence will be a masterpiece.

"Thanks, Quinn." Michael says, "For me, it's like being asked to paint the Sistine Chapel. I started the first piece about six weeks ago. We won't be completing the project for a few more months."

Quinn tries to describe the work he saw, the many extraordinary pieces on display, but Michael interrupts him.

"Now wait, more than half of those are pieces my students create. As June learned the other day, I display them so they can claim gallery status and, hopefully, sales. I get quite a few collectors and designers in here, so their chances of being seen are good."

Quinn describes a small polished wood sculpture for June, one that impressed him. It was a life-size pair of hands cupping some sea shells.

"The shells were actually carved from what looked like quartz or marble. The piece was intricate and quite beautiful. It made me wonder whose hands were rendered there."

After a moment of comfortable silence, June says, "You and Rosemary have a unique lifestyle, Michael. I bet Flora had a ball this weekend."

"Oh, I'm sure she did, but we tried not to overwhelm her with our… um, let's call it 'uniqueness'!" Michael chuckles but maintains a manner of concern. "Not every kid would want this life. The demands on us are different than a normal family… as are our expectations."

"How so?" Quinn's genuinely interested.

"Well, we travel during certain times of the year, to gallery shows and the like. I have to go to other countries to find special mediums for my sculpting, requiring negotiation of fair-trade agreements with local groups – all business, I'm afraid. Rosemary flies to D.C. every so often too, for EPA business." He shakes his head. "Kids don't always respond well to so much disruption in their schedules, especially teenagers. And we have expectations for maintaining the gardens and animals: everybody in the household works!" Michael smiles broadly at that last part, crossing his arms and comically imitating a stern farm boss.

Quinn laughs. "Too bad more parents don't feel that way. I'm a fan of less TV, social networking, and video games with more involvement in something productive."

"Yeah, Rosie and I believe kids need to feel competent

in as many things as possible, especially kids who have lost their original family. An experience like that makes a kid question his or her worth, I think, so we want to build in experiences that enhance a feeling of value. We do the same for our students, only in a more limited arena."

"Sounds like you guys have it figured out," Quinn says, clearly approving. Then he shifts gears. "I guess we three better get back to the party or we're gonna have *our* value questioned."

"We really need to think about going soon," June says. "Flora has school tomorrow."

"Makes sense," Michael says. "But you'd better let Rosemary know about your timeline, June. She wants to transition Flora out of 'party-mode' and make plans for another visit."

Pretty soon these two will be doing my job for me.

"Terrific. I'm on my way to see her now."

The men fall back into conversation. She envies them their comfort.

36.

Wandering through clusters of guests, June finds Rosemary with Flora and... Keely Bruce!

"June, meet an old friend of mine! Keely Bruce, June Hunter."

Maybe not completely star-struck, exactly, but impressed, absolutely. "Wow, it's a real pleasure. You're one of my favorite performers."

"Thanks so much, June, happy to meet you. Rose tells me you do some pretty amazing work, yourself."

She's elegant and beautiful, with a voice like caramel. June struggles to find anything intelligent to say.

"Flora and Keely have a little surprise for you." Rosemary puts her hand on Flora's shoulder, in a maternal fashion. "They worked pretty hard on it this morning."

116

Hmmm, something in a song?

She finds her voice again and says, gently, "That's why I came looking for you, to remind you we need to leave a bit early to get Flora home."

Rosemary turns to Keely and explains. "Flora stays in town and it's a bit of a drive... *and* she has school tomorrow, right?"

She turns to Flora, hands on hips, comically.

Flora nods.

Rosemary grabs June's hand. "Will you please entertain Keely for me while Flora and I take care of some business? We won't be long."

Of course I will entertain Keely Bruce!

"My pleasure."

Keely smiles and gestures to a table. "Let's sit." She takes command, sitting close, creating an atmosphere of intimacy. "Rosemary's great, isn't she? She's one of my favorite people in the whole world."

"She is pretty special." June tries to calm herself. "Flora seems taken with her."

Keely fidgets a little, which seems out of character, then approaches the subject gingerly. "If you need a character reference or anything for this adoption to be approved, I'd like to be considered, June. I've known Rosemary forever, since we were teenagers, and I could vouch for her in a big way."

"I take it you approve of this adoption, Keely?"

Nodding, she leans forward. "I understand there are difficulties surrounding the adoption of a teenager. I won't pretend I know what they all are, but Rosemary and Michael have been schooling me in the DCW requirements and legal process. It seems like the most important thing to consider is a lifetime commitment to Flora, people who will support her and stand by her into adulthood. Right?"

These people do their homework and so do their friends. This makes June happy, kind of, but she still keeps up her guard. She can't be swayed in her final decision, not even if it means pissing off Keely Bruce.

"Keely, this weekend's a trip to Disneyland for a kid like Flora. But living together is different. When the thrill wears off and the emotional baggage kicks in, she'll present any number of behaviors ranging from slightly unpleasant, to illegal, to absolutely horrible. We never know what it'll look like. We just know it *will* happen. At this stage, it's difficult for people to understand what they could be facing later. Imagine stopping at the hospital an hour after delivery to tell your friend that her new baby could grow up to become a drug addict or suicide risk."

June sticks her fingers in her ears and sings, "La, la, la, I can't hear you…" Removing her fingers she looks her in the eye, "Isn't that about the reaction you'd expect?"

Keely has a funny look, somber but there's something else. "I get it," she says. "Denial is first, but potential is what keeps us going. Love and commitment keep us believing."

Coming out of the great singer's mouth, that sounds a lot like the words to a love song.

"Or," June hits it hard across the net, "when the kid strikes out and turns her back on us, we feel so disappointed and hurt and betrayed that we reject the child to save our own spirit from being crushed. Can you imagine what that does to a kid, to listen to a litany of your flaws as the reason why Mom doesn't want you anymore? Most parents don't return their kids to the hospital when they become nasty teenagers. Only adopted kids experience this particular form of rejection. Flora's already been rejected too many times."

Keely is quiet for a moment then returns her serve. "You are probably not aware that I am an adoptee, June. My foster care experience was none too pleasant either, so I deeply appreciate your passion. Where does it come from?"

Crap. Advantage: Keely Bruce.

"I was not adopted myself, if that's what you're asking." She begins her 'why I became a caseworker' speech. "I can't explain why I was drawn to social services as my medium—maybe like singing attracted you. This is the way I express my passion and how I contribute to society. Call it my social identity."

Keely is giving me a look that says, "I think you're full of shit."

"I appreciate you discussing it with me at all, June." She finally smiles. "It isn't like I'm the one who wants to adopt her, right?"

"I believe that the whole circle adopts a kid, Keely, including parents, extended family, friends. I think it's a credit to you that you already care about Flora. Thanks for spending time with her. I know she'll remember this weekend as one of the highlights of her life, largely because of you."

"I hope to spend a lot more time with her over the years." She reaches over and puts her hand firmly on June's arm. "Don't count me out, please, just because I'm a performer. I spend a surprising amount of time here. Rosemary and Michael *are* my extended family."

Before more can be said, Quinn and Michael show up, deep in conversation about 'green construction'. Keely turns away from June and says something that makes the guys laugh.

She sees Rosemary and Flora making their way across the lawn. They're walking shoulder to shoulder, heads tilted together as if sharing a secret. June can see Flora's excited, wound up.

"Time for our surprise?" Keely asks Flora. They grin at each other and disappear into a garden shed.

Rosemary whispers, "I'm the crew for this show... see you in a few minutes." Then she takes off, too.

June suddenly feels like an outsider here. It's the Curse of the Caseworker: invited to work, not to socialize.

37.

The late afternoon light is rosy and washed out. Lanterns are lit on tables and poles throughout the yard, and soft music is pumped in from somewhere. All at once, flood lights highlight the shed and the music stops. The guests hush and turn in expectation.

"Ladies and gentlemen, friends and family," Rosemary is speaking into a wireless mike, "I hope you are all comfortable?"

The crowd responds, people are smiling, raising their glasses and such.

"One of our special guests needs to leave early. It's a school night, after all." Laughter from the crowd. "She wants to say goodnight in her own way, as a special gift to her friend, June. Keely will be her Supporting Lady, tonight. Please make her exit a warm one… ladies and gentlemen, I give you Flora!"

June watches as Flora and Keely step out of the shed and into the light. Both of them are holding mics and in costume. Keely is wearing a man's red velvet smoking jacket and silk ascot, her hair pulled back tight. Flora is wearing a black 1940's-style hat with an eye veil and a big red rose, a full-length black wool coat, and a patent leather pocketbook over her arm. With her Marcel waves and red lipstick, she could be an old-time movie starlet, elegant and composed.

Keely and Flora are facing each other, not the crowd. Keely strikes the key, "Hmmmm…" and Flora joins in, humming harmony.

A pause. Then Flora sings to Keely a cappella, "I really can't stay…"

Keely answers in song.

This is a rendition of a charming old duet called "Baby, It's Cold Outside!", the Louie Armstrong version being one of June's favorites. All she can see is Flora's face, completely transformed.

Her voice, unaided by any musical instrument, is clear and wrenching, but she has just the right hint of humor meant for this number.

She doesn't even see the audience and she is smiling, really smiling, showing all her teeth. The chemistry is obvious, the give and take between them is what you would expect from true professionals, flawless.

Could this be the real Flora?

Finally, the singers turn to face the audience, heads tilted together, arms outstretched, eyes half shut. They sing the last line together in an elegant harmony for a big finish.

The crowd goes absolutely wild. The performance is amazing, delightful, playful, breathtaking even.

So, why am I crying?

38.

Flora's amazed by the experience of performing. Once she and Keely started to sing, the whole world dropped away. The music took up all the space around them and inside of her. Nothing else existed for her, not the party, or the lights, or the people. It was like floating away in a rainbow cloud, mind and body.

Then, at the end of her final note, the applause was an intrusion, abrupt and astonishing. It broke the spell and brought her falling back to the world. The hypnotic that was the performance drained away and she crashed back to earth. It left her trembling and disoriented, but only for a moment.

Something else filled her up right away. In place of the music, came the sound of the people all around her cheering and clapping. It rushed in and illuminated her insides with sound.

"Bravo!" Faces come into focus now, smiling at her and calling her name. She and Keely have their arms around each other. Hugging, taking a bow, then another.

Quinn's helping June get through the crowd and Flora rushes into her arms. "Did you like it? I wanted it to be a surprise, were you surprised?"

She's startled to see tears on June's face. "What...?"

June smiles and wipes her eyes. "It was so good, it made me cry! That was amazing!" She grabs the girl in a firm embrace.

"Look at your fans, Flora," June tells her, releasing her and turning toward the cheering crowd.

Right then, Flora feels herself freeze up, unable to talk or move. Her legs go numb. She teeters.

Oh, please don't let me fall...

39.

June sees the color drain from Flora's face and grips her tightly. She looks frantically for Rosemary, who clearly sees it too.

She nods at June, lifts the mike and says, "Thank you, Flora and Keely, we just loved it. Let's say goodnight to Flora, everyone!"

The crowd claps and shouts accolades. Rosemary signals June and they hustle Flora toward the house, Quinn picking up the rear behind Keely. June can't help but feel like a rock star's roadie.

In the relative quiet of the house, Flora quickly recuperates. Keely takes both of her hands and says, "This was amazing. Now remember what we said?"

She and Flora chant in unison, "Always make your exit on a high note!"

Keely might be one tough cookie but even I think that's pretty cute.

Flora changes clothes in her bedroom. Earlier, she told June she thought it was smart to leave her 'nice things' there rather than take them to the group home. Another sign of her growing trust.

Rosemary takes her by the shoulders, smiling warmly. "Call me next week, Flora."

"I will, I promise. Thank you so much!" She and Rosemary hug for a long minute, tearful but laughing.

Rosemary says, "I miss you already. Now drink this on the way home." She hands her a bottle of mineral water and they head out the door with her belongings. June sees Quinn's already brought up the car.

Last in line for good-byes, Michael walks Flora to the car, helping her into her seat and slipping a sturdy brown bag onto her lap. "Thanks for being here this weekend, Flora. You made every minute a treasure."

June hears Flora choke up and say, "Oh Michael…"

June says her own good-byes and thank-yous as she slips into the passenger seat. They head slowly down the lane, away from the party.

"Well, Flora, I've never been to a party like it," June says. "You really stole the show, singing with Keely Bruce. What a great weekend, eh?"

"Wait." At the junction of the lane and the highway, Flora says, "Could you stop for a second, Quinn? I can't see what this is."

They pull over and Quinn puts on the interior lights. They both turn to the backseat to see her open the bag Michael gave her.

Quinn lets out a gasp. There, in Flora's lap, is the extraordinary piece from Westwoods, the perfectly carved hands cradling delicate shells… signed by the famous sculptor, Michael West.

40.

Inside the quiet of the group home in the minutes before lights out, Flora sits with Gina on the floor outside of her room. Backs against the wall and facing each other, Flora tells her all about the weekend.

"I mean, it's only the first visit so we still have a way to go. But I'm telling you, Gina, it was an amazing weekend with the most amazing people. Is it stupid to feel like they could be my family already?"

Gina has her arms wrapped around her knees, staring at the ceiling. "Don't be ridiculous. I feel like they're your family and I haven't even met 'em. I'm so jealous!"

Flora feels bad then, like she's been rubbing it in her face. "Oh, no, Gina, I'm sorry! How was your visit with that nurse lady, Jan?"

"Fine, no worries," Gina grins at her. "I liked Jan pretty well too, until now."

Flora laughs. "You know this was special, right? It's not like everyday life. I'm almost afraid to find out what 'everyday life' is really like there. Nothing could be as great as this visit!"

Gina doesn't laugh, though, and Flora starts to panic. "Gina? What did I say – what's wrong?""

The other girl looks at her, real serious. "Kids never get tired of Christmas parties or birthday presents or vacations to Disneyland. But that doesn't mean the rest of the time it sucks. Everyday life can be pretty good too."

Flora rolls that around in her head for a few minutes. Life with the Jacobies was mostly quiet, everyday the same. There were no extraordinary days like she had this weekend, nothing she could look back on as a great memory. It was just… nice. Until it wasn't.

"Gina, do you ever talk to anybody else you've met in foster care? You know, like, after they go home or get adopted or anything?"

"I did for a while with one girl, but she went home for good and never answered me after that." Gina says, "Are you wondering if we can be friends later?"

Flora nods. *What if she says no way?*

"We could make a pact, promise to stay in touch no matter what, right? You know, I never had a friend like that," Gina says.

"Me neither," Flora says. "But it sounds like it might be cool."

"Let's do it! First, we gotta meet each other's placement people and say if we think they're ok. 'Cuz if this works out, we'll be visiting each other for sleepovers and all that."

The girls laugh and chatter until Irene interrupts, "To bed, ladies!"

II. JUVENILE COURT

1.

It's comfortable in June's house but she builds a small fire in the woodstove anyway. *Just a little after midnight… I hope I can sleep soon.*

Quinn offered to stay but he knew she'd be working late tonight. He headed home after they dropped Flora at Crossette and June was safely in Tully's care.

They did have a chance to talk about the party on the ride home. Quinn mentioned Flora's fancy clothes, boots, and jewelry. He wondered about Rosemary and Keely, and their plan to make Flora 'an offer she couldn't refuse.' But mostly he noticed how the girl seemed to trust June.

"I could see it clearly in the way she listened to you and in her body language," Quinn said. "She really needs you, I think."

Geez. No pressure. Thanks, Quinn.

Reflecting on the West Picnic, it rivals anything June's experienced in a pre-adoption visit. She recalls riding with a foster child in a private limo to a mansion on the lake, in the ritzy suburbs north of Chicago. That was pretty cool, but nowhere near as emotional as the picnic.

Flora is blossoming right before her eyes. Is it Rosemary and Michael's influence or something else, like Flora's desire for a family, maybe? It could be Flora has tapped into her true talent, performing. Her bliss simply radiated out to all of us in the audience, and even afterwards.

June decides to move slower than originally planned, until she can get a better handle on the dynamics of this situation. Waiting for the other shoe to drop has always been a great strategy, a technique that's served her well in a number of cases. Experience tells her this profound truth: there is *always* another shoe.

Thinking about the court hearing coming up, her stomach clenches. Since this will be in Juvenile Court, the only people allowed in the courtroom are involved parties and witnesses. Flora will only have to see them when they're testifying, then out they go. That's a good thing. It means Flora won't be dealing with a bunch of people in the audience who might try to intimidate or confuse her. It also means no press allowed, a judicial policy designed to protect the privacy of the minor.

June is committed to staying out of Hal and Sarge's way, so as not to mess up somehow and be politically incorrect. She doesn't know all the connections and isn't sure she wants to. But she knows there's more than meets the eye in this case. She's trusting Hal and Sarge on this one, more than she typically likes to do. Trust is totally *not* her strong suit.

I know I'm a bit of a control freak, but who can blame me?

She picks up her pad and starts scratching, jotting down notes and getting her thoughts on paper. This week is a study in contrasts, the success of Flora's visit against the backdrop of being summoned to court. It's hard for a grown-up to swallow, let alone seeing it from Flora's perspective. Her head must be spinning.

Note: *Process with Flora; identify areas of concern, life is not all fancy clothes and singing stars.*

Note: *Talk to Michael and Rosemary about possible role in court.*

Note: *Flora needs prep work for court; see Sarge first thing.*

Note: *ID a 'worst-case scenario' re: court.*

Note: *Keely Bruce wants to testify on the family's behalf (really???)*

Then back to a few of the items on the Court Report, add a detail here and there, circle a few questionable parts as she sees them.

"I want to get to the office early before the noise and stimulation distracts me," she tells Tully. He blinks his understanding. She writes best in the quiet hours before and after work. Besides, she needs Sarge to review her draft and give his input prior to any final revisions.

Next time she looks up, it's almost 3:00 a.m.

Crap! I need to sleep.

Tully pads after her as she shuffles off to bed, a silent sentry keeping her safe from the world.

2.

June arrives at her office around 6:30 after only two hours of sleep, notes in hand. Dora's desk is clean and uncluttered. She usually gets in around 7:45.

June puts a fancy crème-filled donut right in the middle of Dora's desk with a bottle of cranberry-apple juice next to it. Making a tent with a clean kitchen towel from the lunch room, the treats are hidden from view. That's to keep any other early birds from getting tempted by this Monday morning offering. She's going to need Dora and her clerical skills later today, so this is her way of paying homage.

It isn't something I have to do – Dora's always professional – but I like to thank her in advance once in a while.

Spreading the notes out on her desk, she powers up the computer. She wishes, for a moment, that the State would spring for a laptop. Then, just as quickly, she withdraws the wish. It probably helps to keep her worlds separate. Otherwise, she'd be tapping the keys every time a thought crossed her mind, during dinner, at the movies, or watching a sunset.

Never mind. Just get to work!

An hour and a half later, Dora pokes her head in. "Thanks, June. I found my breakfast."

"How could you tell it was from me?"

"Nobody else knows my love of cranapple juice." She shoots her a warm smile. "Oh, and Sarge left a message for you to start the meeting without him. He says he should be in by 9:00 at the latest."

Nodding, June continues compiling her report as Dora slips out. Finishing up, she prints it out and stretches like a cat in the sunshine.

Eyes closed, begin the mantra: breathe in, breathe out. Rats, what happened to my Zen?

She carries the draft to Sarge's empty office and leaves it on his chair, where he can't miss it. Then she grabs a cup of coffee and gets the stuff ready for their Monday Team Meeting.

"Good Morning, boys and girls...and who shall we save today?"

Sarcasm isn't lost on the team. They all know they can't save anyone, except maybe themselves on a good day. Regardless, this relatively enthusiastic group of do-gooders jumps in, reviewing cases and sharing ideas.

"Almost done, Hunter?"

Sarge arrives at the meeting just as she's ready to close. He shares his schedule for the week, asks a few questions about court actions, and assigns a couple of new cases. Not-so-subtle glances are aimed her way when he doesn't assign anything new to June's caseload. No one believes that's a good thing.

As the meeting breaks up, June follows him out. "Did you get a chance to read my draft yet?"

"No, Hunter," he sighs. "I'm on my way there now."

"OK, well, yell if you want me to make any revisions." He shoots a dark look her way and closes his office door in her face.

Dora winces and gives one of those *"Hang in there!"* looks as she answers the phone. Before June turns away, though, she's waving at her, phone tucked under her chin, speaking to someone in her soothing voice. Moving closer, Dora's end of the conversation gives her hope.

"Yes, she was in Mr. Barrett's office, but I'll see if she can get free... no, no, I won't disturb her... Thank you, Mrs. West... hold on, please."

"Rosemary West?"

"Yes, she is in her car and wants to come by, if you are free."

That's gotta be a good sign, right? "Now's as good a time as any. Tell her to come on over if she can be here within the next half hour."

She heads back to her desk, listening to Dora's 'smiley voice' on the phone say, "Fifteen minutes is fine, Mrs. West, I'll tell her."

June flashes her the thumbs-up sign and starts cleaning for company. Dora has Rosemary all set up with coffee by the time I'm ready. "Thanks, Dora, send her over."

She greets her guest and mimes, a phone to her ear while shaking her head means *no calls*. They step inside her cubby hole and sit.

Rosemary apologizes, "I'm sorry to show up on a Monday morning, June! I know how busy you are…"

She holds up her hand to stop the apology.

"Rosemary, your timing is perfect. You were my next phone call. I want to talk about your visit and some other things. You go first. How was the first visit?"

"Oh, June, it was so great. I know we gave the kid a sort of Disneyland for a first visit, but it just worked out that way. Honest! Sometimes our lives are like that."

"Really, it's fine," June says, trying to put her at ease. "Tell me the best part and your biggest concern."

She thinks for a moment. "Well, I know Sunday was really wonderful but that wasn't the best part. Before all the excitement of Keely's concert, Flora and I went shopping together. First, we went to the shops downtown and then to this little café I like. It was very relaxed, gave us a chance to talk. Nothing dramatic, we just gabbed about school, her friends, and the clothes she likes. For me, this was the best part, just talking and laughing. It made me feel… um, like a Mom."

Goose bumps! Maintaining a professional demeanor, June responds, "I'm glad, Rosemary. Now, tell me your biggest concern."

She grows serious. "I hope you don't think I'm being nosy but what is going on with her former foster family? She seems pretty worried. She was sort of vague about them being 'mad' and 'not liking me anymore.' What happened there? Is it appropriate for me to ask?"

June takes a deep breath and tells her everything: the problem with Brendan; the State's decision *not* to file charges; the Jacobie's counter-filing; the hearing on Wednesday. It's a gamble, telling her all this, but she can't NOT tell her.

Rosemary just sits there, looking stunned.

It's time to make her the offer.

"This is your out, Rose. If you and Michael don't want this kind of mess in your home, I will understand. Some wives would be nervous, having a girl with a sexual abuse history living in their home; husbands are pretty vulnerable under those circumstances. In fact, all your college students coming and going would increase your vulnerability, too."

Rosemary scowls, stammering, "You mean you think she might, what, come on to Michael?"

"No, I didn't say that. The truth is, she was either sexually molested or has made a false charge. Either way, some folks don't want to touch a kid like this."

She runs her fingers through her hair and takes a big gulp of coffee. Timing is critical at this point, so June forces herself not to speak. Blank face, blank eyes, to let the woman process this without influence. This way, she can never say they held back the facts or tried to coerce her one way or the other. This has to be her call, hers and Michael's.

June picks up her cup and stands. "Excuse me a second."

She gets a refill and a couple of chocolate chip cookies to bring back. Over the years she's learned that fiddling with a cookie helps some people to think. As for June, she usually needs something to stick in her mouth, to keep her from saying too much.

Back at the desk, Rosemary's been crying. June reaches for the tissues and put on her *I understand* face and a small concerned smile. "You ok?"

"Oh, that poor kid. How horrible for her." Rosemary is angry. "Why didn't you tell me, June? I can't let her go through this alone!"

"Through what? You mean, court?"

"You bet I do!" Rosemary takes out her planner and a pen, "Now, what time is the hearing on Wednesday?"

"I don't even know if the Judge will let you in the courtroom with her, Rose. Let's just slow down a minute."

Rosemary goes still, her voice grim and determined. "Tell me how to do this, June. Don't leave me out here on my own."

June tries to pacify her. "This is emotional stuff, big stuff. You need to talk to Michael. I want you both to think about this for a day or two."

"I don't know what we're supposed to think about, June." She's really pissed off now. "We've already made the decision to commit to Flora. What are you implying?"

Whoa! Deep breath, slow down. She's just upset.

June leans back in her chair and talks low and slow. "Rosemary, I am not accusing you of anything. Honest. I'm trying to be fair. You didn't have this information about Flora before because it just came up last week. I want your decision to be made based on reality, not fantasy."

She copies June by leaning back, breathing deep. "I guess I'm overreacting here, eh?"

With a wave of her hand, June dismisses her emotional outburst. "Nah, you're just processing. This is good."

A smile appears and Rosemary says, "Look, we're not new to parenting someone else's kid. We know it's hard. There is nothing like losing a child to put it all in perspective. You see the value in accepting the child's strengths and weaknesses, rather than fighting them. Time is too short!"

She stops herself to gain control and, after a few deep breaths, continues, "In Flora's case, her window is closing. She's aging out of the system, and we believe this is our time to jump into her life. There are never any guarantees, even if you birth the child. She could grow up to be a professional or a criminal, an artist or a drug addict. Flora doesn't have time to defend her past, June. She's ready to go forward *now*. We will give her that chance, no matter what. That's what parents do, right?"

"You aren't her parents yet," June cautions her.

"Oh, come on, June," Rosemary smiles wide. "You don't really believe that, do you?"

3.

Flora dresses carefully for court, in the outfit Irene helped her pick out the night before.

"Going to court is kinda like a job interview, Flora," she had explained. "You want to look like a nice young girl but not too phony. This blue top is perfect for that, simple and pretty but not over-the-top."

Flora's hands shake as she dresses. She checks herself in the mirror but doesn't really know what to look for. Her face is pale and there are dark circles under her eyes. She decides it will have to be good enough and turns toward the door.

Her backpack sits on the floor next to her bed. Flora decides she won't need it in court. Anyway, her most valuable things are either locked in Irene's office or sitting in her room at Rosemary and Michael's house.

Deep breath.

Everyone says not to worry and just be myself. But which 'myself' is the one they want me to be???

4.

I love the smell of this courtroom, a cross between lemon oil and sawdust. I belong here!

June takes a deep breath. "And so it begins."

"Hey, June." Hal smiles, relaxed and exuding confidence.

"Who's the Designer Suit?" June refers to Jacobie's attorney.

"Russ Monty. He does some criminal work, mostly corporate, never been in Juvenile Court as far as I know."

She files that information under 'good-to-know' and asks, "Who's our Judge today?"

"Judge Paxton's on the bench. Do you know him?"

She shakes her head and Hal continues, "He's new to the rotation, but did some juvenile work as a State's Attorney in the Chicago suburbs some time ago. Reputation says he's fair, not too fond of grand-standing, and usually rules in the best interest of the kid. Sounds pretty good for us."

Rosemary is situated in the third row on the aisle. She isn't in the Judge's direct line of sight, but ready to speak if called upon. Michael sits quietly beside her. Hal gave them the go-ahead to be there and Monty couldn't have cared less.

From her seat in the front row, June turns and gives them a nod. Rosemary returns a small smile that says she appreciates it. Then she pulls out a leather-bound notebook and starts jotting stuff down.

Probably writing down names of all the players, on both sides.

Hal heads for the front of the courtroom where he sits with Flora. The bailiff brings the girl in and escorts her to her seat. She puts a hand on Flora's shoulder, smiling kindly as she says something the others can't hear.

From June's perspective she looks like a little kid, scared and confused. She tries to catch Flora's eye, maybe shoot some support at her. No luck. She's listening intently to Hal, who's speaking softly and soberly. It looks like he's holding June's Report to the Court in his hand.

Sarge had barely touched the report for edits and Hal said it was "comprehensive, as usual." That's probably the highest compliment anyone could get.

I hope Judge Paxton had a chance to read it.

Some judges skim the reports, others don't even bother. Either way, June's prepared. She could recite that thing in her sleep.

Caseworkers would not be privy to Russ Monty's Court Report because they may be asked take the stand. They keep all the parties away from information that may cause them to alter their testimony, probably a good move. But, because June's the minor's State Representative, they let her stay in the courtroom and listen. Anyway, her testimony is all documented in the report. If she were to stray from those facts, it could jeopardize their case.

I'd give a couple of toes to see what Monty's got.

June fidgets in her seat. She'd hate to be blindsided, a favorite technique of hotshot attorneys.

The Judge appears and her adrenalin rushes.

Monty starts off the proceedings. He is smooth and articulate, polished in the way highly paid attorneys always seem to be. June gets irritated in spite of herself, as he rambles on a little about his client's sterling character. He paints Flora as a jezebel, a woman scorned, a destructive and damaged young woman who is a threat to society.

All in all, about what they expected.

Hal goes next. He talks about Flora, why she's in the system, the tragedy of her life, how she has no perceived mental health issues other than anxiety over her future. He closes by referencing the lack of evidence that would criminalize her for anything. Not impressive, but presenting an attitude that says to the Court: "Clearly no basis for a finding."

Then, Monty calls his witnesses.

The football coach is totally biased, Brendan's biggest

fan. He describes him as a role model, a spokesman for the school, blah, blah, blah.

Hal asks only two questions. "During the course of this past year, did you see any negative change in Brendan's behavior, anything that would give you concern?"

That's cool. If he says 'yes', then why didn't he do something about it? If he says 'no', then why didn't Brendan talk to his coach about something potentially serious, or even damaging?

The coach pauses, aware of his dilemma. "Well, his demeanor didn't change in the context of his performance on the field. Brendan has great focus as a player. I don't know about his social life."

"He was offered football scholarships to three prestigious universities based on his outstanding performance this year, is that correct?"

"Yes, he was," the coach confirms.

"No further questions." One down. Nice, Hal.

The current girlfriend, Kelly, has little to offer other than Brendan is "the most respectful boy she has ever dated."

Hal steps up. "Thank you, Kelly, for coming in today. It sounds like you and Brendan have a good relationship."

Kelly smiles and nods. "Yes, we do."

"He treats you well, you said?"

"Yes, he does. He's very sweet." She smiles at Brendan.

"And you weren't at all worried about this girl hounding you?"

The smile disappears. "Uh… I never said she was hounding me."

"No phone calls, no hassles at school, no threats or anything?"

"Well, no, I hardly ever spoke to her. She was only in one of my classes and a study hall."

Hal steps in front of her, blocking her view of Brendan. "So, Flora never phoned you?"

"No."

"Never confronted you, never made a scene?"

"No."

Hal leans in to Kelly. "No problems at all?"

She says, "No, no problems with me."

"How many times did you witness one of those ugly scenes between Brendan and Flora?"

"Well, um, I never actually saw anything. Brendan told me about it, though."

"I see, Brendan told you about it. When was that again?"

"About a month ago, right when they kicked her out. I guess they had to, um, you know, get rid of her, because it had finally gotten so bad."

"Wow. Things got so bad that you never heard a single word about it until after they, as you say, 'got rid of her'?"

Russ Monty jumps up. "Objection, Your Honor..."

Hal puts up his hands, stopping him. "Thank you, Kelly. No more questions, Your Honor."

A few other witnesses yield fairly neutral results. There's the expert witness, a psychologist that tries to paint Flora as a stalker.

Then the buddy who says Brendan complained about her sometimes, but can't remember when he actually mentioned Flora pursuing him. "We all teased him over the years. You know, a good-looking girl living right in his house, how lucky, stuff like that. He pretty much always bitched about it. Nothing specific, just a pain in the ass having a little girl in the house."

One of his friends remembers Brendan used to give her rides to school but stopped last year because he "didn't want her hanging around, getting the wrong idea." He did produce a copy of an email from Brendan, dated six months ago. In it, Brendan accuses Flora's friends of calling the house and hanging up: "...all that little girl bullshit, man! Why don't they just play with their own friends and leave us big boys alone!"

Hal questions the boy further. "Please read us the part

where Brendan accuses Flora of calling and hanging up."

"Uh, no, sir, he was talking about Flora's friends."

"Oh, thank you for clarifying. Could you tell me how you boys knew it was Flora's friends making the calls?"

"Um, well, I don't think we ever could prove it, but girls our age are just more mature."

"So, you never identified the callers?"

The kid shook his head. "No, sir."

Their most credible witness is the minister at their church. He testifies that Brendan had spoken with him on several occasions, outlining his concerns that the girl was making him uncomfortable.

Hal approaches the witness with respect. "Reverend Albert, did Brendan ever specifically describe Flora's actions to you?"

"No, he talked primarily about how uncomfortable he was around her. He used that word several times, in fact. *Uncomfortable.*"

"And what was your response to his discomfort?"

"I advised him to avoid time alone with her, to keep himself busy with his other affairs." The Reverend blushes and stammers, "I don't mean 'affairs' in the secular sense, of course, I meant 'activities.'"

Hal remains respectful, politically correct. He smiles politely. "Thank you for clarifying, Reverend. Did you find Brendan's feelings about Flora in any way alarming?"

Reverend Albert shakes his head. "Honestly, I assumed it was the natural result of these unrelated adolescents living together as family. This is not too uncommon in foster families as the children grow up and enter puberty."

"So you've had experience working with this type of blended family?"

"Yes," the Reverend says. "We have quite a few foster parents in the community, several right in our congregation."

"Did you ever become alarmed at Brendan's situation, Reverend?"

"Yes, but too late. Once I heard about the girl's accusation, I wished I had been more inquisitive."

Hal is kind. "I believe you were honorable and ethical in your approach, Reverend. Let me ask you this. Did you ever wonder if Brendan acted on those *uncomfortable* feelings and did, in fact, molest the girl?"

Monty shouts, "Your Honor, I object! He is asking for speculation on the part of the witness!"

"I'll allow it, Mr. Monty." The Judge turns to Hal, "Mr. Franklin, do confine your questions to what the witness remembers, please."

"I'll answer." Reverend Albert was sitting straight up in the witness chair. "Anyone might wonder if he did it. At some point, *I* did. But then, I never had any indication that Brendan was forceful or aggressive with women. In fact, he seemed quite popular with the girls at church. It just didn't fit."

Hal was not going any further with this one. He established room for doubt, at least.

Mrs. Jacobie takes the stand next, to tell her side of the story — very compelling. Toward the end, her tears begin to flow. "The betrayal was so painful," she sobs. "I loved Flora like a daughter and this is how she repays me…" Classic response, totally expected.

After Monty provides tissues and a glass of water, Hal asks her only one question.

"I see Flora lived 'as your daughter' for about 4 years, Mrs. Jacobie, since she was only 12 years old. When were you planning to make your 'love' permanent?"

Attorney Monty explodes, "Objection, Your Honor, OBJECTION!"

Of course, the Judge, and everyone else, for that matter, is fully aware that the family never intended to adopt Flora. Hal withdraws the question, and the Judge cautions him against such tactics.

I'm actually enjoying this and Hal's doing great.

Rosemary is looking down, writing furiously in her

notebook. It kind of looks like she's crying. Michael, on the other hand, looks angry.

5.

Flora looks detached from the proceedings, eyes darting, kinda spacy. June figures she's scared shitless. What kid wouldn't be? Hal whispers something in her ear and she faces down toward the table, nods. Hal stands, smoothes his tie, and calls his first witness.

The School Nurse, Ms. Demeter, had turned over her records to Hal the week prior. They documented Flora's growing fear of her foster brother over the course of the school year. Her notes clearly outline Flora's requests to stay at school more, to come in early to help out and stay after school until dinner time, all in an effort to avoid contact with Brendan. There was a detailed notation on the day Flora disclosed her molestation, with follow-up notes referencing Nurse Demeter's report to the State, including her discussion with the DCW Investigator.

Russ Monty takes a shot. "Nurse Demeter, when this all started back in September, did you initiate any action on behalf of this young lady?"

"No." The nurse is direct and professional. "Flora's never been very talkative and she was pretty vague at that time. She had no major medical complaints, more like symptoms of anxiety."

"And, as the School Nurse, you are qualified to diagnose and treat anxiety?" Again, he takes a shot.

No." She remains unruffled. "That's why I referred her to the Social Worker. I was seeing her to offer comfort, primarily. As you read in my notes, she complained of periodic stomach pain and headaches."

"Well then, if she was so 'vague', what made you concerned about her relationship with Brendan Jacobie?"

"At first I just thought it was circumstantial, unrelated

teenagers of the opposite sex living together in the same house. Lots of girls get uncomfortable around boys during puberty, even their blood relatives. Flora was generally timid, especially around the boys at school. Later, she started saying things about Brendan, like 'he's so mean' and 'he doesn't like me'. This got more frequent and descriptive and she became weepier and more emotional, which concerned me."

"Could her weepiness and emotional state have been due to, say, unrequited love, Ms. Demeter?"

"She never stated or implied those feelings to me, Mr. Monty," the Nurse responds, looking the attorney dead in the eyes. "But even if she had, once he laid his hands on her it became abuse. That's when I reported it."

Monty moves in toward the nurse. "If this had *really* been happening for so long, Ms. Demeter, why didn't she share it with you earlier?"

Nurse Demeter's face becomes visibly sad as she answers, "I can only assume it was because she had so much to lose."

Didn't she, though! The nurse held up well on the stand, but June feels antsy. This is all taking too long for her taste.

The Music Teacher is Hal's next witness.

"Nurse Demeter told me Flora needed something to do before and after school, but she never specifically said why. I assumed it was about her family situation, you know, being in foster care. Flora has a beautiful voice, a real gift, so I was happy to invite her for extra help." This witness is clearly fond of Flora.

Monty tries to dig, but she just gushes, "Flora never reported anything directly to me. She just thanked me over and over again for all the special attention. She was so appreciative!"

Nothing added by her testimony and nothing lost, for either side.

Hal calls the School Social Worker to the stand.

"Yes, I remember," she confirms the referral from the RN. "I was trying to help Flora get along with her foster brother."

She describes her efforts, during these informal visits, at building Flora's self-esteem and helping to develop her communication skills. This young professional was right out of school and didn't know much about foster kids when she took the job.

Welcome to the world of do-gooders, June greets her silently.

Mr. Monty questions her, and she shakes her head. "Flora never told me about the molestation," she says, fiddling with her jewelry. "Just that she believed he, uh, Brendan, didn't like her."

She says "I don't know" so often that she's just wasting everyone's time. In the woman's defense, her time with Flora was very limited and it sounds like she mostly gave basic social guidance.

Everyone is on edge when Judge Paxton asks to see the attorneys and representatives from the State in his chambers. Not good. The Judge looks pissed.

Sarge is the last one in and, when he closes the door, Paxton gets right to the issue. "What is the point to all of this, Counselors? I'm not even sure why we are here. Mr. Monty?"

"Your Honor, my client has been harmed by the effects of this girl's false accusations. We find her behavior a danger to him and ask that she be assessed in a mental health facility, where she cannot negatively impact anyone else's life in this way."

"All this and you just wanted an assessment?"

Hal steps up, "Your Honor, what Mr. Monty is really saying is that he wants the girl incarcerated in a facility as punishment for reporting her own abuse."

The Judge stops the attorneys from coming to blows and looks at June. "Ms. Hunter, what is your recommendation?"

Growing two feet at this show of respect, June takes a

deep breath and says, "Your Honor, Flora is already seeing a therapist. She has been previously assessed with <u>no</u> restrictions or recommendations for medication. I am working closely with a family that may wish to adopt her, but they have had very little time together. Only one visit, in fact. I would recommend orders for Flora to remain at the Crossette Shelter until it can be determined if the West family is the appropriate placement. During this time, she will continue under the care of her therapist on a weekly basis. Additional shuffling around would only traumatize the child further and impede her ability to attach to the West's or any other family."

Paxton sits up straight, raises his eyebrows. "I see. And how long do you think this might take?"

"It is never easy to predict, Your Honor, but I would suggest a ninety-day period and a status hearing scheduled at that point."

Sarge makes a choking sound behind her.

A big silence while the Judge reads some of the file, then he scowls at June. "Are you an attorney, Ms. Hunter?"

Uh-oh. "No, sir, er, Your Honor."

He looks up and says, "Too bad. Ok, let's get back out there."

Sarge winks at me as we slip on our poker faces and return to our seats.

The Judge takes the bench and barks at Hal, "Mr. Franklin, would you agree to calling Mrs. West at this time? I would like to hear what she has to say, if she sees herself as a viable placement for the young lady."

Rosemary takes the stand with confidence. June recalls that she testifies periodically in environmental cases for the EPA. It shows. She oozes poise, but June still wonders, "Will the Judge believe her?"

"Please state your name and occupation…" Hal takes care of the preliminaries, then jumps right to the question, his only one, "Under the circumstances, Mrs. West, why do you want this young lady placed in your care?"

I glance over at Flora. She's the color of milk, eyes wide, staring at the stand. Rosemary smiles at her and turns, speaking directly to the Judge.

"Your Honor, Ms. Hunter asked me the same question. It is true that my husband and I have spent very little time with Flora, days really. We have read all the reports and spoken to the professionals. Flora put together a little book for us, her story, and we have attempted to try viewing the world through her eyes. We know this is a serious decision. We have made such a decision before, as you know, with much of the same concern from professionals."

Rosemary looks directly at Flora, pauses, then back to the Judge. "I cannot define for the Court what this connection is, or why. All I can tell you is that we have tried to weigh our strengths and weaknesses against this child's needs, and we believe we are able to make this commitment to her. The Court makes serious decisions every day, sometimes with less information. You rely upon others, professionals, but more importantly you rely upon your expertise and your gut to make decisions that impact people for life. I do the same, to a lesser degree, in my job. The planet depends upon my expertise and my gut, so I understand the Court's concern, the responsibility you have here."

The courtroom holds its collective breath as she places her cards on the table. "I am asking the Court to consider this proposal. Put Flora in our care; allow us to demonstrate our abilities and commitment in this matter. We will return to you regularly, every month if you like. If the Court sees any reason to doubt the progress or success of this placement during the next months, we will concede to your decision without contention."

The Judge is staring at Rosemary. There is not a single sound in the courtroom.

After this real dramatic pause, she says, "No one can

truly explain their emotions, Your Honor, but we *can* define our mission."

Rosemary again turns to face Flora. "We see Flora for who she appears to be today and we commit to support her in her efforts to become a happy, healthy, contributing member of society. We accept possible disappointment and frustration along the way, but clarify this by saying that no one's journey is over until life's end. Not Flora's, not ours. Whatever forks in the road, at least we will have an adventure… together. Right, Flora?"

Flora is crying by now, and the Judge is speechless. June can't see Hal's face, but Sarge looks like he was carved out of stone. She just keeps blinking and swallowing, professional-like. The silence is punctuated by random shuffling and sniffling.

Finally, the Judge addresses Rosemary, "Thank you for your candor and your passion, Mrs. West."

Then to the attorneys, "We will recess for lunch until 2:00 this afternoon."

Bang.

I'm still blinking hard, when Hal taps me on the shoulder, "You and Sol, in the conference room now. Send them to lunch, June."

Again, uh-oh.

I send Rosemary, Michael, and Flora to Davey's down the street and tell them to be back fifteen minutes early to report in. They give me the deer-in-the-headlights look and take off.

My friend, Donna, was never even called to the stand.

6.

"All right, Ms. Hunter, how do you propose I pull this off?"

Hal is pissed, due in part to the Judge's 'Are you an attorney' comment. He only calls June 'Ms. Hunter' when he's really, really mad.

"Can't you just order Crossette to keep her for ninety days?"

Hal rolls his eyes and faces Sarge. "Sol, any thoughts?"

"I don't know if it will take another ninety days, based on Mrs. West's emotional attachment." Sarge tries to calm him. "I bet we can have that kid placed in the next thirty days."

Hal is frustrated. "Yeah, ok, but who's going to pay for it? You, June?"

Trying not to smile, she replies, "Easy, Hal! Sarge, can't the State pay them for another ninety days?"

Sarge sits down at the table and leans back, stretching his legs. "That isn't the problem, Hunter. This judge is new, so he doesn't know how things work in Juvenile Court. He can't actually 'order' a private facility to do something like this, any more than he could order YOU to house the kid. We need to get their cooperation over at Crossette. Hal, know any of the power players there?"

Hal drains his coffee cup. "Yeah, but not really well. I guess I could call. Come on, you two, let's go down to my office. At least there we can get someone to bring us a sandwich!"

Sarge and I take a detour so he can step outside for a smoke. "Paxton likes you." He sucks hard on his cigarette and grins.

"Sometimes I get lucky." June grins back.

"Make sure you give Hal some credit, Hunter. He's doing a great job in there."

Realizing that she's been acting a little smug, June's contrite. "Right, Boss! I know he is. Sorry."

Normally, she'd be gloating and wisecracking right now. So far, things look pretty good for Flora's Team.

I'm not sure what it is, though, but something seems off.

Sarge closes his eyes and inhales again. "Looks good for our side about now, doesn't it?"

"Hope so," she tentatively agrees. "Something wrong,

Sarge?"

He opens his eyes and stops her heart by asking, "Hunter, don't you ever wonder if we're *wrong* about this kid?"

7.

By the time they get to Hal's office, sandwiches are already there. June holds up the Snickers Bar she got from the machine and extends it to Hal with a sweeping bow.

"For the conquering hero!"

He chuckles, a bit more relaxed, and waves them into chairs at his desk. They all chomp down a few bites while he fills them in.

"I got a hold of the second-in-command over at Crossette—pretty cooperative. I explained the Judge's direction, told her he is new and all that. Of course, I left out the fact that it was *your* idea, June."

"Sorry, Hal. I really didn't understand the problem I was causing. It won't happen again, I promise!"

He flashes a comic glare her way and warns, "Better not or I'll serve you to them on a platter!"

Through another bite of his sandwich, he continues, "They agree to keep her for a maximum of ninety more days, **if** the Judge puts it in an order **and** the State draws up a special contract. They do not want this to get out, so we need to keep it hush. Also, it had better never happen again! I'll explain to Paxton that they agree to cooperate *this one time*, but not to make it a habit."

June swallows her last bite, wipes her face with a napkin, and pats her belly. "That hit the spot. Thanks, Hal. Hey, I have a question."

Hal looks up from his notes. "What's that?"

"The Judge seemed almost pissed off after Rosemary testified. Any idea what was going on there?"

"Make no mistake, June," Hal raises an eyebrow. "Her

testimony was well-rehearsed and calculated. The way she presented, she pretty much put the Judge in a corner, left him no choice. Most judges don't like to be played that way."

June looks astonished, so Sarge jumps in. "I know you think these people are angels sent from heaven, Hunter, and they might be the perfect placement for Flora, but these are smart cookies. They definitely have you in the palm of their hands. Flora does too."

Now she's defensive. "Oh, hell, why don't I just take the kid down to the river and toss her in?! Let's not find anyone who actually gives a shit about her, no-o-o! God forbid I do my job…"

The guys start laughing at her and poking each other, which grates on her even more. "WHAT?!?"

"You are so easy, Junie," Hal stands up. "You know what they tell you in law school?"

She shakes her head.

"They say, 'Above all, know thyself.' By now, you should know the kind of people who push all your 'warm and fuzzy' buttons. How long have you been in this business, anyway?"

Sarge chimes in, a bit more serious than Hal. "These people are great and you've done a good job with this case so far." He pauses. Then, "Everybody gets over-involved once in a while, Hunter. You aren't immune. This kid does something to you, anyone can see it."

First, she's stunned. Next, she's pissed. Then she explodes.

"Oh, this is just great! I'm biased, you think? Fine, take me off the case, Sarge. I'm done! Find a worker whose buttons can't be pushed."

Good thing Hal's already standing. He cuts her off before she hits the door. "Jeez, June, take it easy. What's got your guns blazing? He said 'Good job', didn't he?"

She knows if she doesn't get out of the room quick, she'll start boo-hooing in front of them. She begs, "Just…

just let me take a walk. Please. I'll come back."

Hal looks to Sarge for direction. He nods and Hal lets her go.

June heads out the back way, where the smokers go, and gulps in the outside air. *I need to get control of myself*, she thinks, *before they banish me to the nursery with the other babies.*

Why do I keep hearing that phrase, 'know thyself' from the people who care about me? Guess I better start paying attention.

She plunks down on a bench that is partially obscured by bushes, and puts her face in her hands to hide the water works.

I am so embarrassed!

Every worker gets this at some point in their career. Something about the kid triggers strong emotions in them, blinding them to the facts. Parents get like that with their own kids, the way Brendan's Mom is probably feeling right now. They get so focused on the issues they share with the kid—vulnerability, abandonment, anything, really—that nothing else matters. All they want to do is fix the kid or her problems, so they don't have to feel her pain anymore. June's therapist calls it "transference".

There's this innovative program in June's State, providing all case workers and supervisors with mandatory mental health supervision. Of course, the State bigwigs use it to cover their own asses in case an employee loses it and goes postal, but it's a great benefit for the workers.

Once a month, June pours her heart out to a therapist who specializes in the stresses and pitfalls of working as a 'happy helper.' In return, her therapist gives her unlimited support and therapeutic guidance. Naturally, it's free.

Some workers are paranoid about sharing anything with a State-appointed shrink, but June figures they're bound by the confidentiality of their profession.

Anyway, if there is a case worker anywhere that doesn't have job-related issues, I'll eat my computer.

Her therapist, Minerva, is one cool lady and they get

along just fine. Minerva actually started out in casework, then left to get her head-shrinking credentials. That means she has walked in June's shoes and knows the hazards.

I guess I'll be calling her tomorrow. That is, if Sarge hasn't already contacted the men in the white coats.

June rubs the frustration out of her eyes, take a few deep breaths, and walks back upstairs with some semblance of her usual cool.

"Better?" Sarge greets her.

She nods, makes a weak attempt to smile, shrugs her shoulders.

"Sorry, Junie." Hal looks like a whipped pup. "I guess I got carried away."

"That's ok," she concedes. "At least you give as good as you get."

Hal laughs and they put it all aside. June wilts in relief.

A quick glance at the clock tells them it's twenty minutes to Show Time.

8.

As they enter the court room, everyone wears that edgy look, including Flora. Hal escorts her to their table after a brief trip to the conference room for a little heart-to-heart. He has to be sure she has no surprises for him, on the off chance Judge Paxton calls her to the stand.

Brendan and his parents sit at the table with Russ Monty. Hal and Flora sit at the other table. Sarge and June sit in the first row, close behind them. Rosemary and Michael sit in the courtroom a few rows back from us. The waiting room has been cleared because everyone else has been dismissed.

The Judge enters.

I don't know what I thought would happen, but I am honestly surprised by what Paxton does next.

"Mr. Monty and Mr. Franklin, I would like to come to

some agreement here. Please approach."

I can't hear all of it, but I'm catching the general drift. After some animated mumbling and arm waving, they both return to their seats.

"Thank you to everyone for your cooperation in this very sensitive matter. These are the Court's Orders:

"First, both of the young people will receive a psychiatric assessment from a specialist. Mr. Franklin will identify the appropriate specialist and each party will arrange their own appointments. All parties will cooperate fully with this assessment."

Brendan's parents whisper fiercely to their attorney, who is holding up his hand in an attempt to silence them.

"Second, I will need a copy of these assessments in sixty days for review, so be timely.

"Third, we will re-convene in this courtroom in approximately ninety days. Once Mr. Franklin identifies the specialist, he will contact all parties to expedite the process and to advise the parties of the ninety-day hearing date."

Paxton pauses in aggravation as Russ Monty actually shushes his clients, startling them into silence. A bit aggravated himself, the attorney conveys his apology to the Judge, who continues.

"Fourth, Flora will remain at the Crossette Shelter for Girls until the State deems it appropriate to make a placement, for a period not to exceed ninety days from today. Mr. and Mrs. West, I will not guarantee placement in your home. That decision is up to Ms. Hunter and her Supervisor, Mr. Barrett. But I will require on-going reports and potential appearances, should placement occur during this period. Do you understand?"

Everyone nods and chants, "Yes, Your Honor."

"Fifth, I will see Flora each month for a status hearing. Mr. Franklin will schedule these before you leave today.

"My last point: Brendan, bringing this case before me might have been construed as your retaliation against this young lady. Understand that the Court could have ruled against you and ordered some consequences for such an act. That being said, I gave you the benefit of the doubt and chose to view this incident in a legally neutral light. As there is virtually no evidence to support your argument, it means that whatever happened remains unclear to the Court at this time. We cannot rule for or against you. Do you understand what I am saying?"

Brendan just sits and stares at the Judge so Monty jumps in, "My client understands, Your Honor."

"Please be aware, however, that I reserve the right to expand these orders should the assessments suggest further action is necessary or advisable. Although I have entered no findings, I will issue this Order: *there is to be no unsupervised or unauthorized contact between the involved parties.* Ms. Hunter, you will advise the Court at once should any contact occur, authorized or otherwise. Thank you." Bang!

Brendan's parents look confused and angry. Brendan just looks angry. Russ Monty speaks firmly in Mr. Jacobie's ear, then drives Mrs. Jacobie out of the courtroom by her elbow.

Hal rises and gestures for us to convene in the conference room. I usher Flora, Rosemary, and Michael in that direction with the reassurance, "Come on. We'll talk inside, answer any questions."

Now that everyone is seated, Hal starts the recap, "The Judge entered no findings today. That means he has left the door open to respond to the assessments in any way he sees fit. I need to identify an appropriate psychiatrist for this. Mr. Barrett, will you assist me when we're through here?" Sarge agrees and jots a note on his pad.

"You may all be asked to participate in the assessment, even Ms. Hunter, so no fooling around. If I give you an appointment you <u>must</u> attend. If you have a conflict, fix it. If you can't fix it, see me immediately because we have no time for this. Everybody clear?"

Dead silence, lots of nodding.

"Any questions about what happened today?"

"Why was Brendan mad?" Flora asks in a quiet voice. We are all silenced for a moment by her timid question.

Hal recovers first. "Flora, I don't know that he was mad. More like he was confused by all of this, but his attorney will clear up any confusion for them. You heard the Judge, didn't you? No contact with Brendan or his family unless we arrange it. No phone, email, text, chatting at the mall, nothing."

Flora looks puzzled, "I never talk to them at all, Mr. Franklin. Why did the Judge say that?"

"I think it was just to be clear, Flora. Sometimes people want to talk about what was said in court and the Judge is maybe trying to keep it simple. This is to protect you, too, from any false accusations. If you don't talk to them, you can't be accused of saying anything wrong. See what I mean?"

Flora seems satisfied. The cloud across her face clears except for that little bit of bunching between her eyebrows.

Rosemary leans in. "Flora, if you have any questions, write them down in your notebook like we talked about. We can answer them all later, when we get together. You did great today! Everything is just fine and we'll take this one day at a time, ok?" Her warm smile and reassuring manner is hard to resist.

I watch Rosemary, her obvious command of the situation, and wonder, "When exactly did I lose control of this case?"

9.

"Hey, Min, it's June Hunter." This call to Minerva is first on her list today.

"June, hi! How are you?"

Her pleasure sounds genuine but that's her job, after all.

"Listen, Min, could you fit me in this week? I know it's already Thursday but the sooner, the better."

Minerva shuffles papers, mumbles stuff like, "Hmmm, ok, let me see…" then exclaims, "Hey, why don't we meet for lunch at my office today? I have appointments this morning, and a meeting at 2:00, but 11:45 to 1:30 is all yours!"

Wow. I must sound pretty bad for her to schedule such a big chunk of time for me… or did Sarge already give her a head's up?

"Great, Min. Do you want me to pick something up?"

"No, we have tons of food over here today, somebody's birthday or something, so we eat for free."

State employees have two favorite words, "eat" and "free". Put those words together and she knows it would be tough for June to resist.

"See you at 11:45. I'll be the one with the napkin tucked under my chin… and thanks, Min."

She wanders into Sarge's office, trying for casual. "I'm going to get my head shrunk at lunchtime today. I put it on the office calendar as 'laundry', just so you know."

Sarge does not laugh. "Hunter, 'just so *you* know' this is not the end of the world. But I'll butt out and let Miss Minerva convince you of that. Meanwhile, Hal is referring everyone to Fallon Clinic for the assessments. You can thank me any time now." He grins.

Fallon Clinic leads the nation in dealing with attachment behaviors and adoption issues. They are privately contracted, charge the moon and the stars for the privilege of their scrutiny, and they are booked for something like a thousand years into the future. How does he do it?

"You truly are The Amazing Barrett! Tell me the story." June plunks into his chair, all ears.

"Remember Barbara Portman who used to work over in Foster Care Recruitment? She left DCW about 8 years ago, finished up a second degree, and went to work for

Fallon. It just so happens Barbara and I went to high school together and she married one of my childhood buddies. Anyway, we run into each other occasionally so I called her."

"Way to work the connections!" June feels like doing a happy dance. "So, when are we set up?"

"You'll have to talk to Hal, but Barb was going to push it through for us. She found our case 'intriguing'."

Who doesn't?

"OK, I'll just stay out of Hal's way for now—and yours, too, Mr. Magic."

June has work to do on other cases, so she grabs some coffee and heads back to her desk. Around 11:00 a.m. she packs up for her appointment at Min's office, about a fifteen-minute drive. It's early, she knows, but before her time with Min she wants to walk on the River Path, a scenic trail that meanders past her building. It's a fragrant and shady place, great for clearing her head before Min starts scrubbing around in there.

When she steps off the elevator, the entire third floor is congregating right there, eating and laughing up a storm.

I'm not used to a reception when I go to see my shrink. It's a bit intimidating.

"Hey, June, over here!" Min acts like June's come for a friend's birthday party, smiling and waving. She stands next to a guy dressed in an expensive suit with a $50.00 haircut.

June offers a weak "Hey," as she wanders over.

Pretend like I belong, not damaged at all. I wonder what that looks like?

"You know Todd, don't you, June? He worked in Foster Care about, what, ten years, was it, Todd?"

The guy looks to be about nineteen years old. She thinks, "The only thing this boy's done for ten consecutive years is wear long pants, for cryin' out loud."

"Do we know each other, Todd?" She figures a quiz is always appropriate for a schoolboy.

He smiles like a shy teen. "Well, I'm sure you don't remember me, but I remember you. You were one of my training supervisors, way back before I went to grad school."

Eeek.

"No, no, it's ok." He pats her on the shoulder, the nervy little twerp. "I looked totally different then, like a shabby hippie with long hair tied back in a ponytail, wire rimmed glasses, and I certainly dressed like a case worker, um, I mean, a student."

Oops, you sanctimonious little shit, now I have to retaliate.

No way that insult was an accident, she thinks. She wonders why anybody would pay this creep to help them.

Pause. Smile. "Ohh, of course—shabby hippie Todd! Well, it's just too bad clothes don't make the man, Todd. Without them, you're just a stallion's recycled oats." His face freezes while his brain tries... to... figure... it... out...

Minerva dumps her cup and tableware, hauling June out of there before Todd puts together the reference to horse shit. She saw it coming. Sadly, he did not.

Behind the closed door of her office, June inhales deeply, filling her head with vanilla and lavender and maybe sandalwood. It always smells so good in here, she thinks, aroma therapy for the case worker's soul.

"Sorry, Min." June sinks into the softest chair, apologizing, "I should have held back."

"Yeah, well, he's such an easy target!" Min's suppressing laughter. "That's why I made you a plate early, before you ran into our birthday boy."

She serves up a platter with every kind of heart-stopping cuisine available, right down to a side of cheesecake, and June laughs out loud. "You have to help me eat this."

She hands her one of two forks. "I thought you'd never ask!"

"Tell me about transference again, Min," she asks

around a bite of fried chicken.

"Ahhhh, the old switcheroo! Who's got it, you or the kid?"

"Me." Forking up a tiny tower of lasagna, she slips it onto her tongue. "I don't know how to fix it and I feel like shit about the whole mess. Even Sarge and Hal could see me screwing up."

"Nothing worse than the big guys watching you slip in the mud, eh?" Min puts down her fork and pats her belly, groaning.

She gets up and pours coffee, sets a cup in front of June. She sips hers and turns to face her patient. "Transference happens when you identify with some piece of the other person's baggage and transfer it to your own, usually without realizing you've done it. It happens to all of us in the helping professions, probably because 'we do what we know'."

"Keep going." Finished stuffing herself, June's intrigued.

"OK, let's take imaginary Doctor John Smith. He was a sickly child with a heart problem, so he saw a lot of doctors as a kid. He gets better enough to go to med school, because he wants to help other kids just like the doctors helped him. Or, so he can show other doctors the right way to treat a sick kid. Get the picture?"

She does. Min continues.

"So, now Doctor John has a nine-year-old patient who tells him, '*Nobody listens to me. I feel like a ghost, invisible.*' Doctor John thinks, 'Why, that is the very same thing little Billy, my hospital roommate, said to me right before he died.' Now Doctor John goes overboard, stays by his young patient's side night and day, so this kid never feels invisible again."

"So, why is that bad?"

"I didn't say it was bad, June. After all, in another circumstance you may call little Billy his muse, his inspiration to save others and become a great doctor. So, how might this be a bad thing for either of them?"

The Socratic Method is June's favorite way to learn, question after question until you find your own answer. "Well, it's like codependence. Caring about others isn't bad until it starts hurting someone. It could be by doing too much for others and neglecting yourself. It could be by demanding that the other person solve their problems your way."

"Right, the baggage isn't the problem; neither is identifying with the other person's issues. It is a matter of degree, in most cases." Min refills their cups. "What happened in your case?"

June lays out the problem from the beginning, how she somehow got over-involved, determined to personally save this girl. Min listens with an intensity that gives her a shiver.

Now that I've explained it out loud, I feel a bit too exposed. And silly.

"I don't know, maybe I'm overreacting to this."

"Don't blow it off, June, it is an interesting phenomenon. It happens to us therapists even more than you caseworkers, because our exposure is more intense— one person per hour. It wouldn't happen if you didn't care. And yet, it can be an enormously destructive occurrence. What do you think could happen that's destructive, in your work with Flora?"

"Umm... I could solve *her* problems by forcing her to accept solutions for *my* issues, maybe? Then I wouldn't really be putting her best interest first, more like recreating my own trauma."

"Right. You didn't work through something important, so you're unconsciously trying to do it by solving Flora's similar problem. It's like your brain sees Flora's life and goes, 'Wow, I remember THIS problem!' and tries to fix it. The crummy part is you keep getting your facts mixed up, like trying to read two similar mystery books at the same time. Once you get real involved in them, you keep thinking, 'Did that happen in Story Number One or Story Number Two?'"

June shudders inside, then steps out there on the ledge. "So, how do I find out which problem is mine?"

Of course, she already knows what Min's going to say.

"Fortunately for you," Min sits back, puts her feet up, and grins, "I happen to know a little something about these things!"

Together, they start the trip back.

10.

"Having your Mom die when you're not quite an adult is shitty, no matter how you slice it," Min says. This is about June's life now, not Flora's.

June knows she never really addressed the issue in her own life because her dad was so screwed up at the time. Busy taking care of him and trying to get herself through school, her body finally said, "Enough!"

When she developed pneumonia and ended up in the hospital, she could finally relax and try to heal. Dad couldn't even bring himself to visit; it reminded him too much of Mom, she figures. Ten days later, she was back to her old routine again, her happy little Psyche having gotten a moment of relief.

June shares with some guilt. "Over the years, whenever I get so overwhelmed that I need help or support, I secretly wish to get sick or break a leg or something. Don't get me wrong, I've never hurt myself or become a hypochondriac, or anything like that. But I thought the thoughts. What does that tell you?"

Min just keeps listening.

"Not going into the whole 'blah, blah, blah' about my dad also perishing in his 50's, I put his death in a tight little box and filed it under 'Later'. Obviously, I have yet to work through my abandonment issues over being an orphan. And now that my son Leo is out from under my wing and halfway across the country, 'being alone' translates into 'being orphaned' once again. My anxiety over finding a path for Flora is something like the concern I have for my own path in the near future, right?"

Min smiles and gestures for her to keep going. "What about this path?"

"I've got a possible career change, the need for some sort of retirement plan, and my love relationship is reaching that 'shit-or-get-off-the-pot' stage."

And...I'm getting older by the minute!

When Min helps her outline the friends and family in her support system, it's pretty sparse. How embarrassing for a professional. June's practice has always been to take care of herself, by herself. That way, she never has to be disappointed or hurt by anyone else.

Facing the second half of her life realistically, she wonders, "What happens if, or when, I can't take care of myself?"

June schedules a couple more appointments and trudges back outside to ramble down the River Path again. She needs time to recover from the session before going back to work.

It's all so simple, too simple. My screwed-up brain can't possibly work better just because I talk about things, can it?

Just then, she notices a Dad, or maybe a Grandpa, sitting there with a little girl. He ties her shoe saying, "Here you go, Princess, is that better?"

The kid beams up at him. He takes her hand and they walk away together, love just oozing out of them. June almost strangles, trying to keep from sobbing out loud. It dawns on her that lately she gets choked up at the littlest things such as a scene like this one, reruns of "Little House on the Prairie", or even a Pepsi commercial.

She recalls something she says to the kids she counsels. She tells them to imagine their emotions are like a water balloon. When it gets too full you have to relieve the pressure, either by letting some of the water out, or waiting until it springs a leak. The first way, you have the control; the second way, it controls you. We always have the choice.

Time to practice what I preach. Inhaling the sweet air of springtime, June picks up the pace, swinging her arms to catch the breeze.

Hate to admit it, but I feel better already!

11.

"That Sol sure can pull strings," Hal is gushing about the appointments at Fallon Clinic. "I couldn't get my foot in their door with a crowbar!"

As pleased as if she'd made the connection herself, June boasts about Sarge, "He's the best. It sure pays to know people."

Who wouldn't be excited? The best practitioners in the nation have agreed to work with her very own Flora.

Hal gives June the appointment dates and times for everybody and they divide them up: June gets Flora, Rosemary, and Michael to their appointments, and Hal has to contact the Jacobie family by phone and registered mail.

"Let's see, Sarge and I meet with Fallon's clinicians after all is said and done, verify their facts, and hash out some recommendations." She reviews the paperwork. "Oh, wow. The first appointment for Flora is next week."

"Hey, I hate to change the happy subject," Hal closes the door and sits down, pointing at what she thinks of as 'her chair' as he continues, "but just to protect you, I did a records search on Rosemary and Michael 'Perfect'. It looks like they are as clean as you thought they were, not so much as a parking ticket for the last ten years."

"Hal, I know these people aren't as perfect as they seem. They can't be! But I haven't been able to find any major issues there. I'll let the Fallon people know about them and see if they can humanize these folks for me."

He shuffles, self-conscious. "Um, I faxed your Court Report over to Fallon. I hope that's ok with you?"

Normally Hal won't send out her stuff without consulting her first. She teases him, "Did you think I might stop you? What, you don't trust me?"

He shakes his head. "No, no, nothing like that! Your work is so complete, better than anything else in the file. I sent it fast before they had a chance to change their minds, that's all. I wanted them to get the positive stuff before Monty sends over all the negative crap about Flora."

June likes that he's protecting Flora. "I get it. Thanks for the compliment. I gotta admit, though, this case has me on edge."

Hal leans forward and looks her square in the face. "Junie, you are the best worker in the State. I'm sorry if you thought I was putting you down. This kid has gotten to all of us, even Sol. I don't know why." He leans back in his chair and throws his arms out to the side. "Everything about this case screams Movie of the Week to me, and that usually means I'm missing something. I can't figure it out, though."

How about that…Hal has doubts!

"I know what you mean," she comforts him. "Let's give this thing over to Fallon Clinic and ask them for a new perspective. Maybe we're just jaded after all these years, eh?"

"You said it." He gets up to walk her out, "Thanks, Junie."

Not prone to emotional outbursts, June surprises herself when she wraps Hal in a great big hug. It feels nice to see someone else mirror my vulnerability back at me, she thinks.

As I leave, I hear him laughing. Sounds like relief to me.

Rosemary and Michael want to take Flora to her first appointment, but June nixes that up front. "No, they will want Flora's history and an overview from me, could take hours. Besides, I would rather Flora not feel any pressure."

"Oh, we would never pressure her!" Rosemary jumps right in, but Michael stops her. "She's right, Rose. Flora needs to feel free to talk without us hanging around in the wings. The kid needs some space for this."

Explaining this to Flora, June finds she is her usual guarded self. "Will you be there, June?"

"I will take you there, and I will tell them why we want an adoptive home for you." Her stomach squeezes at the girl's solemn look. "I will <u>not</u> come in and listen while you talk to them, Flora. That is your time. I can either leave and come back later, or wait outside. You can decide when we get there."

She looks more comfortable now. "Do you know the person I'm supposed to see?"

"No, I don't know these folks. Mr. Barrett knows a lady who works there, but she probably won't be talking to us. The Fallon Clinic is famous, Flora. They're the best people in the country to talk to about adoption stuff." June tries to reassure the kid, knowing how difficult it is for her to trust. "I want you to feel safe with them. They see lots of kids with lots of problems, and I know they will be really nice to you."

She levels a gaze at June and asks, "Do you think they will like me?"

June wishes she was better prepared for that question. "Oh, yeah, I'm sure they will. Does that worry you?"

Looking out the window, she shakes her head. "No, not worry, just, you know, when they have to pick sides, will they like me or Brendan better? He's real friendly, you know. Grown-ups love him."

Every so often she feels a kid's question like a sledge hammer. "Flora, this isn't about picking sides…" She trails off because that's exactly what it is: picking sides. She pauses to re-group.

"Wait, you're sort of right." June starts again, more honestly. "The Judge wants everyone to talk to these people so he can make a good decision. They'll see if they can help the Judge figure out what's best for everyone. Just tell the truth, Flora. That's what I'm going to do."

She shuts up then so as not to blah-blah-blah the kid to death, but a careful glance tells it all. Flora thinks June is full of shit.

The girl shakes her head and looks away.

"That's ok, June. I'll do what the Judge wants. The only thing is, telling the truth is what made everybody mad in the first place."

Bam! There goes that sledge hammer again.

Flora already understands what it took me so long to learn: Truth has many faces. The trick is in knowing which one to show, to whom, and when.

12.

Quinn is riding his big, rumbling Harley ahead of her, slightly to the left near the center line. June is to the right and behind on her sweet Indian Spirit.

The rules of chivalry dictate the man must travel on the outside, or traffic side, of the woman. One could assume that's because the guy's bigger and stronger and responsible for her safety. This protects the woman from horses or cars or being spattered with goo from oncoming traffic or beasts.

When they ride, Quinn always takes the left side, staying protectively a bit ahead of her. June has long since quit arguing that it doesn't make sense today. It becomes like your favorite chair or your side of the bed, more about the sensation of it, the 'rightness' about it, an easy custom or routine.

And it makes me feel cherished, that voice in her head reminds her.

June's motorcycle is special to her in a way she never thought possible. She was always the one who criticized folks with sensual names for their vehicles, joked at the expense of car show junkies, and generally couldn't care less about the make, model, or condition of a vehicle. If she won the lottery, she always said her indulgence would be to hire a personal driver so she'd never have to drive again.

"Too much wasted time, driving, and a lot of aggravation to boot," she told everyone who'd listen until Dad shared his personal insight one day.

"Darlin' girl, why such a whiner about driving?" He shook his head in amazement after one of her well-seasoned tirades. "You have a career that requires lots of driving and you live way out in the sticks, too far to walk to town, but you chronically choose vehicles that are crap. I'd whine too."

June was stunned into uncharacteristic silence.

"Don't just stand there with your mouth open," he commanded. "Find yourself a vehicle that makes you want to laugh out loud!"

The discussion didn't end that night. The following evening found her dad driving her around to look at vehicles. He insisted she drive everything from a Lincoln (luxurious, but way too big) to an ancient Austin-Healy (cute, but too tiny), from a Jeep Wrangler (fun, but a stiff ride) to a Dodge Ram (wonderfully big and comfortable, powerful, but not quite 'laugh-out-loud').

Then she saw it, a photo actually, on the wall of a car salesman's office. "Wow, Dad, what IS that?"

He looked, squinted over his glasses and asked, "Is that a 1940 Indian?"

The guy was so proud. "No, but sure looks like it, eh? It's a new one, a Spirit, a little smaller than the military model…"

June had stopped listening and stepped up to the photo to get a closer look. While their conversation slipped into talk about lighter front ends and sixteen-inch rims, June sucked in her breath and laughed out loud. "That is *so* cool!"

Dad stopped dead.

Mr. Salesguy was too excited about sharing his passion to be pissed over a lost sale. He got on the phone immediately with a cycle shop and, after much excited talk, set them up with an appointment the following morning. That was the only time in the last decade June called in sick to work.

She had never driven a motorcycle, hadn't even been on the back of one since her college days. While she remembered about not fighting the turns and stuff like that, she had precious little to draw from when it came to owning one.

"Get on, let's go!" Dad was helmeted up, wearing a scuffed leather bomber jacket. He handed her a helmet and gave her the ride of her life. She laughed and whooped the whole time.

He bought her that Indian. She bought a helmet, a leather jacket, and riding lessons.

Even today, every time I ride my Spirit I feel his presence, his 'spirit', I guess you could say. And I still laugh out loud sometimes.

Roaring down twisty country roads at sixty-five miles an hour is a kickass tonic for the soul. Snug in leathers, they follow the road west. *Blowin' the dust out*, Quinn calls it.

June's head is in need of a good dust-blowin' after last week:

- o   Testifying in court on three cases.
- o   Placing six kids in foster homes.
- o   Finding an adoptive couple for a lonely little boy with Crohn's disease.

To the lay-person it sounds like 'Social Worker of the Year,' but it wasn't enough. It's never enough. Friday, after a fifty-plus-hour workweek, there were still two dozen families on her caseload whose folders she hadn't even cracked.

Closing the office door behind her, she said, "They can

wait 'til Monday." With only so much to give every week, she finds herself deeper in emotional debt.

This week's Rx for Life:

> *Helmet, leathers, and the power of freedom;*

> *Combine non-pharmaceutical wind-in-your-face speed with the high-def beauty of Midwestern backroads;*

> *Take as needed for relief from heartache, anxiety, and assholes.*

They're headed toward Cassville, a ferry landing on the Mississippi River north of Dubuque. Once over the river on the other side, the ropey road rises and twists through some mighty beautiful bluffs. This is where the demands of her 'other life' go sloughing off in the wind.

Midafternoon, they roll up to the landing and cut engines. June spots the ferry over on the other side and calculates, "About twenty or more minutes before she gets here, don't you think?"

"At least," Quinn agrees.

They dismount, helmets off, and plop down in the sunshine to wait.

"Ah, this is the life!" Quinn is like a cat, stretching and smiling. Not June. She follows the urge to climb river rocks and look for turtles or other signs of life.

"There are so many little fish in here, you can't believe it!" she calls to him.

"Fetching us dinner, are ya?" he jokes. "Now that I think of it, I *am* hungry. How about you?"

Imagining a steak, medium rare, she strolls back to the grassy spot. "Maybe I can find something to tide us over." She rummages in an insulated saddle bag for her old standby, Snickers Bars. "Want one?"

"If we don't eat 'em now, they'll just melt," he says, catching her toss easily. A moment later, mouth full of chocolate and peanuts, he mumbles, "After we get to the other side, let's head up to Bend-in-the-River and get a steak sandwich."

An old shack of a bar and grill, Bend-in-the-River sits high on the bluffs overlooking the Mississippi. It's situated about an hour down the road from a cabin they're renting for the night. The timing is perfect. They'll reach the cabin in plenty of time to watch the sun slip into the west and the moon come up, painting chrome over the water. Spring is June's favorite time of year for riding: warm days, cool evenings, no bugs.

"Sounds good to me. Hey, here they come!"

The ferry makes its way to the landing with a couple of cars, half a dozen motorcycles, and some teenagers hanging over the rickety railing. At about the halfway point they can hear their voices, talking and laughing. It's contagious and June smiles back in their direction. This ferry isn't fancy, no more than a big iron raft with a railing on two sides and a mini tugboat attached, but it transports her from the sharks and predators of her other life to simpler times and pleasanter folk.

Still grinning at the ferry passengers, June declares, "I wish I was the clever guy who came up with this idea. Charging people for a dry vehicle crossing is brilliant."

Quinn stands up and pockets the candy wrapper. "You wish you were a guy?"

Rolling her eyes, she says, "I'm using the global *guy,* like the *man* in 'brotherhood of man.' Hey, did you know even covered wagons were ferried here? But back then they used a system of horses and pulleys instead of a motorized tugboat."

I'm eternally surprised by my own wealth of knowledge. This being the case, I wonder how it's possible I misplace my keys and sunglasses so often.

Quinn kisses her, obviously impressed by her brilliance.
Either that or he's trying to shut me up.

Closer now, the ferry passengers wave and they wave back. They each pull out five dollars. That's ten bucks more than it cost to drive across the big modern bridge, but the simple experience of riding the water is worth a fin or two. Behind them, several cars, SUVs with families inside, and a couple of bicyclists have lined up for the ride. Any latecomers will wait until the ferryman crosses over and back.

"You're right. This *is* the life!" she murmurs to Quinn, who hugs her tight. Then they mount up and drive their bikes on board.

At Bend-in-the-River, they order a pitcher of iced tea and a pitcher of water to rehydrate. At a table by the window, they wait for the food and watch a red-tailed hawk circle and dive for his supper.

"He's a big one." Quinn gazes at the hawk. "Just imagine how much work it is for him to hunt for his supper. And here we sit, waiting to be served."

"Perfect timing," she says as the steak sandwiches arrive, mounded with grilled onions and a pile of sweet potato fries. They whoop so loud that they startle the tattooed waiter, who shakes his head at the outburst. By the time homemade peach pie with hand-churned ice cream arrives at the table, they're euphoric.

Later, gearing up for the final stretch to the cabin, June tucks a full thermos of decaf coffee into her saddlebag and pats an equally full belly. "A flawless day," she sighs. "I need these more often!"

Hitting the road behind Quinn with their hawk riding the currents ahead, June's happy to be alive.

Once they reach the cabin, Quinn asks, "How about a nice hot fire?" He's down on one knee next to the fireplace, breaking up kindling.

"Sounds great. Want a nightcap?" She waggles the silver flask of brandy she packed. He sends her a wink and a grin.

A shot of brandy in a mug of steaming coffee and a crackling fire is a pretty successful recipe for contentment. It works out the stiffness of a long day's ride and sets the mood for a night of tussling fun. Snuggled on the old stuffed couch, Quinn's arms snake around her and he sets another fire, this time of a more personal nature. They don't even bother moving to the bed, making it happen right there, first on the couch and then on the rug in front of the fire, tangled up in a soft, old quilt.

"That's the stuff, darlin' girl," he sighs and stretches out next to her on the floor. "We should do this more often!"

"What, get away on the bikes or have sex?" She teases him.

"Both!" He tickles her in the ribs and grabs her when she tries to escape. Nuzzling her neck, he murmurs, "But given a choice, sex with you is always a trip to the moon."

Quinn waxing romantic shifts June out of idle. She starts up once again, slower, spiraling like the hawk. This time, though, she takes the lead.

13.

In the yard at June's cabin, Quinn's playing catch with Tully. Over on the patio, Ozzie's huge frame barely fits in the big wooden chair but he slumps there anyway, munching on an apple.

"Thanks for keeping him, Oz," Quinn calls out, trying to run with the ball. Tully's faster and Quinn tumbles to the ground, laughing.

Ozzie leans over to look his buddy in the eye, but he's face down in the grass with a dog on his back. "No problem there, Champ. Tully's a great overnight guest: he eats what I give him; he sleeps anywhere; he pees outside; and he's always grateful!"

After watching their game for a while longer, Ozzie fakes nonchalance. "So, how did your little getaway turn out, anyway?"

"Oh, man, it was great!" Quinn gets up, tosses Tully

the last ball of the game, and falls into another one of those big chairs. "The weather was perfect, we ate great, we slept like logs, I peed outside, and June was grateful!"

Both guys are still laughing at their play on words when June pulls up. She grins at the two men who are laughing like little boys, then turns to take Tully back down the lane to the mailbox. The big dog's really getting good at carrying in the paper, thanks to June's efforts. He makes it almost all the way to the front door most of the time.

"Shelley wants to know when you guys are getting married." Ozzie tries to sound casual. "It sounds like she and Ray are gonna set the date soon and she doesn't want to compete with you guys."

Quinn stares at his buddy. "Where did she get the idea that we're getting married?"

Ozzie glances down the lane to gauge his time. "Come on, man, do I look stupid? You and Junie are good together. What's the hang up?"

"You know June; she has a lot of closed doors. She's so involved in this case with Michael West right now, and ..." Quinn sees Ozzie shaking his head. "What??!"

"You better start the conversation soon or she'll be cutting you out. What does she think: you like her but can't commit?"

Quinn's as stunned by his buddy's insight as he is by his boldness. And a little pissed. "Since when did you become a marriage counselor?"

Ozzie laughs. "You can put me off, pal, but June needs more than a 'you know how I feel about you, babe' from you. Better get on the stick before she decides to move on."

Quinn looked embarrassed and he's leaning toward defensive. "Seeing as how you haven't been in a relationship for the past year, you aren't exactly an expert on the subject."

"Maybe you forgot," Ozzie gets quiet, then serious. "But that's why I'm not in a relationship. I waited too long and lost my woman. I just don't want you to make the same mistake."

Quinn feels like an asshole. Of course, he knows about Ozzie's lost love. They had dated for years but Ozzie was never sure he was ready to settle down. She abruptly married someone else about eight months ago and Ozzie hasn't dated since.

"Hey, man, I'm sorry." They watch June coming up the lane with Tully. "I appreciate your concern, really."

As June gets closer, Ozzie put on his carefree face. "We're good. Now let's get Junie out of here and you can buy me a steak sandwich at Chuck's." He raises his voice for June's benefit. "I deserve something for babysitting, right, June?"

"Give me a minute to change, you guys!" June waves and hurries off to the house.

Quinn's never thought of himself as THAT GUY, the one who wouldn't or couldn't commit. He was trying to lay the groundwork, build a good foundation, before he took the next step. He didn't think he was resisting marriage; he was building trust between him and June.

Then why feel so anxious, now that Ozzie's brought it up?

Quinn runs Tully into his kennel and tosses in some chew bones to keep him busy. Ozzie takes off ahead of them to get a table at Chuck's, as June's locking up the house. Watching her get ready to go, he wonders: *Do I really want to spend forever with this complicated woman?*

Wearing a broad smile, June jumps into his truck. "Let's go. I'm starved!"

That smile melts his icy chill a little, but he can't put away the fear he just discovered behind Door Number One, the door to his future, tied forever to this one woman.

14.

"I don't think this is fair at all!"

Brendan's stretched out on the raft, hanging his head over the edge. He stares at his own reflection in the muddy water of the lake.

"Nobody does, man. You're really getting screwed! All the guys think so." His buddy strikes an aggressive pose in the center of the raft, downing a beer with one hand and trying to skip stones with the other, with limited success.

"At least the University has agreed to give me a chance," he grumbles, rolling over onto his back and shading his eyes with his arm. "Our attorney gave those academic assholes a ration of shit and they had to step back. My Dad said they couldn't really mess with me because I haven't actually been convicted of anything, or even charged officially."

"Well, what about the counseling reports?" the kid asks, plunking down on the raft. "Can the University request those?"

"Nah," Brendan sits up, grinning. "They won't even know about it. Confidentiality and all that. Dad says I should just keep my mouth shut and my nose clean for a while. They'll forget about this bullshit once they see me on the field!"

He throws an invisible football to an invisible receiver, and then puts both arms up to signify a touchdown. Both boys make 'cheering crowd' sounds and shove each other, laughing.

"Anyway," Brendan's mood turns suddenly dark, "once I talk to those counselors, man, that bitch will be sorry she ever said anything to anybody."

He scoops some of their skipping stones off the surface of the raft, whipping them ferociously at no one. The boys stare at the spot where the stones hit the water, each thinking his own private thoughts.

The next morning at 9:00, Brendan's dressed carefully

for his appointment in a sport shirt, khaki pants, and a linen blazer, loafers with no socks. The guy at Fallon Clinic tells his mom and dad to meet him afterward in the waiting room, around 11:30, and sends them away.

"Two and a half hours?" Brendan mutters, "What the hell is gonna take so long?"

It didn't take long to figure out. He had to take a test, one of those personality profiles, and he damn sure wanted to give 'em the right answers.

Russ Monty had run him through a brief prep on this kind of test, so he wouldn't be surprised. "It was designed to weed out scumbags, Brendan, not exceptional kids like you."

After finishing the test, the guy leads him into a nice room, like somebody's living room, with furniture, bookcases, and lamps instead of overhead lighting. A view of the garden gives the illusion that you're way out in the middle of nowhere, and the music is soft and unobtrusive.

"Brendan, my name is Rick."

The casual young guy looks to be in his late twenties but moves with the confidence of an older, more experienced man. He's dressed in nice jeans, designer distressed tee tucked into an expensive western-style belt, and well-worn Tony Llamas. Rick must be around 6'2", and Brendan thinks he looked like he should be doing commercials.

"Are you the shrink?" he blurts out, partially due to nervousness but mostly because this guy just doesn't fit the pictures in his mind.

Rick's laughter causes Brendan to blush. "Yeah, but I prefer to call myself a 'Mind-Melder'. What, you expected a fat old lady with moles on her face?" He extends his hand to Brendan.

The guy already thinks I'm a jerk, Brendan frets, but says out loud, "Sorry, man, I just... I didn't know what to expect," and quickly shakes Rick's hand.

Rick shakes his head, "No, no, it's ok. Most people

don't know what 'a shrink' looks like. I've toyed with the idea of growing a beard and smoking a pipe. What do you think?"

Brendan can't decide if Rick's making fun of him or just goofing around. "I…I don't know," he stammers, opting for the safe response.

"Come on, let's sit down." Rick moves over to a big leather chair, "Anywhere you want, Brendan."

Brendan looks around. There's a flowered couch, two striped upholstered chairs, and a straight chair with a padded seat but no arms. He hadn't expected a choice. After a tense moment, he sits upright on the edge of one of the striped chairs, as far away as he can get from Rick, the Mind-Melder.

"This ok?" Trying to be polite, he regrets sounding like a little girl.

Rick nods, dismissing the question. "Has anyone explained to you what we're doing here today?"

While he talks, Rick picks up a folder from the table next to him and hands it to Brendan. It isn't very thick, a slick cover emblazoned with the Fallon Clinic logo. A glance inside assures him that it's just your basic PR stuff, nothing he cares about. He would give it to his parents later.

He hadn't actually answered the question, but Rick kept talking as if Brendan had expressed an interest. "It's pretty straight forward today. I'll just get the story from your point of view. After that, we'll schedule a second session, to fill in any gaps and make a plan."

"What is that? Um, the 'plan', I mean? I thought the Judge just wanted to know what happened." he mangled the folder in his hand as if it were a cobra snake, wringing and wringing in self-defense.

Rick reassures him. "Yep, totally true, but it sometimes takes us awhile to get the whole story. Some people have a lot to tell and others take a while to get comfortable talking."

He pauses for a second, then, "Tell you what, Brendan, why don't we just jump right in here. Tell me what happened that got you here today."

He leans back into his chair, crossing one boot over his knee and opening his arms onto the armrests. He watches as the boy crushes the informational folder with unconscious tension, making a mental note: this kid needs a release valve, something to do with his hands seems to help.

He wants me to talk, Brendan figures, cringing inside and desperate to remember what he had planned to say.

"It's so unfair!" he finally blurts out, way more emotional than he meant to be. "I never wanted her to come live with us in the first place…"

And we're off, Rick thinks. He gives Brendan his 'shrink' face and watches as this tough kid breaks down into angry tears.

15.

June pulls up at the Crossette Shelter first thing in the morning. Flora's waiting outside for her. "Good morning, Flora."

She smiles politely as she hops into the car, but doesn't speak.

Noticing the absence of her backpack, June can't help but smile. *The kid is finally letting go of her security blanket – that's a positive sign!*

They head off to Fallon Clinic for Flora's initial appointment. June says, "They've scheduled me to talk to the therapist first this morning, just to give some background and answer any preliminary questions about the court requirements. Then you'll go in and I'll wait for you."

Flora's quiet, with a face that says, "I haven't a care in the world!" Weird.

"Do you have any questions for me before we get there?" June knows her voice sounds too bright, way too eager.

I guess I'm edgy, knowing how much rides on this assessment.

"No, I'm just going to wait and see," Flora tells her, all calm and together.

"Good, I think that's best," she nods and tries to sound wise. "You know, I'm really looking forward to meeting these people. I told you, didn't I, they are the best in the country, sort of like movie stars in my profession?"

Pause. "Are you nervous, June?" she asks, eyes steady.

Nervous laughter. "No, no, not nervous, but maybe excited. I would love to work at a place like Fallon Clinic someday. I want to see what makes them different from DCW."

She scrunches her eyebrows together in thought, then turns to face June. So serious!

"I bet they get paid a lot more than you guys," she speaks in a very matter-of-fact voice, "and have fancy offices and stuff. I bet they think they're better than us."

What's that – loyalty? "Here's what we'll do, Kiddo. You keep your eyes open, see what you think makes 'em different, and I'll do the same thing. Then, on our way home, we'll compare notes and see what we come up with, good and bad."

Flora nods with that half-smile, almost like saying, "Sure, June. Sure."

"Who knows? You could even see things that would help me do my job better at DCW."

Just about then Fallon Clinic comes into view. The sign and entrance gate are more like an estate than a business, rising elegantly from a bucolic setting with tons of gorgeous landscaping. It actually was an old estate at one time, June remembers. Somebody died and left the main building to the founder, with instructions to open a facility serving adopted kids and their families. Later, as they got better at diagnosing these kids, the clinic expanded to treating related problems, such as Attachment Disorder.

Challenging work, and often not very rewarding, Attachment Disorder kids are difficult to connect with, tend to be resistant to traditional therapy, and are the ones that adoptive parents most often bring back. Without good help, most folks just give up and feel lucky to get out with their sanity intact. These kids can be angry, aggressive, and violent in the worst cases.

June recalls a recent TV special report titled "Kids That Cannot Attach." Of course, they highlighted a little girl who tried to stab her adoptive parents with a butcher knife while the hard-working couple slept. The kid was only five years old.

Her birth parents might have been axe murderers, abusing the poor kid, or at least passing down their violent DNA, but the reporter made it seem like the very act of adoption turned this little sweetheart into a homicidal zombie. June was outraged at the report, portraying these kids as damaged goods and bad-mouthing adoption in general. Hell, it's hard enough to find good homes.

I wonder if that report has been good for business at Fallon.

"Geez, June, give 'em a break," that invisible angel on her shoulder whispers. "You haven't even spoken to them yet."

From the other shoulder, a snide fellow in a devil suit responds, "What difference does that make? Anybody who profits from the emotional trauma of children is suspect."

Funny how she could go from star worship to jaded cynicism in one short car trip. She wonders, is it my professional insecurity or my 'tiger protecting her cub' behavior kicking in?

"OK, Flora, here we are!" June's fake-cheery voice is back and Flora glances at her with a 'get-a-grip-on-yourself' look.

Inside the elegant main building, the receptionist shows them to a beautifully furnished room with a view of a pond, lovely, serene, and just like in the movies. Flora and

June raise their eyebrows at each other.

June picks up a folder with the Fallon logo, some sort of Celtic symbol, and hands it to Flora. "This looks like it has some information about the place. Take it home and look at it later." She stashes another folder in her briefcase for review.

"Flora? Ms. Hunter? I'm Louise, please sit down and be comfortable." Louise shakes with a two-handed grasp, then points to the furniture. "Please, sit anywhere you like."

Smiling, she sits in a wood and brocade side chair while June gives her a fast onceover.

Louise is probably younger than June by about half a dozen years, with short, stylish blond hair and very blue eyes that crinkle a little at the edges of her smile. She sports a pale pink tailored shirt with the arms loosely rolled up to below her elbow and tucked into a pair of casual cream slacks. Her toes are manicured in matching pink, elegant in tan sandals. She has big gold hoops in her ears and an expensive diamond and ruby ring on her right hand. She doesn't wear a watch, causing June to wonder where the clock is. Behind me, I'm certain, she thinks. All in all, Louise is the perfect image of a socialite rather than a therapist.

"Really, call me June." Needing to feel in control, she begins as if they were meeting in her office and this was her meeting. "I'm pleased you were able to see us on such short notice."

Unfazed, in sort of a 'June Cleaver meets Angelina Jolie' kind of way, Louise seems to miss her power play. Truthfully, she just ignores it.

"So am I, June." She leans in as if to share a secret. "I had to fight two other therapists to get assigned this case. I couldn't wait to meet you and Flora!"

"Why?" Flora speaks up in her solid voice, seemingly comfortable and not entirely impressed.

Louise turns to face her. "Flora, I read the Court

Report June wrote and the life story you composed. You struck me as a remarkable girl and I wanted to get to know you better. I will be meeting with Michael and Rosemary West, as well. They seem like very interesting people, and so talented."

Flora agrees with Louise, "Rosemary and Michael are really, really nice."

"Good!" She sits up straight. "Flora, one of the other people who works here is going to give you a tour of the property and explain what we do at Fallon Clinic. While you're gone, I will be talking to June, finding out some basic information. Then, when you get back, we can talk awhile, privately. Does that sound like something you can handle?"

"June already explained it all to me." Flora flashes her loyalty again by turning away from Louise, looking straight at June and sort-of smiling, then asking over her shoulder, "Who will be giving me the tour?"

Louise presses a button on the phone and stands. A young, good-looking man knocks and enters. "Hi, Louise, is our guest ready for the Grand Tour?"

"Come on in, Rick. This is Flora." Louise makes the introductions and Flora blushes wildly the moment Rick clasps her hand.

"Hey, Flora, welcome to Fallon Clinic! Come on, let's check the place out."

As he leads her out of the door, June hears him saying, "I know where they stash the cookies and other treats. If we hurry, I can show you."

After the door clicks shut, June hooks her thumb pointing backwards over her shoulder and levels her gaze at Louise. "Let me take a stab at this. Rick is Brendan's therapist, right?"

Louise changes instantly from indestructible socialite to regular human gal and cracks up. "Right you are! Oh, June, I have heard so much about you. What a thrill for me, to be interviewing you. Everybody's dying to meet you.

Please come say hello to the staff."

She stands up and they slip through a side door into some sort of conference room or employee lounge. June can't believe it. At least half a dozen smiling folks are there waiting to meet her.

16.

Barbara Portman steps up, the first to shake her hand. "June Hunter, do you recognize me?"

"Worked in Foster Care Recruitment, right?" June often drew a blank in these circumstances, an embarrassing little problem of placing names and faces when on the spot. Luckily, Sarge had mentioned her and the gal did look familiar. "Did you work with Donna, or did she come after you?"

"Oh, Donna is one of the best trainers I know." She's animated and positive, making her seem ageless. "She and I worked closely on a few investigations and I can't believe some law school hasn't snapped her up by now. Please give her my best."

"I sure will, Barbara."

Their chat ends just in time. Louise drags her away to a little group of three, holding cups of some pale liquid and smiling broadly in her direction.

"Janine, Ruth, Virginia, this is June Hunter." They all start in at once.

"Wasn't that you on the Boswell case?"

"You probably don't remember, but we met at that training in Colorado!"

"How can we ever convince you to come work for us, June?"

Yeah, flattering, but June's suspicious nature jumps to the front immediately.

"What would make you think I'd be an asset to your program?"

A low, strong voice from her left speaks up in response. "Because there is every indication you are one of the best in the business."

Everybody stops speaking and turns toward the voice, owned by a very distinguished man.

"June Hunter," Louise speaks softly as if on cue, "this is Dr. Drew Fallon."

"Please call me Drew. May I call you June?"

"Of course, please, Drew," She hopes she's not stammering like a school girl.

"Allow me," he extends the crook of his elbow, very gallant. June threads her arm through his as he steers them out of the conference room into the hallway.

"June, this place has been a dream of mine since I got into the 'fix the adoption' business. Did you know I worked for the State, too, many years ago?"

No way, she thinks, but only shakes her head in response.

"Yes, well, I was more of a contract worker than a direct employee. I did have an office at the old building downtown and treated DCW families exclusively."

They walk at a relaxed pace through a maze of hallways.

"When was that? The State moved into the current building about twenty years ago, I think."

"Good memory." He smiles right at her and she notices he has striking hazel eyes rimmed with gold. "Now you'll think I'm pulling your leg, but I met you some twenty-odd years ago, on your first day at DCW."

"What? No." She's too stunned to put terrific sentences together. "That can't be right." They enter an atrium area, quiet and beautiful, and June cringes as her voice echoes back at them.

"Well, you tell me…" He stops walking and gazes out one of the ceiling-height windows. "You were walking through the building with some supervisor. Charlotte, I believe. She was giving you the ten-cent tour and

182

introducing you to every person you passed. My office was on the main floor by the public lounge. Am I ringing any bells?"

He smiles at her like she's a toddler, but all she can do is look puzzled.

"You were introduced briskly and started to walk away, but I asked Charlotte to wait a moment. I explained that I was working with adoptive kids, should you ever need my assistance on a case. You looked at me quite seriously and said, 'Doctor, I believe the staff should have more need of your services than the children. We all have our baggage, don't we?' You winked at me, shook my hand, and then you were gone."

June now recalls the incident as if it were this morning. *How arrogant I was!*

"Oh, my, Dr. Fallon, I am so sorry…"

He holds up the palm of his hand. "June, I thought about you, and your advice, often. Did you know that your comment is what inspired the Employee Therapeutic Supervision Program? I developed it, actually."

She can only stare at him, her mouth nonfunctional for once. Then it dawns on her: *because of him, I get to see Min as much as I want, for free!*

He tucks her hand into the crook of his arm again and continues escorting her through the building. "So, June Hunter, you've been lucky for me both professionally and financially. I have always thought of you as my personal Muse!"

17.

Keely and Rosemary relax in the garden, the rich fragrance of the earth mingling with the soft bouquet of their wine.

"This tour has left me a little limp, Ro," Keely speaks seriously to her friend. "In the Fall, I think I'll take a vacation. Wanna come?"

"Where to?" Rosemary loves to travel.

"I don't know, maybe Alaska, tour the Inside Passage. September is about as late as we could go there, though, without risking crappy weather."

"I can't make any plans yet, not until we know about Flora. She would be back in school by then and so would I." Rosemary shifts in her seat, processing out loud, "Maybe traveling around Thanksgiving would be better, but that leaves out Alaska. How about Santa Fe? Let's think about that awhile."

Keely pours them more wine before she asks, "What do you think about this legal situation, Ro? Are you ok with all of this?"

Rosemary takes a long drink. "What a mess. Flora is pretty calm, but I feel like a mother lion defending her cub. Michael's very level. He says we need to keep putting one foot in front of another until we have answers, that fretting won't bring 'em any faster."

"Is Flora innocent?" Keely's given to bluntness with her friend, a trait Rosemary usually appreciated.

"Keely! I'm surprised at you. You know what happened. Are you telling me you think she fabricated this story? Why?"

"I never said that. Calm down," Keely back-pedals a bit. "I just want to know how YOU feel, that's all."

"Sorry," Rosemary slumps back into her chair. "This court stuff has got me a little edgy."

Trying to relax, she munches a cookie and sips a little more wine. "That boy's parents are trying to protect his reputation, I understand that part. I also think the Judge is trying to cover his ass, getting all of us assessed at Fallon. I don't mind, really. I just wish it would be over so we could get on with the adoption process."

Keely raises her eyebrows. "So, you've made up your mind already?"

"Yes, I have." Rosemary gazes at her friend. "I feel like it's a good match, don't you?"

"I do. I also know that she and I will be able to work together, if you're good with that." Keely smiles. "Dysfunctional kids like us make the best performers, you know. We can slip into a character better than anybody. Lots of practice."

"I'm counting on you to be 'Cool Aunt Keely' and go to bat for me on the days when she hates her new Mommy," says Rosemary, already reflecting on the inevitable separation between her and Flora. "That will happen sooner than later, I'm afraid, given her age."

"I've been in that kid's shoes, Ro." Keely reaches out, taking her friend's hands in her own. "And I know the System. Trust me to help you. Don't forget, you are dearer to me than any sister and I would do anything to keep this family happy and safe. You know that, right?"

"I know," Rosemary squeezes her hands and smiles through wet eyes. "I love you, too. When this is all over, we'll be the coolest family this side of the Mississippi."

"A toast to the lovely and creative West clan." They raise their glasses. "United we stand, against all foes!"

A ringing of crystal seals their pact.

18.

Min and June hunch over the therapist's desk, eating slabs of cheesecake doused in dark chocolate sauce. The one concession to health is the green tea they sip, lemon no sugar.

"Is therapy supposed to make you fat?" June wonders, licking a chocolate drip from her lower lip. "I always thought it was 'stress made you fat and therapy helped you lose it'."

Min scrapes her paper plate clean and drops it into the waste can beside her desk. "Well," she mumbles as best she can with that last huge bite still on her tongue, "I'm prescribing a daily exercise regime to go along with our sessions. Thirty minutes of any aerobic stuff you can tolerate every day. Happy?"

"Seriously?" June can't always tell when she's kidding.

"Yup, totally. I was going to bring it up today, cheesecake or not. I want you to chart each day in this pocket calendar with the time, what kind of exercise, how many minutes, all that. Then a paragraph afterwards with your thoughts for the day."

"You are shittin' me, Min." Her sophisticated communication style just flew out the window.

"Nope, no shit. This will increase oxygen to the brain and production of serotonin for an improved sense of wellbeing, provide time to reflect for peace of mind, and the exercise can only help with the sleep issue. There's a mountain of research to back me up on this, June. I'm not making it up. And it has the added benefit of allowing us to eat rich desserts at our visits."

"When am I supposed to do all this?" She whines like a twelve-year-old. It sounds petulant, even to her own ears.

"Oh, come on, June, you know better than to ask that. This is basic health stuff. You know, I think you should do it during work hours. I'll write a memo to Sol and he will have to see that you schedule it."

Now she's pissed. "First, I am not a baby that needs Daddy to send me outside for fresh air and exercise. Second, I thought this was confidential!"

Min practically vibrates with enthusiasm, while June makes a mental note to cut back on their sugar intake during future visits. "Oh, of course it's confidential. The memo will just say you need to be excused for roughly forty-five minutes daily as part of a prescribed treatment plan. I do it all the time, no problem. Besides, this way you get paid to de-stress."

It's hard to argue with her. As June thinks about it, it begins to sound pretty nice.

Min has already moved on. "OK, now, let's talk about the Flora case. How's it going?"

"It's going. She's still trying to cope with her losses by ignoring them."

"Yeah, well, I was talking about how you're coping. What losses has this brought up for you?"

Oops, stepped right into that one.

"Good catch, Min. Funny you should bring it up, but I was just thinking about this. Flora lost her birth family and her foster family and I see myself going through the same thing."

"In what way?"

Slumping back into her seat, she gets comfy. "Well, I'm an orphan too, since Dad died. My son is grown and living far enough away to be considered gone. And, now, I have to face some choices around retirement."

Min has her professional helper face on now, and her silent listening encourages June to keep going. "I figure I've always made DCW my second family. The work kept me from being too sad or lonely, and I never had to go out and find a social network. But, now, things are changing."

"How so?"

"People keep pushing me about choosing a new job to prepare for retirement."

Min's eyebrows crunch into zigzags. "Who are these people, June?"

"Sarge, Donna, Hal, they've all brought up my moving to a retirement job. Then there's this potential offer from Dr. Fallon."

She almost flies out of her chair. "An offer to work at Fallon Clinic? When did this happen?"

June tells her the story, leaving out the part where Fallon called her his Muse. "I feel kind of overwhelmed right now. I'm finally confident in my work, sometimes even bored, and along comes the idea of all these changes. I feel chained to this roller coaster. I got on by myself and I really enjoy it, but now it won't stop. I guess I'm getting scared."

"Job offers, talk of retirement," Min jots down notes

while she talks, then looks directly into June's eyes. "What else?"

Here we go.

"Of course, there's Quinn…"

19.

As a skilled professional, Louise finds her progress with Flora both rapid and interesting.

Step One: Flora likes to talk while facing out into the garden, so she can avoid eye contact during her most vulnerable moments. Louise wants her to be comfortable and open, so she sets it up that way.

Step Two: Sitting on chairs angled toward the wall of windows, with a low tea table in the middle, offers Flora the security of a barrier between them, disguised as a place to put refreshments. This gives the impression of a social visit as opposed to a court-ordered probe, again for Flora's benefit.

Step Three: Louise moves the table off to the side a little before each visit and angles the chairs toward each other a fraction, as well. Eventually they face each other directly, and Flora still feels safe.

This is the plan, simple and direct.

"Please describe for me the girl named Flora." Louise speaks softly, keeping a casual tone to her voice. "Pretend you are someone else, you are describing your friend Flora to me, and I don't know anything about her."

Flora sits in the chair with her feet crossed yoga-style, and stares out the window wall as if she could see a thousand miles away. "She's almost sixteen, chunky, not very smart in school, with pretty nice hair. Oh, and she likes to sing." Flora nods to signify she's finished, seemed satisfied with her description.

"Now, I don't know this young lady, so I have to ask you for clarification," Louise prepares her for the invasion. "What do you mean when you say 'not very smart'?"

Accustomed to probing school counselors, Flora's not surprised at this line of questioning. "You know, C's and D's in a lot of classes. I don't ... *she* doesn't read too good."

"Oh, that must be hard on her. Does she get help for that?" Louise maintains a casual tone.

Flora's gaze shifts more toward the woman, still relaxed. "Not much help. The school got tired of trying to teach her so they kind of gave up." She puts both her hands on her knees and leans in, almost as if to share a secret, but turns her face to the window as she speaks. "I think they feel sorry for her, sort of."

"Why would they feel sorry for her? Lots of kids have a hard time reading." The therapist appears to dismiss that flaw as a common and legitimate failing.

The girl's eyes come around to study the woman, to weigh her intent, "Well, no, not just that. She's an orphan, too."

"Oh, that's a shame. Did it happen recently?"

Accustomed to playing a role, Flora slides easily into character. She's fully the 'describer' now. Louise gets a rich description of Flora's situation: her allegiance to her mother and detachment from the father she didn't know; the gratitude and love for the grandmother that tried to raise her; and a sense of dependence on June, the caseworker that was trying so hard to help her find the right family.

"Yeah, caseworkers *say* they try, but they don't always help, do they?" Louise tests the water a bit.

Flora almost bares her teeth, defensive enough to slip out of character. "I never said that! June is really nice and she found me a really great new family when my foster parents threw me out."

The therapist now has everything she came for today.

"Oh, I misunderstood. So Flora really likes her caseworker? That's cool, because not all of 'em are so nice, you know?"

Immediately realizing her mistake, Flora reverts back to 'describer' mode, "Yeah, I know. That one caseworker, Cheryl, never answers her phone when kids call, and that Kevin guy was just too in love with himself, always looking in the mirror at his hair and stuff."

"So, what is the best thing about your friend Flora?" Louise seeks a positive ending for the session.

"She really tries hard to get everyone to like her." This falls from Flora's lips as if she were blowing a kiss, a trait she thinks worthy of respect and admiration.

"What a great kid! She sounds like a good friend," Louise fights to look as impressed as Flora seems to feel but her heart deflates painfully, like a balloon suddenly untied.

This child's identity depends solely upon those around her, she thought. *She has no idea who 'Flora' really is inside.*

When she smiles and stands to end their session, chatting casually about next time and having a good weekend, Louise thinks Flora believes her act.

But once out of the room Flora panics, wondering, "Why did Louise look like that at the end? She had that look in her eyes, that funny look."

All the way back to Crossette, she feels sick. She goes over and over the session in her head, reviewing every question and answer, trying to figure out where she went wrong.

20.

Damp and foggy in the woods behind her cabin, June zips up her sweatshirt to combat the late day chill. Tully romps ahead, pretty good about sticking with her, almost never running off after a fox or a fawn. He'll bark, though, and loud, especially if he hears someone coming.

"Thirty minutes a day isn't so bad," she tells Tully, rubbing his head as he dances around her. "I need the exercise anyway."

Writing a stupid paragraph about my thoughts every day is what really bugs me, she complains in silence.

The pocket calendar Min gave her sits on the kitchen table in June's house. It suddenly dawns on her: *Quinn could be in there right now, casually reading my most personal thoughts!*

Calming herself, she focuses on the Quinn she knows, historically respectful about invading the privacy of others. But in light of the first possibility, however unlikely, she moves it along and heads for home.

Tully bounds through the brush that thins into grassy space where the path opens into June's yard, and barks with great enthusiasm. Quinn parks the Harley as they come around the bend. He sees them, waves.

"Hey, I never even heard the bike," she yells, waving back. "You get a tune-up?"

"Actually, I did it myself this afternoon." He rubs Tully to keep him from jumping. "Want me to do yours?"

"Oh, that would be great." She throws her arms around his neck and waggles her eyebrows. "And after that, you can do my bike."

"Hah!" He kisses her with vigor. "Is that an invitation to spend the night?"

"Only if you take me to dinner first, Mister."

"No need." He pulls a bundle out of his saddle bag, waving it in front of her. "I brung the fixins, ma'm!"

By the time the charcoal is glowing ash, June's got the ribeyes marinating in garlic and lemon, a salad tossed, and the table set. Quinn pours her a big goblet of white merlot and pulls up a chair for her by the grill.

"A toast to Spring!" Salute and sip. "Ahhh!"

Quinn sizzles the steaks while regaling June with funny stories about his work week. She snatches up her calendar as he fools with the grill, and drops it into her purse with no written record for the day. Too bad. Her thoughts bounce around like Ricochet Rabbit, hitting every possibility for Quinn and their relationship.

What more do I want from him? What more could he want from me?

After dinner, dishes, and a cozy tumble, June rolls out of bed quietly and curls into her chair to watch the moon. They neglected to fire up the woodstove, too busy firing up each other, so it's a little chilly. She pulls a throw around her and listens to the sounds of her life. Quinn breathes evenly in a satisfied sleep and Tully snores softly next to the bed. Only she is restless.

Grabbing her purse, she fumbles for her Thought Calendar. Flipping on the lamp, she snuggles back into the chair and begins to write:

Just like my job, I have hit my comfort zone with Quinn. It is all so easy now. We know each other so well. But, just like my job, I am sometimes restless and frustrated. I want to make plans, but don't know how—include Quinn or plan on my own? I want to buy that cabin in the mountains for my retirement, but what does he want to do? And if I make a decision without him, will he see that as rejection? Worse yet, what if he doesn't really care? Despite my cavalier attitude, I have to admit I want more than the convenience of a comfortable partner. I want a real partner to grow with, who wants to grow old with me.

I know the only thing to do is talk to him about what I want, what he wants, too. I'm afraid to rock the boat right now, tho, especially when I feel so confused about my career. How do I remain steady when everything seems about to change?

Re-reading what she wrote, June rolls her eyes. "What a drama queen!"

Flora's case has made her think about living alone forever, never being truly attached to anyone again. The risk of making it permanent doesn't seem too intimidating when things are going well, but what would it be like when they couldn't escape back to our own homes and lives?

She tries to think clinically. *Truthfully, I would love to spend the rest of my life with Quinn, but taking that step would mean everything changes. Besides, he hasn't asked me!*

It strikes her now that the demon chasing away her sleep these days has nothing to do with work. *If I were to describe that demon, she is disturbingly familiar, a sad, lonely, regretful old woman. The future 'me'.*

21.

Sarge and Hal are fairly comfortable with the report from Fallon Clinic. June's dying to see, but Hal is adamant. "The Judge considers you a party to the case and, as such, you are not to review any material prior to acceptance into the court record."

In plain language, if she knows what the shrinks are saying about her, she can bend the facts in her favor by acting differently until the case is decided. June's main concern, of course, is that the report implies she's a bad caseworker and this will go on her permanent record.

Those grade school threats really stay with a girl!

The only thing he'll say is, "I see you're giving them your usual high-quality stuff, June."

At least, that's what Hal says. When she prods, Sarge just gazes at her like a skunk in headlights—if you don't want to get sprayed with something ugly, you'll just have to stop, wait, and stay out of the way.

Flora, on the other hand, has become a genuine chatterbox. "Keely is coming in on Thursday and we're all going to the Santa Fe for dinner. I just love that Spicy Shrimp and Avocado thing with the Spanish rice, and oh, June, have you ever had Fried Ice Cream?"

These run-on sentences are a new habit of hers, especially when Keely Bruce is coming to town. Flora completely adores her and they spend lots of time together on voice training. Small wonder the kid now aspires to be a jazz singer.

To be truthful, June finds herself a bit jealous of Flora's relationship with Keely. It's not only the fact that she's hanging out with an authentic super star, one June fawns after herself, but the bald admiration she shows the woman.

What am I, these days, Wonder Bread?

Curbing the green-eyed chick, June gushes, "Wow, Keely has come in to see you almost every weekend, hasn't she?"

Flora's face pinks up. "Oh, it's not just to see me! She comes in to see Rosemary and Michael all the time. They kinda keep it a secret, though, so her fans don't bug her."

"Well, you sure are the lucky one, Kiddo." June winks at her. "And I promise to keep her secret!"

June sits down in the chair next to the couch in the sunroom and gesture for Flora to sit, too. It's time they get serious about tomorrow's court hearing.

"Let's talk about court now." This subdues the girl. "And what we want to tell the Judge."

"Do you think he will ask me to go up there?" Eyes wide, she looks surprised.

"Well, it is certainly a possibility, and I don't want you to be taken by surprise." Remembering Hal, June asks, "Hasn't your attorney met with you about this?"

"Not yet," she says, relaxing a bit. "I'm meeting with him an hour before court tomorrow."

Surprised and a little pissed that Hal hasn't discussed this with her, June says, "Oh, well, good thing you said something. I guess I'd better come get you early."

"No, Rosemary and Michael are bringing me." She is casual, but then looks up at June, questioning. "That's ok, isn't it?"

"Of course." She chuckles and pats her shoulder for reassurance. "I just wasn't aware of everyone's plans, that's all."

Crap! June's getting what she and her do-gooders call "small feelings." *It's like I am not even a player, or at least not an important one.*

Instead of entertaining such emotions, June puts on her professional face and says, "Now that I know what everyone's doing, I think we need to write down what you want to say to your attorney and the Judge tomorrow, ok?"

Flora makes a "Whatever!" face but agrees.

"Great. Now, what do you want to tell the Judge about the past month?"

June take notes while Flora outlines her recent activities. The girl paints an electric picture of activities and interactions, one meant to impress the Judge with the new direction her life is taking. When she finishes, she stops, takes a long deep breath, and turns to me. "This really isn't what he wants, is it?"

Good catch, Kid! "What do you mean?"

"He wants to know how I'm dealing with … you know, the touching, Brendan and my foster parents, that kind of stuff."

"So, what…you don't want to tell him that?"

She looks at her hands. "I don't know what to say. Nothing is different, really. I talk to Louise about it and I think she's coming to court tomorrow, too."

"So, everyone has a different piece of information about you and it seems funny to be asked what you think. Does that sound about right?"

"I don't know what I think, June." Her eyes fill up and her voice squeaks. "I just want to do the right thing so I can get a family."

Whoa.

"Flora, I think I can explain what's happening to you right now, because I've helped a lot of other kids with the same problem. Want me to try?" June wants Flora's permission to invade her emotional plane. The kid looks miserable, but agrees.

June dives in. "When you have bounced around for so

long, home to home, family to family, never knowing what will happen next, you develop sort of a bad habit. You spend so much time trying to figure out what everyone around you is thinking, doing, wanting, that you stop thinking for yourself and about yourself. Could that be what's happened to you?"

This is a rather sophisticated concept for a younger teen but it seems like she's asking to go there. June has counseled an awful lot of women struggling with the same problem, living their lives for everyone else and slowly forgetting who they are. Sadly, many of those women don't want to hear it.

When your identity is 'whatever someone else wants you to be', it goes against the grain to carve out a piece of 'just you'. It takes a person who's ready to become a grown-up, willing to take responsibility for themselves instead of always turning it over to someone else. Most of the time, the woman is in so much pain she has only two options: change or check-out. Too many of 'em check-out. June doesn't want that for Flora.

"Maybe I am busy thinking about what everybody else wants," she says, "but if I don't, won't they just get rid of me?"

"I won't lie to you, Flora, it is a risk. But when people find out you are fooling them, just pretending to be the Flora they love, how do you think they'll feel about you then?"

She stares out the window for a long time. Then, in a quiet strained voice she says, "That's what 'Mom Jacobie' said to me, June. She said I only pretended to care about them."

Damn! Not where I wanted her to go.

This kid is so full of hurt that June can only open her arms to her. Flora leans in, crying full out now. All a caseworker can do at this point is keep their own feelings in check and find a way to put the kid back together again. After a few moments of anguish, she chokes back and sits up.

Grabbing the box of tissues from the table, June pushes it into her hands.

"Flora, let me tell you something. Most people are much older than you before they start to understand this stuff. I'm proud of you just for talking about it."

She wipes her nose and tosses the tissue on the floor. "Big deal. I still don't know what to do about it!"

Her anger is a good sign. It means she's ready to move on, so June says, "Well, if you want me too, I can give you a few ideas…"

They talk about the process of learning *who we are*: building an identity, exploring what we like and don't like, and finding people who fit in with that identity. June tells her how to create choices, and they set up this "exercise program" to develop her "identity muscles":

- o First, she will ask herself a question each day, examining her likes/dislikes;
- o Second, she will write the question down in her school planner; and
- o Third, she will record her answers, all of the likes/dislikes, throughout each day.

"How about this one for today?" Flora says, actually excited about it. "*What do I like/dislike about Michael and Rosemary?*"

"Good one!" June encourages her, "That's really two different questions, though. Just make sure you answer them separately, maybe even work on one today and save one for tomorrow."

Flora's already made two columns, *Likes* and *Dislikes*, when June says, "Remember there's no wrong answer in this exercise, just what you like or don't like. If you want, we can go over them together and I'll show you how to figure them out. Then, after a while, you'll be doing it all the time and you won't need any help at all."

"Maybe I could try another question to start," she says. "Something easy."

"How about, what's your favorite color?"

She starts writing in her columns, laughing at her own thoughts.

22.

Sitting in the Courtroom, June has time to reflect. Pleased with her progress, she's been watching Flora build her own identity after so many years of being a puppet. In spite of her struggles at school, the kid is really smart too, lots of insight. She just needs to start using it for her own best interests. Hell, a lot of folks could take a lesson from her.

When the Judge asks Flora to stand up and "fill him in" on what's transpired in her life since the last court hearing, June fidgets in her seat.

Did I prepare her enough? Did Hal?

In these situations, caseworkers give the kid some tools and hope they do more than shuffle around and say, "Um, I don't know." Kids are like that sometimes.

Flora rises from her seat next to Hal, poised and confident. The adults are all taken by surprise when she gives Judge Paxton her very cogent speech.

"Well, Your Honor, this month I found out something about myself. I've been trying to get everyone to like me so I could have a family, you know, like all the other kids. I never cared about what they did to me or how they treated me, as long as they would like me enough to let me stay.

"Yesterday I realized I didn't even know what my favorite color is or which cookies I like best. I always wanted what THEY wanted. I didn't pick for myself because I didn't want anyone to think I'm stupid or get mad at me. I just pick what everyone else picks and they're happy with me. But when people find out you're faking, they aren't happy with you anymore. They think you lied, and then they hate you."

She takes a moment to swallow a sob, then runs on, talking fast.

"But June, uh, I mean Ms. Hunter, she's teaching me to pick for myself. I told her it feels scary, so she's helping me. She says she won't have to help me for long, because pretty soon I will like it and will want to do this by myself. That's what grown-ups do."

She starts to sit down, but jumps up again, "Oh, um, I picked … it's purple, my favorite color, I mean. Like the sky was last night when the sun was already down but it was still a little light out, that kind of purple. June said I might change my mind sometimes, but that's ok, so today I pick purple!"

She smiles wide and sits down.

23.

Judge Paxton is doing the same thing everyone else is doing, choking back emotions. Even the Jacobie family is blinking hard. The rest of the room is either sniffling (the women) or clearing their throats (the men). The big burly bailiff, a former cop who tolerates little nonsense, is blowing his nose with great gusto into a crisp white handkerchief while the Judge gulps a glass of water. Finally, he speaks.

"Thank you, Flora. It sounds like you have been working hard this past month. Keep up the good work."

He coughs a couple of times, then barks, "Mr. Franklin, Mr. Monty, Mr. Solomon, Ms. Hunter. Give me thirty minutes to review these reports. Then you four meet me in my Chambers. The rest of the parties are excused. The Court thanks you for your appearance today. Mr. Franklin will notify you all with next month's hearing date."

Bang!

June whispers in Flora's ear, "Nice speech, Kiddo." Then, winking at Rosemary and Michael, she makes the 'I'll call you' sign and rushes out of the courtroom after Sarge. He flies down the stairs toward the smoking area with her flying after him.

"Sarge?" She asks, "What did you think of our girl's speech?"

He only glares as he pulls hard on a cigarette, "She was real compelling, Hunter, a regular drama queen."

Uh-oh. "Something wrong?"

He pulls in smoke and blows, leaning back against the brick, "I hope I'm being paranoid, but I suspect Paxton thinks this was rehearsed. First, we had the 'Rosemary West Show' last month and now this. I can't tell if he's pissed about all the drama in his courtroom or just anxious to get on with it."

She hadn't prepped the kid and the implication caused a swell of anger. "Geez, Sarge, I can't help it if Flora's diving into her personal growth head first. If he asks, I'll be happy to explain to Paxton what I'm doing with her." Grinning, June concedes, "She did sound like a zealot, didn't she? 'Ladies and gentlemen, a little course in Self-Help 101 for my friends in the back row!'"

Sarge calms down, even smiles a bit. The cigarette is doing its job. "Ho, ho, ho. Just don't get defensive if he admonishes you about this. And please don't take credit for her showmanship. Be ready and give him your 'calm professional' routine, ok?"

Sarge's uncharacteristic pleading gives her the willies. It stimulates an abnormal compulsion to cooperate. "Sure, ok, Sarge. I'll be my best 'Suzie Social Worker'. I won't embarrass you. I promise."

He hauls himself off the wall, grinds out his smoke, and actually puts his hand on her shoulder. "I know, I know. I've been out of the courtroom for a while, and I forgot how much it wears me out. When this started, I was hoping this crap would be over with before Memorial Day.

Now it looks like we could be here through Christmas."

"Things are moving along pretty quickly. Really, they are. What do we know about Brendan's side of the fence?"

He heads toward the door, checks his watch. "Let's go, I want to be early for this. I don't think the boy has given us a couch-side confession, if that's what you're hoping. All I could get from Barbara is the kid's pretty angry, especially about his future. You know, keeping his scholarship, this getting on his record, his parents' reputation, all that. No surprises as far as I can tell."

They're about ten minutes early, so Sarge goes to visit Hal. June plunks down in the front row to pull her thoughts together.

Deep breaths, in, out. I'm calm, professional, respectful.

Two minutes of deep breathing and she reaches Zen.

Paxton is doing his job, I'm doing mine, all is as it should be. Unlike Sarge, I feel pretty good. Ready for anything.

They sit in straight chairs, four across, in front of the Judge's gigantic wooden desk. Sarge, June, Hal, and Russ Monty. Fidgety, throat clearing, nail chewing, sweaty. The Judge could award them the Nobel Prize and they'd still feel like this, your basic conditioned response. "To the Principal's Office, you hooligans!"

The Judge sits and glares.

"Ms. Hunter, let's chat with you first."

Oh, shit. "Your client's speech was quite moving. Could you explain to me what the blazes she was talking about?"

Everyone turns to June, eyebrows raised, blinking with expectation.

"Of course, Your Honor." Breathe in, breathe out. "As you know, children in foster care often spend most of their time observing others, trying to interpret all the unspoken rules.

Who's really in charge?
What do they expect from me?
How do I know when I've crossed the line?

Stuff like that. After a while, they start to lose track of

201

who they are and base most of their decisions on what everyone else wants, likes, or expects."

"I understand that," he says, "but what was the part about 'picking' things?"

"Right. Well, the way I help kids build an identity is a three-step process. First, they learn to identify things they like or don't like. Second, we identify wants and expectations for the future. Third, we design plans. They set goals and the steps to achieve them, as well as what happens if we don't or can't get there."

They all stare, dead quiet, so she keeps going. "Say we identify that you like, um ... flowers. Great! Next, we would decide if you want to try to grow flowers, study flowers, draw pictures of flowers, whatever. This part is to incorporate positives or 'Likes' into your life. So, if you want to grow flowers, the next part would be to plan how. If you're good at school, you could study horticulture. If you're not a good reader, maybe get a job in a flower shop and learn arranging. Then we set up a plan that is logical. Maybe you want to own a greenhouse, so we apply logic: join 4-H, learn some gardening skills, apply for a part-time job at a nursery, take a class in business at a community college, etc."

A deep breath and she brings it home. "So, when you wonder who you are and if you have value, you can say, *I am a person who enjoys flowers. I have developed the skill to grow them and sell them to others for their enjoyment. This gives me joy and has value.*"

She sits back in her chair. Breathe in, breathe out.

Her three colleagues turn to look at the Judge. Judge Paxton keeps looking at her, deep in thought.

Finally, "Thank you, Ms. Hunter. That was simple and direct, and seems to be very appropriate." He starts jotting a few notes and asks, "Now, tell me whose technique this is and what do we call it?"

Oh, man! Now I have to tell him I made it up.

"Your Honor, this is just something I do with the kids

on my caseload, especially the older ones. It isn't any great counseling technique or anything. I sort of developed it over the years, using what worked and discarding what didn't. It hasn't been published or anything. It's just a tool."

She thinks she hears angels singing when he says, "Huh. It sounds like a quality approach."

The Judge speaks to each of the guys at length while June sits in stunned silence. At some point he dismisses them and she wanders out of the Courthouse.

Not speaking to anyone, not even Sarge, June drives home, changes her clothes, get on her Indian, and hits the road. The Judge's questions have instigated some heavy duty, Flora-type thinking about her own life.

What do I like about my life?
What am I missing?
What do I want for the future?
And how the heck am I going to get there?

III. TRANSITION & ANALYSIS

1.

Sweet Sixteen is a milestone in any girl's life. June and the others had been planning ways to celebrate, some gesture for Flora. In light of the recent drama in court, June was adamant that any birthday celebration be low-key. All Flora needed was for Judge Paxton to see her as a party girl. Russ Monty would love to make a mountain out of any little molehill he could find, proving that Flora was not remorseful or some such crap. In the end, they each did their own thing, planning a more substantial celebration when Flora was fully cleared of all charges and the adoption could take place.

June held a small cookout at Crossette, inviting Gina and the four other girls currently residing at the shelter. They grilled steaks and the girls made a birthday cake. It was sweet, really. They sang "Happy Birthday" and each gave her a gift: a cute key ring for when she learns to drive; a mirror for her purse; a used CD of a popular boy band; and more stuff like that. With her foster care money, June bought her a nice three-piece set of luggage in purple paisley. She loved that, a huge improvement over the standard black plastic garbage bags.

As a personal gift, she gave Flora a copy of the Dr. Seuss classic, *Oh, The Thinks You Can Think!* Inside the front cover, she wrote:

"Flora, this is one of my favorites—I have a copy on my own bookshelf. It reminds me to always 'think great thinks!'

Happy Sixteenth Birthday,
June Hunter."

Flora stared at it long enough to cause June to wonder

about insulting her with such a babyish book. Then she looked up at her, all serious, and said, "I'll try to 'think great thinks', too, June."

Geez, the kid weirds me out sometimes.

Rosemary and Michael had a nice celebration, too, at a dinner theater near Milwaukee. She loved it, of course. Rosemary got her some terrific jewelry, made by her artist friends, of course. Michael really knocked her socks off with his gift, a handmade bronze shovel with an elegantly carved wooden handle. Flora laughed and laughed, because inside the card was the invoice for about three dozen fruit trees, to be delivered to the Westwoods Studio at the end of June.

Evidently, Keely had contacted Flora earlier in the month, planning a birthday dinner in Chicago. It was to be just the two of them and they dubbed it the "Sisters Celebration." June thought that was awfully sweet, especially knowing what it would mean to Flora in terms of feeling accepted. Besides, being picked up in a limo and transported to Chicago to meet up with Keely was very cool! So, later, when the shit hits the fan—when Sarge's screaming his head off, and Hal's blaming June, and the Judge's ordering an immediate hearing—June's got nothing to say. After all, she did approve the party.

How was I supposed to know about the 'big surprise' Keely Bruce had secretly planned?

Chicago Tribune, Friday Tempo Section, Page One

Chicago – Last night at Willy's, Chicago's trendiest North Side jazz club, Keely Bruce launched her talented new protégé in a surprise appearance at the club's weekly event, Open Mike Thursday. I was fortunate to be in the audience for this memorable moment in modern jazz history.

Jazz superstar Keely Bruce, walked into the club,

unexpected and without fanfare, around 7:00p.m. during dinner rush. After a light supper with her young friend, she casually stepped up to the mike and introduced herself to the stunned crowd. Thursday night at Willy's caters mostly to regulars expecting to hear seasoned local performers and a few unknowns trying out their chops.

Willy's house band backed Bruce stylishly on a couple of jazz classics, as well as her recent hit, "West of the Stars". House guitarist, Jason James, shared the spotlight in a tight and eloquent acoustical rendition of "Blue Moon".

Then the young songster, introduced simply as Flora, stepped up to the stage and performed three numbers: The classic ballad, "Someone To Watch Over Me"; "Black Coffee", a lesser known but powerful blues number; and "Baby, It's Cold Outside", a comic jazz duet performed with Ms. Bruce.

This journalist hates to jump the gun, but the kid has mighty powerful pipes and an emotional style that defies her years. If last night was any indication, audiences will be clamoring to see her. For the record, Flora is a knock-out. No pink teenage princess, she is a pale brunette resembling those porcelain starlets of the 40's, all smoky eyes and shoulder-length Marcel waves.

Query: What is her age? Unable to secure details, I can tell you they rushed out of there by 9:45 pm. Note: Willy's is closed to minors at 10:00 pm sharp, no exceptions.

Query: Where does she come from? Not revealed last night, but word is out that Flora is the soon-to-be adopted daughter of renowned artist and sculptor, Michael West, and his environmentalist powerhouse wife, Rosemary West. It seems Ms. Bruce is an old school chum of Mrs. West and a regular companion during her off-tour season.

Query: When will we see more of Flora? Bruce's manager remains unavailable but I promise, readers: when I know, you'll know.

–by Art Cassidy, Tribune Music Columnist

Staring at the newspaper, June mumbles, "I am so screwed."

2.

The lay person might think, "What's so bad about the kid getting her big break? Sounds like good news to me!"

Unfortunately, the finer points of the law outline it differently. As the representative of the State Office of the Guardian, June knows she's in BIG trouble.

First: She approved a trip to Chicago where the kid was unescorted and was meeting up with someone who has no State clearance. Keely Bruce thinks of herself as a member of the West family, as do Michael and Rosemary, but from a legal standpoint she is nobody. In the eyes of the Court, this would be roughly equivalent to sticking an unescorted kid on a bus for Chicago to go party with Mick Jagger and the Rolling Stones.

Second: The kid was performing publicly in a club where liquor is served. Yes, the law says that minors can be present as long as the club is serving as a restaurant; once the kitchen no longer serves dinner, it is officially "a tavern" and the "no minors rule" is enacted. But the State requires legal approval for a Ward of the Court (that's Flora) to work in a tavern, among other places. Technically, Flora was not "working", but just because she didn't get paid doesn't mean June's out of the woods.

Third: The article in the paper would violate the Ward

of the Court/minor's right to privacy, except for two things: she was performing openly in a public forum and the reporter never mentioned her last name.

Technicalities.

Of course, the guy reported she was a foster kid about to be adopted, naming the semi-famous people who were adopting her, so her cover is blown no matter that the letter of the law was followed.

Last: Per instructions during their recent court hearing, they were all supposed to be keeping a low profile surrounding this case.

Would it be redundant to say, "I am so-o-o screwed"?

"I will be contacting Mrs. Rosemary 'I-Am-Above-The-System' West with a subpoena!" Hal's practically foaming at the mouth. "Let her explain to the Judge how she could let this happen."

"And where the hell were YOU when the kid went public, Hunter? Attending a Keely Bruce Fan Club Meeting?" Sarge is equally pissed, evidenced by such a low blow.

"Do you really think I knew about this, Sarge?" June's shaking now, mostly furious, and a little scared. "Keely Bruce set me up! She's a 'System Kid' so she knew *exactly* what she was doing."

"What the hell does that mean?" Sarge is fuming, but that last statement slows the flow of anger. She definitely has their attention now.

"Keely told me she is an adoptee." Hal and Sarge both stare, dumfounded. "She knew this kind of public display would be completely inappropriate and I would never approve it if I had known in advance."

Hal groans. "So this is her way of putting the screws to us. If we don't go ahead with the West adoption now, this case will be a public spectacle. The State becomes a villain, standing in the way of the kid's accomplishments and her would-be family's happiness."

"And since Flora is so young and talented," Sarge

chimes in, "how can we prevent her from this opportunity for certain success?"

"Most teenagers in the System never do better than a minimum wage job," June summarizes. "With Flora's distinct lack of achievement in school, her other prospects are pretty dim."

We all look at each other in silence for a few seconds before Hal mumbles, "Paxton is not going to sit still for this kind of manipulation, Junie. He's gonna think you're trying to force his hand."

She sinks into one of Hal's chairs and leans her arms on his desk. "That means we have to be ready for him." She looks from Hal to Sarge. "I don't plan to lose my job *or* my reputation because Keely Bruce outsmarted me. Tell me what you guys think of this idea…"

3.

June thought she was ready for this Monday morning command performance in court, but her shaking hands, dry mouth, and weak knees tend to differ.

Using her obvious distress to her advantage, she goes back to her theater training in how to manage stage fright. The human brain is basically lazy and others will interpret your actions the way you lead them. Hide your fear behind an angry facade, for example, most people will see only the anger. However, you must be consistent and believable in all actions, no mistakes. Any inconsistent remark or act will stand out enough that most observers will sense something is not right, even if they aren't sure why.

She and Sarge worked all weekend to finish her Report to the Court, examining every point carefully. He now sits at the table beside her, appearing still as angry as he was Friday morning. Their body language has been carefully orchestrated to indicate a breach in their working relationship. He has moved his chair slightly, so their arms do not touch, and he is angled about fifteen degrees clockwise away from her. They do not speak or make eye contact.

June's projecting the image of a case worker struggling to be professional in spite of her obvious anger. She sits square with the table and upright, shoulders tight, both feet on the floor. Her report is in front of her next to a clean legal pad. She squeezes her pen and taps it in aggravation. Just a little, not too dramatic.

The Report to the Court is clearly focused on the adversarial relationship between the West family, including Keely Bruce, and the State. The writing of the report was skewed to imply that every unintended slight or accidental infraction was a clear indication of the West family and Keely's lack of respect for the Court and DCW. Sarge and June both signed it, to imply that the recommendations were orders from above, not necessarily June's idea. Perhaps this will salvage some of the trust built up between June and all of the folks she's trashed in her report.

Judge Paxton is clearly unhappy, but a little uncertain. He's trying to determine who is responsible for this mess and who to blast for being irresponsible. However, the Report to the Court surprises him. He is wary. He ignores protocol by conducting the questioning himself. He directs Hal to put Flora in the attorney's conference room, so she can't hear the interchange in the courtroom.

"Ms. Hunter, would you have me believe that you had no knowledge of this Chicago trip until it was reported in the newspaper?"

"Your Honor, as my report indicates, I was aware of an innocent birthday dinner to take place at a restaurant in Chicago. This blatant disregard for both State regulations and the direction of the Court came as a complete surprise to me."

Rosemary and Michael are sitting in the middle of the room, a row behind me. Observation of their body language and sharp whispers indicate they are floored by June's attitude. They do not have direct access to the Report, but will hear any references that the Judge or anyone else might make, as well as her recommendations.

"Mr. and Mrs. West, what do you have to say about this incident?"

Rosemary tries to stand, but Michael puts his hand on her shoulder and rises. As June turns to look at them, she works to keep a poker face. Rosemary looks devastated but Michael is strong and determined.

"Your Honor, we deeply regret any action that might imply an adversarial relationship with the Court or DCW. It has always been our desire to cooperate fully with Ms. Hunter, Mr. Franklin, and all the parties involved."

"Then how do you explain this incident, Mr. West?"

"Perhaps I should be the one to explain, Your Honor."

We all turn to see Keely standing next to the bailiff, wearing a dark blue suit and crisp white blouse, looking every bit like a New York attorney.

"Ms. Bruce, I presume?"

Keely nods at the Judge and responds, "I am."

"Please join us, Ms. Bruce. If Mr. West doesn't object, perhaps you should be the one to describe the incident." Michael raises his hands surrendering, sits down. Keely steps to the front of the court room, separating herself from Michael and Rosemary. She stands directly in front of the Judge's bench.

"I have no excuse for what I did, Your Honor, and ask the Court's forgiveness. As an adopted child myself, I was caught up in the idea that I would be giving Flora a wonderful opportunity, a chance to shine. I know how few those moments are for a child like Flora, and how often we adoptees are disappointed by life."

The Judge interrupts, "Certainly you are aware of the privacy laws meant to protect Wards of the Court, Ms. Bruce."

"I am, Your Honor, but for a moment I was distracted

by the joy Flora has been experiencing with her singing. Had this club been in a smaller town, with no reporter present, this appearance might have gone unnoticed. A number of performers sang at the club that night, but to my knowledge no others were reviewed. This opportunity could have occurred at Flora's school talent show or in a local audition for her community theater. She does have a remarkable voice, but the chance that any singer will get 'discovered' at an open mike performance is slim to none … take a performer's word for it."

Judge Paxton actually smiles at this. "I understand the odds, Ms. Bruce. However, most open mike performers are not accompanied by a superstar."

A tentative laugh ripples through the court room. "I concede to Your Honor!" A smiling Keely pauses, then looks serious. "Please understand, sometimes it's difficult for me to remember I'm anything but that lonely little girl, waiting for someone to like me and take me home. When I'm with Flora, I remember my own experience. I want only to give her something more than disappointment."

Keely clasps her hands together, like a praying child. "That night was not planned, Your Honor. If it had been, there would have been a huge press turn-out, and possibly other musical stars present. That's how PR people handle such things. When we saw it was an open mike, we just wanted to have fun like normal people at a normal birthday celebration." Keely's head bows and she says sadly, "Just for a moment we forgot that neither of us is truly 'normal', Your Honor. I'm so sorry."

She's brilliant! But is the Judge buying it?

Paxton scrubs his face with his hands and lets out a huge sigh. "Anyone else have anything to add?"

Of course, no one dares move a muscle.

It's easy to see the Judge is looking at my Report, on the last page, where the following 'Recommendations' are spelled out.

<u>Recommendations</u>
If the Court finds that the disregard of State law has been committed with deliberate intent, it is our recommendation that the following orders be entered:

1.   That Keely Bruce be reprimanded by the Court for child endangerment.
2.   That the Court order no unsupervised contact between Keely Bruce and the minor.
3.   That Keely Bruce participate in and successfully complete Foster Parent Training Classes.
4.   That Keely Bruce participate in Family Counseling Sessions at the Fallon Clinic, addressing her relationship with the minor.
5.   That Rosemary and Michael West be reprimanded by the Court for complicity.
6.   That Rosemary and Michael West be required to repeat Foster Parent Training Classes.
7.   That Rosemary and Michael West be limited to weekly supervised visits with Flora at DCW Offices.
8.   That Rosemary and Michael West continue Family Counseling at the Fallon Clinic, to address their lack of cooperation with the State.

"Mr. Franklin, Mr. Barrett, and Ms. Hunter, I'll see you in my Chambers in fifteen minutes."

Bang! The Judge exits the Bench.

Hal gets up and addresses the court room. "Everybody, please excuse us. I will meet with you after we have our meeting with Judge Paxton. Please remain in the area." He lets Flora join the group in the lobby and we duck into the conference room.

As the door closes, Sarge mutters, "You ok?"

June nods and sits on the other side of the table, just in case anyone comes in.

"Well, she certainly mollified the Judge." Hal grins,

keeping his voice low. "That Keely is one great actress."

Sarge scowls, "But what do you think Paxton's thinking, that Keely Bruce is full of shit?"

"Maybe." Hal sits down. "Even still, she makes me feel all soft and squishy inside. How about you guys?"

They all agree. Even knowing she was full of it, they still bought her story, emotionally. She really brought it home with the 'normal' thing. Of course, she's absolutely right. *And* she apologized with gusto, important to any judge.

"OK," Hal opens the door. "Let's go and good luck to all of us."

Judge Paxton is a big man, even more intimidating close up at his desk. Mimicking naughty school kids once more, they line up in their seats in front of him.

"Let me start by saying, if Flora was my daughter, I would be pouring champagne and toasting Keely Bruce right now. I was very unhappy to see this young lady's pre-adoptive status laid out in the press, but the advantage of her standing in the 'popular court' does not escape me. This is an appealing profile, 'poor orphan kid with great pipes turns superstar'." His voice gets louder, "And yet I am unwilling to let Keely Bruce, or anyone else involved in this mess, exploit this girl. Do you understand me?"

All heads bob in silence.

"Ms. Hunter, based on your recommendations I'm wondering if electrocution would be severe enough action for you?"

Hal coughs and chokes, Sarge turns his face away, and June can only stammer, "Uh, um … Your Honor?"

"Come on, these recommendations would be typical for kidnappers or child beaters." He glares at her. "But, for the record, I get your point. I assume we were all angry and frustrated by the press involvement, and Friday I was looking for someone's head on a stick. Given a weekend to cool down, most anyone might reconsider their viewpoint. I know, I did." He leans in to look her right in the eye.

"What do you really want to see happen?"

Breathe deep, this is your chance.

"I think it would be appropriate for Ms. Bruce to attend Family Counseling sessions at Fallon, as she is both a potential 'big sister' to Flora and her career mentor. I'd like to see her reporting to the Court, getting approval prior to taking any action. Of course, she should submit to the State background check process, just like anyone else spending time with a Ward."

Scribbling notes, he looks up. "That it?"

"Yes for me, Your Honor." I look at Sarge, "However, Mr. Barrett may have some additional insights."

"No, that would be acceptable to me, too, Your Honor." Sarge relaxes now.

"Hal?"

"Judge, in light of the lack of malicious intent, I think these simple cautions would be appropriate."

"Hang 'em quick, hang 'em high, eh?"

When Paxton winks, they laugh in nervous relief.

Saved our own necks yet again.

They reconvene and the Judge chats with Keely, Rosemary, and Michael, emphasizing his concerns about the exploitation of a Ward of the Court. He issues his orders, practically word-for-word the way June relayed them in his Chambers, with one off the record addition: an autographed copy of Flora's first gold album. He calls Flora into the room and reassures her that everything is fine, that she just needs to be more careful about public appearances or media involvement. He explains how people can take advantage of her and how the Court is determined to protect her from that. He tells her how proud we all are for her, and how she should be very proud of herself. He also cautions her and everyone else by stating if Flora's grades suffer, he will intervene, star or no star.

Keely stops June on the way out of the court room. She doesn't even speak. She just shakes her hand and gives a look that says they are partners in this thing. June smiles and asks her to call the next time she's coming into town.

Later, they all gather at Chuck's: June, Sarge, and Hal, laughing at how scared they had been, how cool the Judge was, and how they pulled it off once again.

Quinn joins the trio after he got June's "the coast is clear!" call and raises his beer in a toast. "To Harry Paxton and Keely Bruce, may they forever be your champions!"

They laugh and drink, but then June asks, "Hey, since when do you call Judge Paxton by his first name? Do you know him?"

"Good friend of the family ... didn't I ever mention that?"

Quinn Harimann continues to surprise me.

4.

Brendan was surprisingly comfortable with his therapist, the sessions at Fallon as productive as Rick could expect. Nearly ready to prepare his summary for the Judge, Rick would first need to sit down with Louise and confer on the status of her work with Flora.

"I could have lots of girls if all I wanted was to fool around." Brendan was most certainly bragging but trying to make it sound more factual. "I'm tellin' ya, man, those cheerleaders are seriously hot to trot!"

"They really get into hanging out with athletes, eh?" Rick restates the fact, encouraging.

"Yeah, but it's more than that. Some of these girls are real competitive, collecting 'notches on their headboard' just like guys do."

Rick acts surprised. "Wow, no kidding? The tables sure have turned since I was in high school. What do the guys think about all that?"

"A lot of the guys think it's pretty funny, you know, that girls take sex as such a challenge. The guys all know when one of them's looking to hook up, so they play along all innocent and surprised, like. Everybody knows if the guy wasn't totally cool in the first place, none of those babes would be beggin' for it like they do." Still bragging, pretty smug. "And if the guy ignores 'em later or 'calls a spade a spade'… well, they cry like babies. What the hell do they expect? A guy to fall in love over a toss with a shorty?"

"It sounds like everyone figures they deserve it."

"Well, if the girl can't handle the truth, she shouldn't be hangin' it out there for guys to take." Disgusted now, Brendan says, "Like if some girl gets fat, for instance, nobody's surprised when the guys call her 'Fatty' or 'Miss Piggy' or whatever. So, if shorty is spreading her legs for everybody, she can't be surprised when they call her 'The Mattress' or 'Eagle' or worse."

"You had a couple of steady girlfriends during the past year. Were you serious about them?"

"Naw," he shakes his head, arrogant. "Both of 'em were pretty nice, good looking and all. It was ok to have one girl for a while, but they both got all clingy after a few weeks and I had to get out."

"Sounds like the girls find you irresistible," Rick teases.

Brendan's blush is a surprise. "I don't know about that, but I do ok."

"When I was in school, there were basically two kinds of girls: girls you fooled around with and girls you dated. Is it still that way?"

Brendan ponders this for a moment. "I guess most guys want to date a 'nice' girl eventually, one your parents like, you know, when you're ready to get married. But after you date one for a while, they put a lot of pressure on you to 'love' them, not just fool around anymore. I'm not interested in getting married, not now. Most of the guys I know aren't even interested in dating 'cause they're going away to school next year."

"But what's the difference between having girls to 'fool

around with' and a steady girlfriend? It used to be that the steady was the *only* one the guy was sleeping with…like that was sort of a commitment to be exclusive, you know?"

Brendan shakes his head. "Not really anymore. Going with a girl is more like saying she's your favorite. Guys will still hook up with other girls, but not as much and not as openly."

"We were always worried, back then, about getting some girl pregnant. What do you guys worry about: AIDS or getting pregnant or what?"

"Guys don't really talk about it much." He knits his brow. "Mostly the girls are on the pill or keep condoms in their purse. You hear stuff, like one of the cheerleaders supposedly got an abortion last winter, but I think that's pretty much just gossip."

"Have you ever seen a guy put the moves on a girl who doesn't want it?" Too obvious, for sure, but good to test Brendan's response to such direct questioning.

Brendan had been slumped in an easy chair with his legs stretched out before him, arms up and crossed behind his head. At this question, he sits up straight and looks sideways at Rick, clearly suspicious. "I saw this guy working a hottie, convincing her she wanted it until after it was over and she freaked out…yeah, I've seen that. And I've seen it where a girl yells 'Stop!' half way through, and the guy lets her go. Nobody likes it when things get messy but sometimes it happens where a girl changes her mind."

"Is that what you think happened with Flora?" Rick figures the kid can't say he was tricked into answering. Brendan obviously knew this was coming.

"Pretty much." Brendan's standing now, staring out the window. "She was always wanting to be with me and hang out with my friends."

"Was she in love with you, do you think?"

"That's what she said." His jaw's set and he's actually gritting his teeth now. So close!

"Wow, she did?" Rick leans in. "What happened then?"

"I told her to stay the hell away from me, or I would tell my Dad what she was trying to pull."

"Did she freak out when you told her that?" Rick keeps at it.

Brendan keeps looking out the window, back to Rick. "Yeah, she cried, but not much. She knew I wasn't interested."

"What did your Dad say?"

He turns, glaring at Rick, hands fisted and face red. "Every time I told him how she was acting, he said she wouldn't be around forever, that I should just ignore her if I couldn't be nice. Big help that was!"

"If he really wanted to help, what should he have said?" Rick notes Brendan's tears before he turns back to the window.

"He should have sent her back! I told him and told him. Why didn't he just send her back?"

Later, Rick led Brendan to the lounge and brought Mr. Jacobie into the office.

After some initial discussion, he asks, "In the beginning, Mr. Jacobie, how did Brendan seem to feel about Flora coming to live with you?"

"He was just entering high school back then, preoccupied with his own life. I don't think he gave it much thought, honestly. After the foster care classes, he never brought it up again. Not until we got Flora, that is."

Rick nods. "That sounds pretty typical for a teenage boy. When Flora first came to live with you, how did he feel? Was he surprised you actually did it?"

Jacobie laughs. "Yes, I think he was. It seemed like those classes never really prepared him the way they were supposed to."

The classes were a tool, Rick thinks. *It was your job to prepare the kid.* Out loud he says, "Oh, that's too bad. How did he react?"

"He was annoyed at having to share his space: his

bathroom, his TV in the family room, his computer, that type of thing."

Rick smiles, "Again, pretty typical. What kid likes to share?"

"Right." The man's more confident now. "We expected some of that behavior. He seemed to adjust pretty quickly after she was placed."

"So, he never really had any problems after that, then." Rick knew it was a leading question, more of a statement, but was interested in Mr. Jacobie's perspective.

"No, not really." Still confident. "Other than having to give her rides later, once he had his license. You know how older kids hate it when they have to drag around the younger ones. I guess his friends made fun of him back then."

"I bet," Rick grins, rolling his eyes and mimicking a complaining kid. "'So-o-o not cool', eh?"

Jacobie agrees. "We just ended up leaving the girl to ride the bus to school and my wife drove her to any extracurricular activities if she needed a ride."

'The girl's' name is Flora, Rick thinks. "Sounds like a good solution. It was smooth sailing after that, then? Everybody happy?"

"Except for my wife," he shakes his head and smiles benevolently. "Poor thing had to take that girl to school early all the time and pick her up late, too, for music classes and the like. But I'm sure she didn't really mind. She wanted her to know what a normal life could be like and to fit in with the other girls."

Rick's ready, putting on his compassionate face. "Mr. Jacobie, most teenage kids are pretty secretive, trying to separate from their parents and all that. It's too bad, though. If Brendan had communicated his concerns about Flora a year ago, maybe you could have intervened and avoided this mess."

Mr. Jacobie looks grim. "I have thought that very thing a dozen times, lately." Shaking his head again. "If only…"

5.

Rosemary fusses with the sandwiches, arranging and rearranging them on their plates, moving little bunch of grapes and lettuce leaves around them with fluttering fingers.

"Come on, Ro, it's over for now." Keely sips her wine and calls to her from the table. "Quit wrestling those sandwiches and bring them over here!"

She brings the sandwiches then, sitting down with her own glass of wine. "I feel like I'm walking on a frozen lake during Spring melt, you know? How did things get so messed up?"

"It isn't messed up now, not anymore." Keely takes hold of her friend's hand and gazes into her eyes. "Believe me when I tell you, I know how the System works. I have thrown myself on the mercy of the Court and the Judge has forgiven me. Still, I put them in an uncompromising position. They cannot back out now without looking like a bunch of insensitive oafs."

Rosemary's unconvinced. "But what if they still think…"

"Listen," Keely interrupts. "Even June knows it. This adoption is a done deal, barring any new developments, just as soon as that judge ties up his end of the business. He has to finish what he started, but I guarantee it won't be long now."

Rosemary holds her forehead in her hand, chewing a bite of her lunch, "Oh, Keely, I wish you had left well enough alone. I had it covered, really, I did! Things were going along beautifully."

"A little insurance never hurts." She's smug as she bites into her sandwich. "And the best part is, you and Michael were completely innocent. Everyone knows you didn't have anything to do with it. It was all the fault of that mixed up adoptee, Keely Bruce!"

Rosemary sucks in air, letting it out slowly to calm

herself. Maybe that's the problem, she thinks to herself. I don't like to be out of control of the situation. Having Keely execute one of her elaborate plans is like living in a food processor: once the button's pushed, it's impossible to fight the maelstrom. Keely is good at chaos, she thinks. Much better than I am.

Rosemary decides to shake it off, move forward. She attacks her food with resolve, barely chewing before swallowing, just getting done with it.

"All right, then." She slugs down the rest of her wine. "Let's forget it and talk about what's next."

They're lounging on the deck, talking and laughing, when Michael shows up.

"He's home early," Rosemary murmurs, as Michael shoots them a cursory wave and stomps into the house.

"Is he mad at me, too?" Keely doesn't sound concerned, as much as surprised. Michael's pretty much a 'live and let live' kind of guy, rarely judgmental.

"Oh, I wouldn't say *mad*," Rosemary's hedging now, a little guilty about letting Keely in on their marital conversation. "He is concerned you're letting your feelings about the System effect our situation with Flora."

"Hmmm." Keely glares at the door. "Well, is he going to talk to me about it, or is he just going to stay pissed off?"

"He's not pissed off, I told you." Rosemary leans forward to put her face between Keely's eyes and the door. "Please don't start with him, Keely! Let me handle this."

Michael chooses that moment to step out on the deck. "Hi, ladies. I'm on my way to Fallon. I promised Flora I would pick her up after her session with Louise today." He plants a kiss on top of Rosemary's head and smiles blandly at Keely. "See you two at dinner."

After the goodbyes, Michael drives off and Keely unwinds a bit. "At least I'm still invited for dinner."

Rosemary notices she's holding her breath. Blowing it out in relief, she says, "And you two will play nice, or no dessert!" They laugh, each secretly hoping no permanent damage was done to their self-made family.

Michael stands in the waiting room at Fallon Clinic, observing the grounds through the huge windows. It's starting to green up now, new leaves the color of a fresh pear in sunlight. He's thinking about the fruit trees and getting them planted soon.

A crisp young lady speaks from behind him. "Mr. West, Louise and Flora are ready for you."

He follows behind her down the hall to Louise's office, where Flora wraps him in a bear hug, "Michael, you came!"

"Of course, I came. I promised you, didn't I?" He squeezes her tight and leads her to the chairs to sit down. "Hello, Louise."

"Glad you could make it, Michael," Louise greets him. "Flora's been on the edge of her seat all session."

"Did the trees come? Can we plant them this weekend?" Flora interrupts, eyes wide and hopeful.

Michael laughs at her enthusiasm, considering the transformation that has occurred in her since their first visit. Was it only a matter of weeks since then?

"Yep, we're good to go," he assures her. "But we can make our plans later. What are we talking about today?"

"Not our favorite topic, is it?"

Michael watches as, in response to Louise's question, Flora reverts to that distant, removed young lady of weeks ago. She shakes her head and stares at the wall behind Louise, silent.

"What are we talking about here, Flora?" Michael always tries to address her directly, not talk about her when she's sitting right beside him the way so many professionals seemed to do.

"Death," Flora croaks. "Any losses, actually, but mostly death."

"Hmm, creepy," he nods, deliberately looking out the window. "I remember when Amanda died... we were supposed to be expecting it and all, but I was still devastated. How could such a beautiful four-year-old child, someone I loved so much, die? I didn't get dressed for a week."

Flora's eyes regain her focus and her mouth falls open. "Really? You??"

This gives Michael permission for eye contact and he takes it, locking on to her stare. "Uh huh, me. Every time we lose someone special, we lose a piece of our heart. That's the piece we gave them when we fell in love."

Flora seems to be melting away, the edges of the box where she locked up her feelings is weakening, getting too soft to keep them inside.

"Funny, though." Michael stays locked on to her eyes, not letting go. "You don't remember until much later that you have a piece of them too, the piece of their heart they gave you. It allows us to laugh at funny memories or enjoy remembering what it was like when they were with us— still are, actually, and always will be. That's when we stop hurting so much and remember how happy we are that they were a part of our lives."

The light dawns almost visibly in the room. "So we're happy that they lived, more than we're sad that they died?"

"Think about eating the biggest, best ice cream sundae in the world. At first, you're sad it's gone, but if you really, REALLY enjoyed it, don't you talk about how fantastic it was, remember how delicious it tasted? You forget how sad you were when it was first gone."

Silent for a long moment, then boldly, trusting, she asks, "But what if you ate it really fast when you were little and you hardly remember how it tasted?"

Michael grins wide. "All you have to do is look in the mirror…a sundae that big stays with you, in every cell in your body."

Flora laughs at Michael pinching his love handles. Then he turns to face her, taking both of her hands in his. "Amanda was with us for such a short time, Flora, but look..." he leaned his face close, smiling, "...see these crinkles here?" He pointed to the laugh lines in outer corners of his eyes, "She gave me these to remember her by. The thing is, I have to smile to see them."

Michael hopes tonight Flora will look in the mirror, discovering somewhere in her beautiful face the traces of the gifts her parents had given her not so very long ago.

6.

Quinn and June have a serious case of Spring Fever, a bit late this year. This weekend they're working outside at June's cabin: weeding the vegetable garden she'd let Quinn plant a few weeks ago, tidying up perennial beds, and cleaning and sealing wooden outdoor furniture. Not big on fooling with annuals, June does love flowers. She's conceded to this conflict by growing hostas, hardy rose bushes, and easy stuff like begonias, geraniums, and coleus every year for her outdoor enjoyment.

"How about growing some herbs again this summer?" Quinn is a patient cook, much more patient than June, taking time to pick his seasonings from the garden while stirring and chopping and preparing a meal.

"Plenty of room over here and not too far from the back door." June recalls the time she put the vegetable garden so far away from the house that she could never muster the energy to go pick anything. The ruin of that garden site was her badge of disgrace for the whole harvest season. Friends still joke about it.

"Even though we put lettuce in the planters, maybe the herbs can fit there as companion plants." Quinn figured that one out, putting decorative planters with lettuce growing right outside the door, where they sit and relax. Every day, it's easy to remember to cut and rinse a salad, a gift from the earth in those early days before the 'real' vegetables come in. "As the lettuce dies off from the heat

225

the herbs will fill in the space."

"Yeah, I love that!" Not only because it's an excellent idea, but because it's Quinn's. "Let's put in a few different types this year. I can bring some of them inside once the summer growing season ends."

They carry on like this for quite a while, Tully chasing butterflies and June chasing domestication. She hadn't noticed until now how comfortable they are in this house together. She struggles to remember the last time they spent time at his place.

June tries to view Quinn through a future lens and imagine what it would be like to live day in and day out together. Right this minute that sounds sweet and romantic, but she knows too well what marriage can turn into: a natural disaster of monumental proportions.

Do I really think I can do it again?

Doing the same thing over and over but expecting a different result is one definition of crazy. She gets that. Her first marriage was an exercise in crazy. She trusted and trusted, completely ignoring the ugly yellow build-up of evidence that her partner was not worthy of her faith in him. The worse he got, the clearer the evidence of his cheating, the harder she tried to be a trusting and worthy partner. In the end, neither had any respect left for *her*.

But what would I change this time around?

She begins noting the ways she's changed: I've learned to respect myself and others more; I 'say what I mean and mean what I say', at least most of the time.

It's hard for cultivated good girls to say what they mean if it isn't so nice. To this day, June hates when someone is mad at her, even a waitress or store clerk. She's always trying to fix it. That *is* what she's good at, after all, fixing things.

When asked what she wanted to be when she grew up, her answer was, "I'm going to make the world a better place!" Her generation's flower children were full of Peace and Love rhetoric—she just couldn't get any for herself.

"Hey, Junie," Quinn interrupts her reflection. "I'm getting hungry. Do we have anything to throw on the grill?"

"I'm marinating those pork chops for dinner." She drops her shovel and work gloves on the spot. "In fact, I'm opening some wine. Want some?"

"Beer for me." He wipes his face with a bandana and quips, "I'll pick up out here, if you'll deliver."

Cute and clever. "Ho, ho, Word Master. One beer coming up. Not only will I deliver it to you now, but I may deliver later…" Waggling her eyebrows, she finishes, "…if you're nice!" His laughter follows her inside.

In the kitchen, she gets out a cold bottle of beer, pours some crisp German Riesling, and stops for a moment at the window. She observes a grown man, well formed, tempered by tough times and softened by the warmth of friends.

What am I afraid of?

Later that night sitting next to the woodstove, June thinks again the man now sleeping in her bed. It's as if I have never been without him, she thinks, a sense that he's grown into a part of me. The real question is: *Could I give him up?*

A rush of relief bubbles up. Finally, June thinks, I know what I want.

7.

Min and June walk along the River Path together, a prelude to eating the fruit and yogurt they have waiting for them back in the office.

"So, you feel like you can move forward in your relationship with Quinn now?" Min is breathing easily, while June pants like an old dog.

"Yes, I really do," she gasps. "I can actually see a future with us."

"Has he suggested a 'future' together, June?" She always does this.

Stopping to catch her breath, June says, "You know he hasn't, but I think I'd like to open that discussion with him now."

Min cooperates with her need to rest and points to a bench up ahead. "Let's go sit for a minute." The minute June's ass hits the wood, she asks her, "What if he doesn't want a future, or at least not the same version as you do?"

"I have considered that possibility, Min," she replies, cringing at the thought of such rejection. "But I would rather know where we stand than keep ignoring the elephant in the living room."

"Well, you two have been together for three years, so I think you should have a sense of where you're headed. At the very least, you should be able to compare notes."

She agrees. "Like I said, I want to open the discussion, not hold him at gunpoint."

Min laughs. "Good for you! Keep me posted. Meanwhile," she takes a quick slug from her water bottle. "What do you hear from your son?"

"Leo?" June wonders where this is going. "He's working on his Doctorate in Denver, teaching some classes at the university. He will probably visit in early August. That's when he usually has a couple of weeks free, before the Fall Semester starts."

"What does he think of Quinn?"

"As far as I can tell, he likes him just fine." She gives this a quick thought, but doesn't feel much concern. "Leo's grown now. He doesn't get too involved in my social life."

Min gets up to stretch. "June, you might want to at least chat about the possibility with him. I like to bring things full circle. Kids and husbands are linked, even if they are all grown adults. Anyway," they start walking again, "nobody likes surprises, least of all if the surprise is your Mom getting remarried."

Man, that girl can really complicate things.

By the time they get back to her office, June's about done talking. Not Min. They gulp down water and grab some coffee to shore them up for the afternoon.

"So, what are you thinking about your 'retirement job', June?"

"Wow, you're covering all the bases today." She groans. "Do we have to?"

Min's relentless. "We still have about fifteen minutes. Let's not waste 'em."

"OK." June wiggles into her overstuffed chair, spooning yogurt and berries into her mouth. "The way I see it, I have three options: I can move to Training and Recruitment; I can go work at Fallon; or I can stay where I am."

Min's all business now. "The first decision, then, is to do something or do nothing."

She's right, of course. "Yeah, I get that. I'm pretty good at doing nothing. If I make no decision, then I can't make a bad choice, right?"

"That old perfectionist is rearing its ugly head again. 'If I can't make a perfect choice, I make no choice at all.' Right?"

Sounds good, logical, even. "I don't have to choose right now, do I?"

"No," Min scowls a little. "But let's talk about that. Are any of your 'action' choices time-limited?"

June hates when Min's right. "Yes, my first two options are time-limited."

"So, we need to eliminate them as viable choices before we can say with certainty that 'no action' is your best move. Pick one of them and we can review it."

"How about the Fallon Clinic option?" June starts with the real stunner. "Drew was very persuasive and working there could be an exciting challenge. Adoption work is right up my alley and the money would be fantastic."

"Why not jump at it?" Min is strangely encouraging.

229

"Um, well, let's see…" June struggles to come up with a good reason to reject it. "The most obvious point is that Drew hasn't made me a formal offer yet. He just wanted me to entertain the idea of working for him. The weird part is, I'm afraid of failing there. Everyone thinks I'm so damn brilliant that my mistakes would stand out like neon."

"You believe your reputation precedes you and they have you on a pedestal. Lots of responsibility comes with those high expectations." Min looks her square in the eye and says, "So you think you can't do it."

Geez! "No, I never said that! I know I can do it."

"Then, they expect you to do a good job and you have no doubts that you can." June figures she's just trying to piss her off. "Let's move on to the Training and Recruitment position."

"Oh, ok," she says, trying to shift gears as her head spins. "The pace is slow so it's a lot less stressful, Donna is a total joy to work with, and these positions rarely open up."

"And this would be an easy job for you?" Min interrogates her.

"Oh, yeah, I could do it with my eyes closed, but I don't think it would be boring." Already defending this possibility, June gets a jump on her 'devil's advocate' approach.

"So, this job needs to be filled and fast?" Min asks.

"Yup."

"Sounds to me like both opportunities fulfill certain needs and desires for you, sort of two sides of the same coin." She scowls again, but then lights up. "Hey, how about this? Accept them both."

What the hell? "Huh? How can I do that, Min? That's ridiculous!"

"No, no, listen," she's leaning forward and just about vibrating. "You take the Training position, and contract part-time with Fallon. The Training hours are fairly consistent, right? A couple of days a week you could work on Fallon cases, bank some serious cash, and still be satisfying both sides of that coin."

June's already calculating in her head. "Training classes are evenings or sometimes on weekends. Maybe I could work out a flexible schedule with Donna…"

"June, this is a real possibility for you." Min's totally excited. "Why don't you talk to Donna, talk to Drew Fallon, and maybe talk to Sol, too? Then, next week we can start designing and implementing your transitional plan. Sound good?"

"Sure… next week." Wandering out of her office, June looks for the train that just hit her.

8.

Michael and Rosemary and Keely sit around the kitchen table, each with their own agenda and each with one eye peeled toward the patio. The big glass doors offer a clear view of Flora weeding the flowers in the wooden containers near the shed.

The Fourth of July had passed quietly for the West Family and Flora; there was the parade, a home cookout, and fireworks in town. For the rest of the weekend, everyone was careful to detail what they want to do and with whom, so no one could get mad or mess up.

Michael leads the family meeting. "I don't want there to be any more 'accidentally on purpose' mishaps, so I am suggesting we do everything in pairs when it comes to Flora."

"That will be hard for me," Rosemary murmurs, almost meek. "When she and I are here together during the day or on weekends, you might need to be at Westwoods or even out of town."

"I guess it really only applies to outside activities, field trips, that sort of thing." Michael's clearly softening.

"Are you two going to chaperone me when I'm giving her lessons?" Keely's angry, since the meeting was called following her 'surprise' courtroom appearance. "I don't think you need to protect her from me, if that's where this is going."

"No, no," Michael's calm, but firm, gazing directly at Keely. "I believe the Judge was convinced that this incident was unintentional on your part, and that we were not involved with you in some 'plot'. However, we cannot take any risks this close to a decision about the adoption. Don't you agree?"

"Right, I guess I do," she concedes. "And I see the value of trying to keep two heads in the game at all times, right now. But that still doesn't resolve the lessons in the studio."

"I have an idea about that," Michael ventured, "but I haven't had a chance to run it past you, Rosie."

"Let's hear it now." Rosemary leans both arms on the table, curious. Keely mimics her, focusing on Michael.

"Well, the old machine shed out back has a separate electrical system to it and insulation in the office area. If we completed the insulation and put in a heating system, couldn't we build our own music studio on site?"

Rosemary's eyes shine. "We hardly use it for equipment anymore, so that's no problem, and we just put a new roof on it last year. What do you think, Keely?"

Keely's hesitant, calculating in her head. "The remodel won't be as bad as the equipment costs; recording and sound equipment can be extreme. But I could use it as a business expense, even the remodel, if you write me a contract. Problem is, it would require a separate driveway and a permit, I think."

Why don't I check with Quinn on the permits and all that?" Michael says. "This way you never have to worry about booking studio time or running into media people when you're in town. The phone has been ringing off the hook out at Westwoods."

"We had a few media calls here, as well," Rosemary says, "but since our home number is unpublished, it hasn't been too bad."

Keely bows her head. "I'm sorry about that, you guys. My agent has been swamped too, but hardly anyone has my private cell number. I've been a little concerned about taking Flora into town for her lessons. This could be a fantastic solution."

"A solution to what?" Flora enters the French doors, pulling off her gardening shoes and gloves, dropping them on the woven mat.

They all look up. In their excitement, none of them heard Flora enter.

Michael smiles at her. "Come on in, Flora, we have an idea to share with you…"

Later, pressing up against each other in bed, Michael and Rosemary discuss the plans they put into motion that day.

"You are my hero, Michael West." Rosemary snuggles and squeezes him until he laughs out loud.

"Wow, you're easy to please," he chuckles into her neck. "If that makes you happy, wait 'til you hear my next great idea."

Rosemary sits up so fast he nearly falls off the bed. "Another idea? What is it?"

"Oh, boy." He flops flat on his back, arms behind his head. "I guess I should have prepared more for this one. Do I get graded?"

"Come on," Rosemary demands, jabbing him lightly on the shoulder. "Don't make me punch it out of you!"

After a short but delightful tussle, Michael shouts, "I give up! I'll tell you!" They both sit up, propping pillows behind their backs.

Rosemary listens, astonished, as Michael outlines the business idea from start to finish. After about forty-five minutes, he sums up his 'presentation' with a qualifier, "If you think this is completely crazy, I'll just drop the whole thing right now."

She had been listening to him carefully, trying to absorb all the details. Now she could only blurt out, "It's a fantastic idea! What in the world made you think of it?"

Michael dipped his head and rubbed his chin, smiling a tiny smile. "Remember <u>Flora's Story</u>, where she talked about the peaches? I just could never get it out of my head that the one positive image she held of her mother was her favorite baby food. She didn't even remember it herself; her grandmother told her. I just wanted to bring everything full circle for her."

"To honor her mother that way, Michael…" Rosemary choked back tears. "I didn't realize the depth of your love for her, already."

They embrace then, tightly, exploring a new dimension of their love for each other, trusting that the new life they were bringing into their family would enrich all of them.

9.

"So, they're gonna build a music studio right there, and Keely will give me lessons at home, and if we want to record anything we can do that, too, and…"

"Hold on there, young lady." June chuckles at her enthusiasm. "This is all very exciting, but when is this going to take place?"

"Right away," she takes a deep breath, tries to slow down. "Some building and equipment guys are coming over next week to draw up plans, Michael says. I don't know for sure how long this stuff takes, but just to know it's really happening… Wow!"

"You aren't kidding with the 'Wow'. When this family gets an idea, they don't mess around, do they?" They're sitting in the sunroom at the Shelter and Flora is bringing June up to speed.

"No, they don't," Flora gushes. "Michael says my

grades can't drop even the tiniest bit or the music stuff will have to go on hold. Not the school choir, just the outside stuff. He says it's like a job or a sport, if it interferes with my school work, we drop it. He says school has to be my biggest focus because you can't get very far without a diploma."

Way to go, Michael!

"And what do you think?" She tries to sound neutral.

"I think he's right, kind of." She frowns a little. "We looked at the newspaper want ads, and he showed me all the different jobs that say 'high school or GED'. I wonder if music is a little different, though."

June figured this would come up and she was ready. "What do you mean?"

"Well, you don't really need a diploma to sing, I don't think." Still frowning, she's not entirely sure of herself. She tries to play devil's advocate. "But I bet there are lots of famous singers that didn't finish school."

"I'm sure you're right, some famous singers don't have a lot of education." June plays her favorite card. "Do you know Willie Nelson?"

"Oh, sure." She perks up. "He's not just a singer, he writes a ton of songs and he's in the movies, too. And he does a lot of charity stuff like Farm Aid."

"That's the guy." She leans back, acting casual. "You would think he would be, like, a zillionaire by now, wouldn't you?"

"Yeah-h-h...?" She senses a punch line, puts a question into her answer.

"Well, the people he trusted to take care of his financial stuff basically stole all his money and didn't pay his taxes." June shrugs. "He pretty much lost everything a few years ago."

"Are you kidding?" Flora is astonished.

"No, I'm not. Too bad he didn't pay more attention and learn more about money and taxes and business. Maybe if he did, he could've seen what was going on before it was too late." Not really recalling the facts of Willie's predicament, she knew she was winging it on the details but believed she conveyed the spirit of the story.

"You mean they ripped him off?" She was having a hard time digesting this.

"Yep, that happens a lot to famous people, even good ones like Willie." June put on her sage face. "The smart ones learn as much as they can about business, and even get involved in the handling of their own finances. That way, it isn't so easy to take advantage of them."

"Man, that is so uncool!" She shakes her head. "If I ever get to be famous, I'll need to learn all that stuff, huh, June?"

"You had better learn it before you get famous. By then it could be too late."

She gives her that wide-eyed look. "Really?"

"Yes, really. Many of them have other businesses on the side, just in case they don't stay famous. Remember when we went to that football player's restaurant last month?"

"Oh, yeah! When he retires, he can have that for his job."

"That's the idea. Most people who get famous don't stay famous for their whole life. At some point, they need a different way to support themselves."

She gazes out the window. "June, what if Keely wasn't famous anymore? What would she do?"

"Well, she went to college, remember?" Bring the school thing back full circle. "She could do a lot with her college degree. For example, she could teach jazz studies at a university. Or she could start her own business, a recording label, even."

"Right…" She trails off, deep in thought.

"Enough about Keely and Willie," June jumps to their self-esteem work. "How about Flora?"

She pulls out her notebook and opens it to a well-scribbled page. "I've been working on my Likes/Dislikes assignment, June. You know what I think?"

"What's that?"

"I think it's hard to tell people what you don't like."

She laughs out loud. "Oh, boy, can I relate to that! I've been working on it for years. Lots of people don't like conflict, Flora. And the hardest people to be honest with are the ones you love the most."

She scrunches up her eyebrows. "That seems backwards, doesn't it? Like, they should be the easiest people to be honest with, since they love you."

"Here's how it works. The more you love someone, the more you don't want to lose them. So, if you worry they might not like something you think or do, you may try to cover it up or just not tell them at all."

"Oh, I see. Like, if your friend asks if you think her new jeans are cute, you don't tell her they make her look fat."

"Exactly." Now to the meat of it. "Let's say Rosemary wanted you to be a teacher. She keeps bringing you information about colleges that have teaching degrees, she tells everybody that you would be a great teacher, and every time you show her how to do something, she says, 'Oh, Flora, I'm so proud of you! You will be the best teacher in the world!' The only problem is, you don't want to be a teacher."

The idea that anyone thinks she would be great at anything is obviously a tough concept, but that she could or would let Rosemary down seems to hit the mark. "Oh, wow, June… what should I do?"

"Let's think for a minute about what kinds of things you might say," I get out some paper to make a list.

Flora comes up with a few things:
I don't think I would be a good teacher.
I don't want to work in a school.
I don't like school that much, so I don't want to be a teacher.

June helps her add a few more:

Would it disappoint you too much if I wanted to be (an astronaut)?

Being (an elephant trainer) excites me more than teaching right now.

My grades in school are much better in (floor mopping) than in more academic classes.

Could you help me find out what it would take for me to become (a deep sea diver)?

Flora gets a kick out of my crazy occupations, but is learning about helping another person to see who you really are by being honest. She sees the value in knowing what you like and helping others to like you as you really are, rather than put on a false front.

Going back to her Likes/Dislikes list, June asks if she would be willing to share about Michael and Rosemary. She writes:

Likes	_Dislikes_
Michael:	
Thinks I am smart.	*So busy all the time.*
Seems to know what I want.	*Makes me figure things out*
instead of telling me.	
Rosemary:	
Loves to do things with me.	*Worries about me too much.*
Helps me with my homework.	
Wants to be my Mom.	

That last one brings her up short, until she remembers the kid needs to rebel against somebody and Rosemary is the safest person around. This is a good sign, means Flora is progressing developmentally in her adolescent need to pull away from 'family' and establish her own identity.

I just hope she and Rosemary can work through it without

hurting each other too much.

10.

Ray, Tera, and Pete stare at Michael, each registering different emotions. They sit at their round table, the big oaken slab where they conduct their serious business, papers spread out between coffee mugs and half-eaten sandwiches.

Pete is the first to speak. "Michael, what makes you think I can manage this place? I've taken some business classes, management mostly, but I have absolutely no experience outside of Westwoods."

Michael encourages him. "It isn't your ability I'm concerned about, Pete. You've been managing this place about fifty percent of the time anyway. It's your desire that concerns me most. I don't want to push you into something you don't really want to do."

"I can see it, Pete," Ray grumbles. "You were always the one with the business ideas."

Then Tera, "And you've always been the best with the customers. Can't you just imagine Ray doing it, snarling at the clients or storming out on them?"

They all chuckle at that image, even Ray who takes pride in his ornery demeanor.

"The important thing to remember," Michael continues, "is that I will still be around. This is a co-op, so we would have weekly meetings. And I will still hold fifty-one percent of the managing interest. You will not be on your own, ever."

Tera jumps in, "Michael will still be teaching students here, too. Right, Michael?"

"Right!" Michael pulls out a binder for each one and hands them out. "Look this over. It's the draft of the business plan for the co-op. The tabs are for the different sections: green for Westwoods, purple for the orchard, peach for the new business, etc."

"When do you close on the orchard, Michael?" Ray seems almost excited about the plans, a rare emotion for him.

"That won't be until next month, but I have to confirm that with the bank." Michael pages through his binder to the section with the purple tab. "All of those details are covered in the section about the orchard. I picked you, Ray, for this project since you had a history with the agricultural end of things, and because you were my initial contact with the greenhouse."

Tera, a bit intimidated, asks, "I get why you picked both of the guys for this, Michael. But … what about me? You didn't want to hurt my feelings by leaving me out?"

All of them turn toward Michael, then, trying to gage his response. He shakes his head, "Tera, your insight has always been a force here, along with your creativity in brainstorming and planning. You are a 'big picture' kind of person. I need that… we need that." Michael looks to the others, who nod their agreement. "Besides, you work well with Flora. I look forward to you teaching her how to manage us guys with such grace."

"As you can see," Michael is the teacher again, "this plan requires you all to develop your business skills, studying the finer points of management and finance. That part of the agreement is pretty clear, so if you don't want to pursue that line of education, you need to tell me right away. No hard feelings if you want to back out."

After a thick pause, while the three students collaborate silently with each other, Pete faces Michael, "I think I speak for my colleagues, Mr. West, when I say we would be crazy to pass up this opportunity."

Tera smiles brilliantly and declares, "We would follow you anywhere, Michael."

They all turn to Ray, who cups his chin in his hand. "It appears you've made us an offer we can't refuse, Sir." He turns to the others with outstretched arms. "Let's do it!"

They each dig into their binders, then, scribbling notes and drinking cold coffee until the color drains out of the sky.

11.

Sarge fiddles with his silverware, arranging and rearranging the pieces on the green cloth napkin: spoon, fork, knife; spoon, knife, fork; fork, knife, spoon.

Holding the menu up front of her nose, June provides a little barrier between them. She can count the times he's taken her to lunch at a 'real' restaurant and he never ordered a beer before. Since he's acting so weird, June orders a glass of 'good' wine. Hell, she figures, he's buying.

The waiter brings the drinks, a bread basket, and a vegetable tray with dip. He pauses to see if they're ready to order.

"How about we make it easy on the fellow, Hunter?" Sarge takes control of the situation, finally. "Two steak sandwiches, medium rare, and two dinner salads." He raises his eyebrows and glares at her. She nods and hand over the menu. She wasn't looking at it, anyway.

He raises his glass of beer, declaring, "To us, Hunter. A great team deserves a treat," and takes a nice big swig.

Stunned, she raises her wine glass, sticks her nose in it, and breathes deep. "You're the best, Sarge." God, that's good! She closes her eyes for a tiny second and savors it, because she can tell what's coming is not good. When her eyes open, he's looking at her.

Don't say it, Sarge, whatever it is.

"OK, I'm just gonna say it, Hunter, and not keep you in suspense."

I said, don't say it!

"I got a call from Dr. Drew Fallon last night, at my home number if you can believe that guy. He wanted to know how I would feel if he made you an offer of

241

employment."

"He what?" She almost drops the glass. So embarrassing, that he would call my boss to ask permission.

"It wasn't an insult, Hunter, it was professional courtesy. He wanted me to know his intentions, but was trying to respect me by talking to me before he acted."

"What... what..."

"Now, listen close. What I told him was this: I told him I was retiring in ninety days and, if he would wait to take you until then, I'd give you a letter of recommendation that would impress the Queen of England."

Whatever she could imagine the bad news was gonna be, it wasn't even close. She still hadn't picked her chin up off the floor when her salad appeared.

"A couple more of these, Pal." Sarge gestures at the drinks and winks at the waiter, who smiles discreetly and vanishes. "Drink to my future, June," he picks up his beer, "and to yours, wherever you roam."

He called me June.

She just stares at him, trying not to cry, and gulps her wine like a gal in the desert. Sarge mixes French and Blue Cheese from the dressing caddy. June's finally able to croak, "Retire?"

"Yup, retire," he announces heartily. "In December, I'm taking the ol' ball and chain to New Zealand and next summer we're going to Nova Scotia. This is the return of romance, girlie! I can't wait to do something nice for my wife after all this time."

"So, what, are you wealthy, now, traveling the world?"

"Not as wealthy as you're gonna be, working for Dr. Moneybags Fallon," he answers dryly, trading the waiter his empty for a full glass. "He owes you, anyway, for stealing your idea and getting rich on it."

Did everyone know about her Therapeutic Supervision idea?

"He didn't exactly 'steal' the idea, he just developed it

into a viable program." She scoffs at Sarge giving her all the credit. "But how did you know about that? I only just found out, myself."

Sarge laughs, "I worked with the guy, Hunter! He did everything but jump up and down that first day he met you and begged us all to support this idea, when and if he got it all together."

She's still shaking her head in amazement when he says, "If you don't write the book on it by yourself, maybe you can collaborate with the good doctor."

Book? What book?

"Quit acting like a schoolgirl, Hunter, and drink your wine," he orders. "You need to write the book on this idea and explain why you thought it was necessary. Get Fallon to give you the rest: the research, how it works, what other experts say, and all the clinical crap. Then you sum it up with your expert opinion as to why other agencies should adopt your program. Get some credit for your ideas and reap the benefits, as well. You're a terrific writer, you know. Ask Hal, he'll back me up on this."

The only thing I know for sure at this point is, I'm going to need more wine.

12.

Keely lifts the box overflowing with wires and stuff and shoves it onto a shelf in the office. Flora clears off the rest of the table and they sit down, spreading out her music sheets before them. The machine shed would be a studio soon, but for now it was just a big messy building. Still, it felt good to work here.

"Oh, this one has to be your finale, Flora, it's your most powerful piece," Keely sticks a colored tab on top of the page, just over the title.

"We're still doing this duet, aren't we?" Flora bends over the sheets, concentrating.

They're going over the numbers she would record on the CD they're planning, a compilation of old jazz tunes and ballads. Keely and Flora would both perform on this album, but the primary purpose is to introduce Flora to the music world.

The Westwood Recording Studio would not be up and operating for some time, but putting something like this CD together is a major project. The actual recording and mixing are almost the last steps. Keely already has an agent and a producer involved. The most important piece right now is to outline the project for presentation to, and approval by, Judge Paxton, as Keely was ordered. Flora's out of school for the summer but time flies and they still have lots of work to do. Keely's Midwest appearances for the fall and her Holiday Tour are coming up fast. Her break for the summer lasted far longer than originally planned.

Hashing out the order is fun, but after a while Flora keeps losing track of what they're doing. Sometimes she simply stares off into space, not responding to Keely's rapid-fire conversation.

"Hey, Kid," Keely drops her papers and pen, leans back in her chair, and stretches, "You seem to have 'left the building' on me. Need a break?"

Flora looks up, blank. "What? Oh, sorry Keely. I guess I do need a break."

They grab something to drink and wander outside, following the fence line. Jeeves the dog keeps them company, happy to be trotting along behind them in the summer sunshine.

"Something bothering you, Flora? You seem pretty distracted today," Keely deliberately faces her eyes forward as they walk, so as not to threaten her with a direct gaze.

Flora stammers a bit, then blurts, "What was it like for you, Keely, when you turned eighteen? Were you with your adopted family? What were they like?"

So, thinks Keely, *she finally feels safe enough to ask for my story.* "I lived in a whole bunch of foster homes during my teenage years, Flora. Kids my age were not on the 'most wanted' list, you know what I mean? In those days, anyone who wanted to adopt could find a cute little baby to take home, because most young mothers gave up their babies. And to be honest, I was not the most lovable kid, carrying a big attitude fueled by tons of anger. I was getting kicked out of homes on the average of every three months."

Flora hangs on Keely's every word as she continues, "I remember sitting in my case worker's office when she told me basically we had run out of homes, and that I would have to go to Division, sort of a combination group home/jail for kids like me. I was pretty freaked out but trying not to show it, when the big boss came in to talk to me. I didn't say much, but she asked me some questions and I tried to answer her respectfully. I remember I thought she was pretty cool. After we talked a little, she suggested we give this one 'special' foster home a try. She told me straight-up that this was my last chance and if I couldn't make it with these folks, I deserved Division!"

"Wow," is all Flora can manage.

Keely seems lost in her history. "I had heard some pretty rough stories about Division and was terrified to end up there, so I decided to give these foster parents a fair shake. My new foster parents, Mom and Pop Griffin, were a lot older than most, more like grandparents to me. They really didn't plan to adopt. They wanted me to have young parents, like all the other kids at school. After a while, though, they did adopt me. Mom and Pop knew they were my last chance for a real family. That was the best thing that ever happened to me."

Keely hadn't spoken of the Griffins for quite a long time, and is surprised by how much emotion she feels. "Anyway, a good education was real important to them, so they spent a lot of time tutoring me, stuff like that. The Griffins were friends of Rosemary's parents, who ran a boarding school. They helped Mom and Pop get me a scholarship to college."

"Where are they now, your Mom and Pop?"

Keely hesitates a bit too long before answering, "Pop died while I was away at school. After that, Mom kind of fell apart, ended up in a nursing home. She passed away right after I cut my first album. She was so proud of me!" That does it. Keely covers her mouth to hold in the sob.

Flora's hands fly up to her face, her mouth in a big 'O'. "I'm so sorry! Please don't cry, Keely!"

She can't help herself, though. She wraps her arms around Flora, as much for her own comfort as to reassure the girl. "No, no, it's not bad crying, it's good crying. I just haven't talked about them in a while, and I was remembering how wonderful they really were to me."

She pulls away from Flora, holding her shoulders in her hands and smiling through her tears. "Thanks for letting me remember."

Composing herself, Keely starts walking again, this time with her arm loosely around Flora's shoulders. "They gave me a very special gift, Flora, one that has carried me through some pretty lonely times."

"What is it?" she gazes up into Keely's face now, like a small child.

"Their love taught me that I own a place in this world, that I belong. They said it's my responsibility to expand that love by developing the gifts and talents born in me."

She stops walking and turns to Flora, "Pop told me there are three steps to becoming truly happy: #1 - Use your talents to better the world; #2 - Love only those who are worthy; and #3 - Accept love freely. How about that?"

"Pretty cool," Flora murmurs.

"You could say he gave me a map to follow," she smiles, remembering.

"A map, so you never feel lost." Flora's eyes drift across the pasture. "And you can always find your way home."

"Here is the best part." Keely closes her eyes, face to

the sun. "The last time I visited Mom before she died, she said: 'Remember, Keely, when your life is guided by love, you are never lost.' I try to pass that wisdom on to others."

"With your songs," Flora smiles. "I get it now."

"At first it was with my songs." Keely turns to look at Flora. "And now it can be through you."

Flora scrunches up her face, confused. "Me? How?"

"Well, if I'm worthy of love, so are you." Keely grins at her. "And as far as our talents go, wait until the world gets a load of us!"

13.

June pulls out her phone and it vibrates relentlessly as she and Quinn come through the door of the cabin. She says, "I hate this damn thing. I was the happiest when no one could reach me."

Quinn says, "Yeah, I remember. You fought getting a cell phone because you didn't want people to bug you. But now you can text me whenever you want, no matter where you are, and I'll come running. There is an upside."

His silly grin makes her laugh. She doesn't like to admit it but sometimes she turns off her phone and drops it in her purse. It's her way of secretly rebelling against life's intrusions.

She and Quinn are just getting back from a ride. The watery light stretches late into the evening, making for a pretty cruise on our bikes especially around the lake. This was one of those times she turned her phone off.

"Whoa! Looks like you're in demand this evening." Quinn eyes the phone over his shoulder as he and Tully wrestle. "Work, is it?"

Oh, man, I hope I don't have to go in," she grouses. "I'm all mellowed out."

Zipping out of her leather jacket, she kicks her boots into the corner. "Seven voice messages is pretty rare for me…" she says, her anxiety beginning to climb. "OK, one from Leo, Sarge, Ozzie… a couple are from numbers I don't know."

"Ozzie's probably for me, I'll call him back. Tully and I are going for a run in the woods before it gets too dark." He pulls on a sweatshirt. "Go ahead and check your messages… if no one's on fire, come on out."

"I'll be along in a minute, fire or no fire," she yells, picking up the phone and waving it in the air. "I'm off duty!"

He laughs as they take off outside, Tully barking and Quinn whooping. June picks up a pen and pad, and listens to her messages.

The first one is from her son, Leo, telling her he can get a good deal on airline tickets in August, "So we need to decide on a good week for you to take off, Mom." That makes her smile.

The second is from Ozzie, looking for Quinn. No problem, he just needs a ride tomorrow, his truck is leaking oil.

The third is from Ozzie again, apologizing, "Sorry, Junie, I know you hate these things, but tell Quinn I found the leak and patched it up. Don't worry about picking me up tomorrow." He knows her pretty well.

The fourth and fifth are hang-ups. She hates those. It always feels like a serial killer is checking to see if she answers or something. Chances are better it was a telemarketer but anxiety makes her more dramatic than usual.

The sixth is from Sarge, just letting her know about a change in the court date for Flora. They moved it from ten days out to three days from now.

Great.

Of course, as busy as she's been, she hasn't even started her Report to the Court. Now it's due in 24 hours.

The seventh call is kind of a shocker. Drew Fallon says, "Sorry to bug you at home but didn't want to put you in an uncomfortable position at the office. Could you meet with me after Flora's court hearing, around 5:00 p.m. at the Upside Grill? I'd like to buy you dinner and discuss our possible collaboration." Then he left three different phone numbers to call him to confirm, at June's convenience.

While not totally surprised he's trying to reach her— Sarge gave her the heads up—she's stunned he's moving so quickly. The changes are coming hard and fast, and she's struggling to keep up.

She pulls on a sweatshirt and heads out to play, thinking, *Wait 'til Quinn hears this*.

After a brisk walk, she catches up to them already heading back to the house. "Ozzie called you twice: first time, truck leaking and needs a ride tomorrow; second time, truck fixed, disregard the ride."

Quinn laughs and shakes his head, "That boy is no mechanic. Maybe I'll call him anyway, just in case. What other fires did you put out?"

She fills him in but hedges on her thoughts about Fallon's call. "I'll let you listen for yourself."

After he plays it back, he raises his eyebrows and whistles low, "This is it: *The Big Offer!* What're you going to do?"

Slouched in her chair by the wood stove, she covers her face with both hands. "I don't know."

"OK, don't panic. Let's go over this and figure out what you want to do. You don't have to give him an answer right away, you know. Let him wait, think over his offer."

She sits up, a little relieved. "Yeah, you're right. I have three days to think about what I want, and I can give it some thought after I find out what's on the table."

She fills him in on Drew Fallon's professional courtesy call to Sarge and her boss's retirement bombshell.

"So, he's finally retiring. It's the end of an era." Quinn looks at me hard. "You feeling a little shell-shocked?"

"Sarge and I have been together for a long time." Eyes

welling up just talking about it. "I don't think I want to break in a new guy."

"How about if you're the new guy, June?"

"Huh?"

"Come on, Junie, don't you think that's 'Plan A' over at DCW?" He gives her that 'it's so obvious' look. "They couldn't find a better replacement."

"I never…" Shaking her head. "I couldn't!"

He cups her shaking hands in his. "Settle down, now. I'm only saying it's gonna come up. You need to be ready for it. The way I see it, that job is 'All the power, none of the glory'—right up your alley."

Puzzles, I don't need. "What are you saying?"

"June, you have the experience, the reputation, and the wisdom to pick and choose at this point in your life. They all want YOU, for a change. It has to feel good, knowing you don't need them and they all need you."

"That doesn't help, it's too much pressure." Brain feels like spun cotton. "I still don't know what to do."

"Darlin' girl, for once try this." He makes a silly face. "Pick the one that seems like the most fun!"

Where have I heard that before?

14.

Fallon Clinic: Report to the Court

Case #J04162019
Assessment and Summary

Due to inconsistencies in reporting details about the alleged sexual molestation, it is the determination of the therapist that improprieties have occurred involving the care of the Minor in question (Flora).

While it is not possible at this time to determine the full depth or nature of the improprieties perpetrated on the Minor, it minimally extends from a general disrespect of the Minor by family members. This disrespect was evidenced during therapy, by family members regularly referring to the Minor as "the girl" instead of by her name; the family's view of her as "not normal"; seeing their role in her life as helping her to "appear normal"; and the family members' primary expectation being the Minor's "gratitude" (or lack thereof) for all that the family offered her by her association with them.

Brendan Jacobie

Brendan's desire and motivation throughout the four years was for his parents to "send her back". Interestingly, Brendan described incidents in great detail, while family members omitted significant details or described them quite differently. There is no doubt that deliberately falsifying details surrounding the Minor was occurring for the benefit of both the therapist and the Court. It is not clear at this time, however, who is lying and when.

Brendan maintains a deep resentment for the Minor. His anger at her for her intrusion into his life, as well as at his parents for their willingness to allow such an intrusion, is still quite palpable. In addition, Brendan holds an abiding hostility toward females of all ages, especially those with whom he must interact regularly. His narcissistic viewpoint allows him to be quite aggravated and even offended should a woman behave in a way that is not satisfying to him. This hostility is acted out both verbally and sexually, but it is unclear as to whether he has ever become violent. He does not extend this generalized disrespect to males, although he is very clear about his peers needing to be "worthy" of his companionship.

His impression of relationships with the opposite sex is concrete: either a girl is meant for a sexual relationship or she is meant for "marriage". He clearly views women as neither his peers nor friends. The behavior of Brendan's social circle is shallow and cold, viewing sexual relations as a recreational sport. Their focus is on domination and control over others, rather than developing peer relationships. A prevailing dissatisfaction is deeply evident, but Brendan reports that he and his peer group rely upon sex, substance abuse, or sports to alleviate this angst. Brendan reports he looks forward to college as a more satisfying period, leading to a powerful career and conspicuous consumerism. His reference to the time in adulthood when he will be able to "buy anything I want" is extraordinarily immature.

It is possible that Brendan's general feelings toward women have been colored by this recent experience; yet, there is no indication of any compassion or respect for the Minor. His overall belief is that the inferior and manipulative nature of females led to such a ridiculous accusation, and is therefore invalid.

In summary, it is evident that the emotional climate in this foster home would be toxic for any female child, especially the Minor in question. The possibility and likelihood of abuse is high in this environment. However, this assessment did not uncover any clear evidence of sexual or physical abuse.

Minor #J04162019

Flora, the Minor in question, has demonstrated her ability to compartmentalize her emotions regarding the death of parents and caregivers, the loss of her foster family, and her fear of an uncertain and lonely future. Her ability to fully form a personality of her own has been impaired by her need for protection, sustenance, and approval. This impairment is typical of children in the foster system, most pronounced in those who are older (i.e., less likely to be placed in an adoptive setting or where parents are missing or deceased). Testing revealed no mental illness or pathology. Intelligence testing did indicate some delays consistent with academic performance, but no learning disabilities or delays were identified. Results indicated a tendency toward profound sadness, but this would fall under "Circumstantial Depression", rather than a chronic condition. Given the Minor's traumatic history, this condition would typically be treated in therapeutic sessions, and likely surface at developmental milestones. Post-Traumatic Stress Syndrome has not been ruled out at this time.

The Minor's efforts to maintain her foster placement, while tolerating her perceived abuse, are indications of her weak personal identity. Her lack of control over her environment clearly influences her decision to do "whatever it takes" to preserve her placement. During therapy, the Minor outlined her efforts to gain the emotional commitment of a family and to establish some sense of security, first with her extended family and then in foster care. Her persistent failure to secure and maintain a family has undermined her esteem further. The Minor views herself as lacking power to predict or influence her life, both past and future. This perceived deficit creates a "Victim Mentality", where she believes that she deserves 'bad' things to happen to her as she is inherently 'bad', and she may even create such situations herself.

In light of this mentality, it is surprising that the Minor participated in efforts to avoid her alleged perpetrator, such as leaving for school early and going home later. It is probable that the Minor's desire to be 'liked' by the school staff (her most consistent nurturers) was stronger than her need to maintain a secure placement. It may also be true that she did not recognize the potential for these opposing forces to eventually collide, as she views most authority figures as collaborators in her care.

It remains unclear whether the Minor has the capacity to plan and carry out a complex manipulation, such as setting up her foster brother with a charge of sexual molestation without actually reporting him herself. She did not seek support of the adults in her foster family; on the contrary, she maintained a "polite but distant" demeanor with all family members, as verified by her previous foster mother, Mrs. Jacobie.

The Minor's ability to seduce her foster brother, only to accuse him of sexual molestation after the fact, appears unlikely. Her consistent description of details leading to the incident, as well as her overriding desire to remain in the home, does not logically support such behavior. The Minor's tendency, during therapy, to blurt out questions and insights as they are formed would indicate a difficulty with devising a plan in her head, then secretly implementing the plan to fruition, and finally maintaining her consistency and composure during interviews by this therapist, the Police, DCW representatives, and the Court.

The Minor's somewhat flat affect during the initial interview has diminished gradually. At times she appears exuberant and unrestrained, behavior typical of females in her age group. She reverts quickly to that detached demeanor when challenged to reflect upon painful situations or when she feels threatened by sources outside of her control. This is not unusual for children who have experienced a disrupted attachment process. Her rather rapid progress is unusual, however, and is generally seen after a long trust-building period with a consistent nurturing adult.

Adoptive Placement: Michael and Rosemary West

This match appears optimistic for the Minor, Flora, and may be her first child-caretaker relationship based on mutual respect and affection. Trust has been formed in a short time, not an easy developmental step for the Minor.

Michael and Rosemary West appear to have a realistic view of the Minor's psycho-social profile. Their expectations of this adolescent are based on contributing to her development and her future, rather than what she can contribute to their happiness or well-being. While Mrs. West does have some hope of a typical mother-daughter relationship, Mr. West sees his role as a loving teacher or mentor. He expressed his view thusly: "We will never be her mother and father, but we will be her 'parents'; in fact, we have already been parenting her, a role she seems eager for us to accept. After all, what is a parent, but a teacher and a guide, concerned most with launching a happy, healthy human into adulthood?" This approach is at least non-threatening, and at best what the Minor needs most to develop appropriately and productively. She will also need continued therapeutic support, with which Mr. and Mrs. West intend to cooperate.

In summary, the Minor does not appear capable of the complex manipulations necessary either to lure her foster brother or set him up for false charges. At the same time, she does not appear to have any mental disorder or illness that would threaten self or others. She struggles with attachment issues consistent with losses and rejections during her young life, but has thus far embraced the therapeutic process. She appears to have developed a healthy relationship with the potential adoptive family, and willingly participates in both difficult and painful emotional tasks in therapy with their support.

Recommendation

It is, therefore, the recommendation of Fallon Clinic that the Court proceed with placement of the Minor, Flora, with Michael and Rosemary West, for the purpose of adoption. Until the adoption is finalized, Fallon Clinic will continue pre-adoptive counseling for the West family, including the ersatz extended family member, Keely Bruce. At the time of the Adoption Hearing a long-range therapeutic plan will be presented for Court approval.

Respectfully Submitted,

Dr. Drew Fallon, CEO Fallon Clinic

§

Basically, the therapists reported that Brendan is messed up and hostile toward Flora but there is no actual proof he did anything wrong. They also think Flora is dealing with issues typical of foster kids, but is not a danger to anybody. Legally, this means she cannot be locked up, like the Jacobie family wants. Russ Monty figured that was what the decision would be, but his clients are pretty unhappy about it.

June tells Hal, "I can only speculate, but if Brendan were my client, I'd tell the parents how lucky he is. The Court could easily have ordered extended services like counseling, or on-going court supervision based on a report like that. If he were my kid, I'd be rushing him into therapy right now, before he turned into a wife beater or worse. Off the record, his attitude had to come from somewhere, and his father seems to approve of the kid's behavior. Oh, well, we can't fix everybody. Still, this kid gives me the creeps!"

Even though the Judge didn't ask for it, the therapists at Fallon went one step further and recommended the West family for adoption, and agreed to continue providing services to the family afterward. One less hurdle to jump.

When Judge Paxton asks for June's recommendation, she says, "Place her immediately, thereby giving them permission to commit to each other."

He looks sternly at Flora, and asks, "What do you think, young lady?"

Flora shows the Judge that poise she reserves for performing. "I want to live with Michael and Rosemary. They're helping me learn to be a grown-up…" she turns briefly, and looks at them, "…and I am pretty sure they love me, Sir."

The kid is learning how to work a crowd, I'll give her that.

Rosemary is sniffling, Keely blows her nose, and even June's misting up—getting to be a habit, where Flora is concerned.

Judge Paxton does all the expected things such as ordering monthly reporting to him, requiring Court approval on any career moves for Flora, and sets expectations for follow through on directives from Fallon Clinic.

Then he says something very kind. "Pack your bags, young lady. You're going home today."

Michael and June exchange looks. Struggling to maintain his composure, he grins and winks his thanks.

In the lobby, she feels obliged to tell them, "It isn't over, gang. This is great, but it's only the first step. The Adoption Hearing for finalization is months away." Nobody's listening—just as well.

While they're all merrily milling about, June pulls Sarge off to the side and asks, "Is it alright with you if I go see Donna this afternoon? I have to meet with Drew Fallon this evening and I want to have a vague notion of where I stand here."

"Hunter, before you make a decision about them, have you considered taking over the unit for me? No one is more qualified than you and it would give us time to make a good transition, you know, break you in. It would mean a big raise, too, and I think I can give you a solid recommendation." He chuckles at that last comment.

"Sarge… do you think I should?" His bombshells are beginning to get on her nerves.

He smirks. "Hell, Hunter, I don't think anyone should have to do this shitty job. That isn't the point, now, is it?"

A big sigh is all she can muster in response. Waving, she makes her exit without another word.

15.

June tiptoe's into Donna's office, breathing deep of the lemongrass cloud. Her secretary says she is at her desk, no problem. June asks not to be announced so she can surprise her.

"Pretty low-key in here. Is this what the taxpayers deserve: tea and classical music?"

Donna looks up from her papers and lights up. "Hey, June, what a surprise! What are you doing over here?"

"It's the court decision on Jacobie's complaint against my foster kid." She solemnly hands over a copy of Fallon's Report to the Court. Donna shoots up from her chair, scanning the document.

Donna's still standing at her desk as she finishes reading. "Wow, June, this is fantastic news! Congratulations!"

June gets comfy, feet on the desk.

Donna sits back down and says, "Tell me everything. I felt so bad when they skipped my testimony at the hearing, but it looks like you had all the bases covered without me."

She gets the lowdown while fiddling with their file. "We'll have to meet with them and all, but it looks like the

Jacobie family is out of the fostering game."

June agrees. "Yeah... even if the decision had been in their favor, I doubt they could ever be objective. I know I could never trust them again." They share a solemn nod.

"Is this copy for my file?" She waves the report in the air.

"Yup, all yours. I'll get you the final court orders when Hal sends 'em over next week." June decides to lay her cards out. "So, what's new in your neck of the woods?"

I'm only testing the water here.

"Oh, wow, you probably haven't heard my news." She leans forward all excited. "DCW is restructuring my unit, adding a whole new component. We will now be called Support Services, and we'll take over all the supportive functions for foster care and adoptions. This allows to us work much more closely with the casework teams. We'll even be handling contracts, like with your buddy over at Fallon Clinic. I'm so thrilled."

More changes. This means the position she offered last month may be off the table.

"So, what does that do to the structure of your team?"

"Not just 'team' anymore, June... teams! This expands my unit by about 50 percent right off the bat, and maybe more later."

"Then, are you still looking to fill that Trainer position?"

Donna freezes, the light finally dawning. "Are you kidding me? Don't you dare play with me, June. If you want to move over here, you just say so right now."

Saying it out loud for the first time, she says, "I'm ready to make a move, Donna. Not for public knowledge, but Sarge is retiring and I think it's my time."

Donna throws up her hands and shouts, "Yahoo!" then she grabs her friend in a big hug.

"Wait! You didn't say, about the position. Is it still open?"

"Forget about the Trainer job, June, that's small

potatoes. The social work gods are smiling on us today. I need a Service Coordinator to run my new division, the one I just described to you. It would be right up your alley: assessing, approving, and providing services to foster and adoptive families." Donna runs over to her file cabinet, yanks out some papers, and hands them to me, "Read the draft of the job description and see if you weren't born to do this job!"

By the time June leaves her office, Donna has secured her commitment to officially apply for the position and scheduled a formal interview. Her last words: "I won't even entertain any other candidates, June. *You* are my Services Coordinator! Start packing up your office."

A parting look that says, "Don't rush me," is ignored. As June exits, Donna is actually dancing the hustle.

She totally cracks me up.

The message to Min is a bit cryptic. "Making progress on my homework. I'll bring the treats tomorrow."

June heads over to the Upside Grill, a swank urban restaurant appealing to the professional crowd. The lighting is dim, the music is soft and classy. Instead of the usual restaurant clatter, all she can hear is the tinkling of crystal and murmur of genteel conversation.

It's a good thing I'm dressed for court, she thinks, because everyone in the place has on a suit.

Walking through the lobby, Dr. Drew Fallon appears at her elbow, smooth as silk. "June, I am so pleased you were willing to see me."

A white-shirted waiter escorts them to a private booth. On the table is a bottle of an expensive white merlot. "I hope you don't mind, June. I understand this is one of your preferred wines, so I took the liberty of ordering it ahead."

How could I 'mind'? I won't even give him the satisfaction of asking how he knew.

"Very thoughtful, Drew. Thank you." I take a lesson

from Flora and play to my audience.

They chat a bit about the case and today's outcome. Of course, Drew is already apprised of the Judge's decision, but wants to know how June feels about the situation.

"That boy is a fire keg ready to go off any time, if he hasn't already with our young lady." Careful not to use names in a public place, June naturally respects the rules of confidentiality. "I worry about leaving him unchecked, but there is no evidence that would allow for court action. We have to let this one go."

Drew nods, listening intently. She continues, "Our side of the case was positive. The adoptive placement takes place today, the State pays for their treatment with your team, and everybody gets the help they need for a successful adoption." A pause to relish her excellent wine, then, "I hate being in the dark about what really happened between Flora and Brendan, Drew. Loose ends make me uncomfortable. I do believe that this is the best outcome, however, in spite of it."

He leans in. "What makes it good, June... the placement?"

Up to the test, she explains. "Not just the placement, Drew, although the West family appears to be fairly healthy, emotionally. The most positive part is that support is in place before, during, and after adoption, when this girl is transitioning into adulthood. Most of the kids I see get left on the curb at age 18, or maybe held over for minimal services until they're 21. A 'healthy kid' from a 'healthy family' struggles with early adulthood, but these kids are barely equipped to wake up everyday. No foster or adopted child should be without services until they've stabilized."

"But that stabilization might never occur, June. Don't you agree?" He's quizzing her and she knows it.

"True, but any competent counselor could help these young people develop a plan." She hopes she sounds more like a professional than an evangelist. "Once the plan is in place, they could help the kid set up a solid support system, including therapeutic services and how to access them. Adulthood is a crapshoot, Drew, for all of us. These kids simply need a little more guidance getting there."

"What about the responsibility of the adopting family? Shouldn't they be expected to maintain the support for the child?"

She's a little more passionate now. "Look, it's no secret that many of these adopting families may not be a viable support system when a kid's in crisis, at least not without help. They often just throw up their hands. It isn't that they're necessarily cold or insensitive, they're mostly frustrated and just plain tired. And I'm only talking about the adoptions that haven't disrupted before the kid reaches 21. I haven't even mentioned the kids who have been living with reluctant relatives or in foster homes because no one wants to adopt them." Breathe, June, breathe.

Drew shoots her a broad smile. "There's the June Hunter I remember: 'Defender of the Weak' and Robin Hood of DCW!"

They both laugh at that vision, June wielding the sword of honor and conning money from the fists of bureaucrats.

If I end up as Donna's right-hand woman I'll be doing a lot more of that, finding money for the best services available. Sounds almost as frustrating as case work, now that I think about it.

Drew finally takes the ball into his court, describing at length the vision he has for Fallon Clinic. They are digging into fantastic desserts, something dark, chocolate, and gooey, when they finally get down to the business of June's future.

"I would welcome the opportunity to bring you on board, June, in almost any capacity. Have you given it some thought?"

"I have, Drew, ever since you gave me the tour of Fallon," she admits. "I would like to present you with some ideas I have for my possible involvement, and get your feedback..."

She outlines the plan she designed last night from 2:00 to 5:00 am, when sleep evaded her. As Drew scratches out notes on a little pocket pad, she reflects on all the changes in her life recently.

Seems like Flora has influenced everyone she touched. I'm sure she has no idea she's become a catalyst for change in so many lives.

Drew is astonished by the book idea. While he reviews a copy of the proposal, she assures him it's just a draft. "Give it a quick review, Drew, and jot down some thoughts if you like. I don't have any more to share with you today, at least nothing typed. Most of my work is still scribbled on napkins and post-its. But if you're interested, I can get you a more formal proposal in a couple of days."

"This is fantastic!" He flips papers with excitement. "I am sure we could put something solid together, June. I'll dig out my research and we could meet in a week or two to review it. By then I'll have a rough contract drafted, as well. How does that sound?"

"Great," she says, collecting her stuff. "You can call me sometime next week to set it up."

He pauses to gaze at her. "You are a real deceiver, June. To chat with you, you seem completely aloof to the possibility of working together. Then you hand me all this!"

Giving him her Zen-smile, she says, "I guess I've come to realize I have lots of options, Drew. These projects would be great fun but if it doesn't work out, I'll put my energy elsewhere."

I float out of the restaurant feeling like I am right where I should be, for a change.

16.

Quinn and June sit outside the cabin, drinks in hand, watching the moon rise. The air is pleasantly cool for this time of year. Relishing the fragrance of summer blooms and enjoying the night sounds of frogs and owls, June relays the day's events to Quinn. Until she does, there'll be no sleeping for her.

"What a day." He puts down his empty beer bottle and stretches. "You win your case, get job offers from Sol, Donna, and Drew Fallon, and negotiate a possible book deal. How do you feel?"

"Mostly I feel relieved." She stretches, too. "All the uncertainty is gone now and everything seems really clear."

Tuned in to each other, they pick up the empties to head inside. "Any loose ends?" he asks.

"I still have to let Sarge in on my plans," she says, holding the door for him. "Donna has me set up for an interview and I need to look over the job description. I know there will be some challenges, but the advantage of a newly created position is: I can tailor it to suit me."

"How about Fallon?" Quinn's already on the couch, Tully trying to climb into his lap. "When do you two sit down again?"

"He's calling me next week to set up our meeting." Falling into her chair, she's finally winding down. "I have a ton to do, preparing for that. The outline I did last night was way too simple."

"Lots on your plate right now." He acknowledges her expanding load. "Hey, did I tell you Michael West called me?"

Quinn's won the bid for the building remodel that will ultimately be the Westwoods Music Studio. He fills her in on Michael's plans for the new business, making Westwoods a co-op and bringing in his students as 'co-owners'. Quinn's eyes are full of light as he describes his role in the project.

"What an amazing idea for expansion! Does Flora know about all this?"

"No." He shakes his head. "I'm not sure I should even be telling you. Keep this stuff under wraps until they announce it officially, ok?"

"This fall is going to be jammed." She kicks off her shoes, moving to join the boys on the couch. "We better eat our Wheaties!"

Quinn pushes Tully off his lap and pulls her over to snuggle. "You said it. Hey, I know what might help."

"What's that?" she asks, snuggling in close.

He sets a small box in the palm of her hand. "Let's become partners, you and me."

June's a bit slow to respond after the day she's had, just staring at the box. Finally, hands shaking and holding her breath, she opens it. The oval champagne diamond is set in a white gold band, with baguettes on either side— beautiful, amazing, terrifying.

"We can do this, Junie. We make a damn good pair, I think." He is so reassuring, speaking softly into her hair.

When she can breathe again, she stammers, "Oh, Quinn, do you think… what if…"

"I know, this is a big step." He sits her up and looks directly into her eyes. "But we're some of the smartest people we know! Other couples make it work. We can figure it out together."

He takes the ring out of the box. "Take my ring, Junie. I love you like crazy and you love me, too. We've got a lot of good years left. Let's give life a run for its money!"

June pushes past what is left of that wall of fear as Quinn slides the ring on her finger.

"Let's do it!" She laughs and cries, and they start celebrating right there on the couch.

I have lots to share with Min tomorrow. When she gives me an assignment, I don't fool around!

IV. PLACEMENT

1.

Michael seems electrified, sparks of excitement surround him as he brings in a tray of refreshments. Sipping coffee, June looks around at the others.

Am I the only one who can see this?

Rosemary flutters amid waves of happiness in the wake of the court decision. Keely hums to herself in the kitchen, putting baked goods on a platter to serve the rest of us. Flora perches on the edge of an ottoman next to June, her closed-lip smile designed to keep her joy from shooting out, like a fire-breathing dragon. Tera, Ray, and Pete chuckle and whisper in the corner.

June feels like the wet blanket of the group. Swallowing great mouthfuls of the rich coffee with cream, she relishes this one moment of quiet before becoming the voice of reason.

Once everyone has refreshments in hand and sits down, they will turn to me for whatever is next, still ecstatic with their joyful news. Maybe, just this once, I could let them bask in their happiness for a bit. Maybe, just this once, I could savor being the hero before morphing into the "DCW Drudge" who only wants 'em to jump through hoops.

She takes another swallow of the excellent coffee and decides to give 'the good guy' routine a shot.

But the Universe intervenes again, just in case she's thinking she has any kind of control over the situation, when Michael stands to address them all.

"Everyone, in the wake of our great news yesterday, I would first like to officially welcome Flora to our family! I know, I know, she isn't formally adopted yet, but the decision to place her here with us is a significant one. It's even more special knowing the charges leveled by her previous placement were dropped by the Court and we're

266

free to proceed with our plans for adoption!" Everyone cheers.

Michael smiles at his happy audience. "In a few minutes, June will be explaining all the dreary details of what it will take to make this arrangement permanent. Before she does, though, I have something to share. In honor of Flora, and to demonstrate our commitment to her, we would like to formally announce our plans for a new business venture: Flora Fare, Organic Food for Children!"

Michael reaches under the coffee table to produce a large cardboard sign with a bigger than life-size photo of Flora, her eyes gazing down at a glowing peach cupped in her hands. This is the new Flora Fare company logo.

"Ohhh!" They all gasp. It's simple, elegant, and beautiful.

Michael continues, "Flora Fare will produce natural and organic baby and toddler food, grown right here in the Midwest. We will be focusing first on infant fruits and vegetables, with plans to expand the line as we become more well-known. At this time, I have contracted with two organic orchards in the area, for apples, pears, and—what else—peaches. About three miles from here is a reputable food processing facility and I'm currently in negotiations with the COO. Rosemary has already begun some of the legal work for government certification as 'organic' and 'natural'." He smiles at the tearful Flora. "Of course, we will eventually produce some of our own fruit right out of Flora's newly planted orchard."

Silence. Astonishment. Then laughter and smatterings of "Oh, wow" and "Can you believe it?"

He holds up both hands. "Wait now! This is a five-year plan, giving us all time to create a sound and productive business so don't get too excited. The process is only beginning. We'll know more by next spring if the whole thing is viable or not – it takes a few years to stabilize an organic operation."

Rosemary jumps up next to him. "Me next! Westwoods is becoming an employee-owned corporation with the woodworking studio, custom carpentry, the art gallery, the orchards, and Flora Fare all under one umbrella. Pete will be managing the woodworking and carpentry division. He has been successfully apprenticing in this role for the past two years. Ray's agricultural background will come in handy as he'll be overseeing the operation and development of the orchard, including the selection of wood and fruit crops. Tera will be working directly in Flora Fare after she graduates, developing some of the marketing plans and business strategies. Flora can even intern with her part-time, if she likes; we'll see in a couple of years. Currently, both Tera and Keely will assist Flora in the development of her educational strategies."

Flora's speechless, simply staring at Rosemary and the others. Rosemary puts her hand on Flora's shoulder and continues, "Of course, the Music Studio is an independent operation at this time, but we could bring it into the corporation at some point in the future. Meanwhile, Keely will be managing the music duties and hiring the staff, while Michael will be working on the business end with her. Of course, she'll also manage Flora's musical training, while introducing her to the basic expectations of operating a studio. This will be hit and miss for a while, as Keely's touring schedule is quite demanding over the next nineteen months, but we'll all work together to make this happen as smoothly as possible in her absence."

Michael props the logo on top of a side table. "Naturally, I will continue to manage the art gallery and educational component, incorporating students as interns into all areas of the corporation. Rosemary will supervise and coordinate Flora's education and career decisions, in addition to doing anything she wants in any part of the business!"

Rosemary puts her hands on her hips. "And I am resigning from my current contracts over the next three months so I can be the boss of you all!"

That sort of breaks the ice, and everyone laughs. They yuck it up, everyone talking at once and offering congratulations. June is amazed at the progress of the project, as well as the creative, dynamic people who are spearheading the concept. She's feeling a bit like the red-headed stepchild in the room when Michael pipes up, "Oh, hold on folks, one more thing…"

They stop and sit back down, murmuring and chuckling happily, when he says, "June, I have one last surprise especially for you."

Huh? This takes me off guard, especially when I see who is coming through the doorway.

Michael addresses the group. "For those of you who don't know him, Quinn Harimann is one of the area's most respected carpenters and contractors. He has a great eye for beauty and functionality, and has a keen interest in moving 'green' projects into our region. This is the perfect time, politically and economically, to move forward. I have asked him to partner with me on some of our more challenging assignments, as well as to sit on our board. The pay won't be great at first, Quinn, but everyone's prosperity will be tied to the success of the others. In light of this, we should be rich in no time!" The room fills with laughter.

Quinn grins at June. "Surprise!"

Eloquent, as usual, June babbles, "How… When… Why didn't you…?"

He takes her hands speaking quietly, "I wanted it to be a surprise. Besides, it sounds like fun and that's our new policy, eh?"

Looking around at all these people throwing caution to the wind, June thinks, I am in pretty impressive company. Going with the flow, she raises her coffee cup in a toast, "To Flora Fare, Westwoods Corporation, and the newly expanded West family. I trust you to always send the message that life is not just about 'doing', but about 'living', fully and with joy."

Pete rises quickly. "To living!"

"To living!" The toast becomes a vow, a commitment.

June suddenly feels part of something bigger than herself, something new and exciting and beautiful. Goose bumps signal scary territory for her but she slips back into the Zen thing, connecting with the others and going with the flow. She ponders this new life while devouring something chocolate and, just for today, slides her briefcase of dreary paperwork out of sight.

2.

They take up the whole back room at Chuck's Grill, laughing and singing and eating themselves into a stupor. Chuck has outdone himself with barbequed ribs, southern fried chicken, and who knows how many pounds of boiled shrimp.

June looks around and realizes that most of the folks here are Quinn's friends, or were his friends first, before he became a 'we'. She's never been the best at socializing, so friendships have mostly come from her work environment—it shows. Sarge and his wife are there, so is Hal. Donna, Shelley, and Dora, her secretary, made it, too.

Ozzie and Quinn have their heads together in the corner, and every so often they laugh, deep and hearty. At that moment, Quinn turns his head to face her as if she called his name out loud. He winks, puts his hand on Ozzie's shoulder to signal his move, and heads for the front of the room to address the crowd.

"Thank you all for coming tonight! We told you that this little bash was to celebrate the end of a great summer, but we deceived you a little bit." He put out his arm, inviting June to join him. It's suddenly like everyone is holding their breath, dead quiet.

He grabs June around the shoulders and she pretends

to swat him away. The crowd laughs, then hushes up. "June and I figure we're only at our half-way point in life, with lots to do and the wisdom to choose appropriately. But we don't want to fly solo into the second half, wishing we had someone to whisper our secrets to or to hold us when we need it most. In that spirit, we're celebrating a new partnership today, one that ought to shake up a few folks. Ladies and Gentlemen, today I am the happiest man in town... June Hunter has agreed to be my Bride!"

As they say, the crowd goes wild.

She relishes the applause a minute or so, then steps up to be noticed. They settle back down again and June speaks off the cuff. "Like Quinn just told you, I believe I'm a bit wiser now. That being said, I'm a touch more gun-shy than I was twenty years ago. I always figured to face my second half of life quietly with my boy, Tully!" Big laughs. "How could I have known that the Universe would throw such a gem at me as the amazing Quinn Harimann? And if you hear a noise in the distance, it will be us, raging at the passing of time and laughing at everything we can. Feel free to track us down and join the party of a lifetime... if you can keep up with us, that is!"

Now, that wasn't so bad. I had told Quinn I would speak without notes, from the heart. Judging from his great big kiss, I must have made it work.

"When's the wedding?" Is shouted from several points in the room, and Quinn fields that one.

"June and I have delicate work situations that could be negatively influenced if we plan the wedding too soon. So, bear with us. We look for certain special events to occur before we actually tie the knot." Of course, he's referencing his collaboration with the West family and the pending adoption. They can't have a conflict of interest issue messing up their wedding, after all. "We promise to keep you all posted as we nail down our plans."

"Don't you worry, I'm not letting him out of it," she jokes, holding up her left hand. "I've got a ring and witnesses, and legal connections if he tries to run!" She points at Hal who throws back his head and roars, while Ozzie holds Quinn by his collar as he pretends to struggle.

Just then, the juke box goes dead as the room abruptly goes black. Confused yells and questioning voices diminish into cheers as Chuck brings in a two-tiered cake with sparklers on the top, lighting the room in a fantasy glow.

June slips into reverie:

Well, we did it. It's official now. I look around the room, pondering the origins of the concept of marriage. It signified the union of two families and their assets, building a strong front against both enemies and natural disasters. Sort of the 'two heads are better than one' principle. It makes sense. Our combined 'assets' are in the people gathered here for us. If a strong front is what we want, we certainly have it, a safety net of support and wisdom and love.

I read somewhere that the diamond ring was chosen as a symbol of marriage due to the stone's value, great strength, and brilliance. Together, Quinn and I have been able to accomplish something neither of us could on our own: we have created a family, valuable, strong and brilliant, one that reaches out and impacts others around us.

I'm starting to think this might be fun!

3.

The fall colors are glorious, perfect for drives to the country. June meets with Flora regularly to help with the transition to her new family life. She's a little jumpy after Flora's complaints about how hard her mid-terms were, but today all will be revealed.

Flora spreads all her papers out in front of us on the table, keeping the most important in her hands for June to read first.

"Can you believe I got a B average this quarter?" she crows, sparkling like sun on the lake.

"You worked really hard, Flora, and you deserve it,"

she tells her, plunking down the fresh baked cookies picked up from the bakery. "I got these to celebrate!"

They munch the treat in cozy silence, Flora relishing her success before getting serious. "Rosemary helped me so much, June. Before this, I could only get C's and D's." She looks up at her with eyes wide. "Besides, Michael says I have to keep my grades up or forget the extra stuff, you know, recording music with Keely and working at Flora Fare someday."

They're alone in the house. Rosemary and Michael are both working and Keely has gone back on tour. She comes back in a few weeks to hold her annual local concert, kicking off the holiday season. This particular concert benefits a different area charity each year. This year it will be funding counseling programs for families of foster and adopted kids—big surprise.

Keely has gone public about her own difficulties as a foster child and adoptee, presumably to take the attention off of Flora. When she thanked the press on national television for respecting Flora's privacy, and promised them she would bring them more of Flora's music as soon as the child was ready, the media went crazy. Documentaries and news programs across the country started covering the difficulties kids face in foster care and adoption, as well as the plight of children in the arts who are exploited for their talents. Keely became the overnight guardian angel of kids everywhere.

She sure knows how to turn lemons into lemonade. From now on, whenever someone says, "Adversity builds character," Keely is the character I'll think of first.

"Hey Flora, we haven't had a moment alone since all these changes took place. How are you handling all of this?"

"I'm ok, June." She sits back in her chair. "Now that I'm doing better in school, I can relax a little."

"How about your counseling sessions… still going ok?"

"Oh, yes." She speaks eagerly. "Louise is kind of picking up on the stuff you were having me do. She calls it 'building a future from the inside out' but it's really more like fixing my insides."

"Explain to me what you mean when you say 'fixing your insides.'"

"I remember when you were helping me put together my life story, you told me I was like Dorothy in the Wizard of Oz." She gets this faraway look as she explains. "She had everything she needed inside her all along, she just needed help figuring it all out."

June reaches back to those early days with Flora, feeling immediately sentimental. "I remember."

"Well," she continues, intent on getting it right. "You said she got the help she needed from her friends and they were like her family. My insides were all messed up, but everybody is helping me figure it out. It's kinda like having a whole bunch of parents."

She looks out the window for a second, then back at June. "No matter what stupid things I did before, or how I liked people who treated me bad, everybody is helping me fix it so I don't keep doing that stuff... I'm 'fixing my insides', see?"

"I think so." June repeats it back to her, just to be certain. "You didn't learn how to pick the right kind of people or act in a way that was good for you. Now you are trying to 'fix' your thinking so you make better choices. Right?"

"Right!" Flora gives her one of those composed smiles. "Back then, you even told me I should go into business. Do you remember?"

She does remember. "If I'm not mistaken, it had to do with how you negotiate a deal. You do know how to ask for what you want in the most disarming way, Flora."

They both laugh about that.

"I guess I'm a bit worried, though, that this is all too much, too fast," June tells her, laying her cards on the table. "The music career, the new business, all this legal mess, getting a new family… it would be a lot for anyone, Flora. My head is spinning and all I have to do is talk with you about it."

She doesn't laugh in spite of the joke. "It is pretty exciting. Before you met me, June, nobody ever looked at me. I was like a ghost, invisible, watching the world like I wasn't even in it. Now people look at me and listen to what I say, so I need to think hard before I talk, you know? I don't want to make a mistake."

Boy, I know what that feels like. It's a pretty big burden for such a young lady.

She bites into a cookie and continues, "Rosemary says life is like a roller coaster. You can't just watch it fly along, you have to get on the ride if you want to feel something. Some parts are scary and some parts are really exciting and fun, but you never know if you don't get on board."

June shakes her head in wonder. "You know, Flora, I've been thinking the exact same thing lately."

V. ANNUAL FOLLOW UP & CASE CLOSING

Do you ever see a shadow out of the corner of your eye and, when you turn to look, it disappears?

Flora West graduates from high school next month. June keeps close contact with the West family, and cautiously considers them among her friends.

I have to be a bit careful, though. Friends made as a result of my kind of work might easily drift into a non-paid 'therapist and patient' sort of relationship.

Rose and Michael respect June's position, for the most part, and have retained their own family therapist at Fallon to deal with rising developments. They tap into her expertise for direction once in a while, but not more than any of her lay friends might. In return for their respect of her boundaries, June tries to act like a regular human when in their company. You know, no lectures or unsolicited sage advice. Keep focused mostly on outside interests such as music, art, and living in the country.

June finds herself cruising up to Westwoods on her motorcycle when the weather is nice; sometimes she and Quinn both go. The West Homestead is storybook bucolic, and they're always interesting companions.

Quinn's business arrangement with Michael is a source of great excitement for them both. They're currently working on a huge resort/spa/educational center that is being built in the area. There's a ton of green technology going into this place, and they plan on holding conferences and workshops that focus on healing the planet. Some very famous investors are involved and Quinn is not the least bit intimidated.

Good thing, because I find myself star-struck at their very names. This resort could change the make-up of the whole area, kind of a "Miraval of the Midwest".

Meanwhile, June takes off on her Indian Spirit every chance she gets, enjoying the country roads before this area turns into a tourist free-for-all.

The engagement is a happy one but wedding plans remain off the table right now. June and Quinn are still in the brainstorming stage, like "Hey, what do you think about such-and-such for a honeymoon?" and "This is delicious; we have to serve this at our wedding reception." With all the changes going on, they haven't gotten too concrete yet. Things will slow down soon and they're committed to getting the show on the road after the first of the year.

An old saying comes to June's mind, "When nothing changes, nothing changes." It refers to stagnation limiting our ability to grow, and it seems like everyone she knows is growing at the speed of light these days. There is a lot of excitement and fun in this supercharged atmosphere. She finds herself wandering around, chanting, "Change is good; change is good!"

Scavenging her collection of memorabilia, June rummages around for material to make Flora a graduation gift. She thinks, "A little Scrap Book or Memory Box from our early days together might be nice." She's wading through a mountain of disorganized crap in the hopes of finding a few worthwhile scraps.

I'm no artist; I'll have to rely on my wit and creativity for this one. I don't know exactly what I'm looking for, but any cute or positive items are candidates for inclusion.

She finds a photo of the Crossette Shelter, the place they first met. She sets aside a copy of Flora's report card from that semester, the one with a dramatic improvement in grades and a positive progress evaluation from her music teacher. June makes a note to locate the music for "Over the Rainbow" since this was referenced in the teacher's report.

After graduation this summer, Flora moves to Chicago to study music; Keely got her set up. It almost seems moot, since they're releasing a CD this month called *Springtime Flora*, in which Flora and Keely perform jazzy renditions of classic love ballads together. However, Rosemary is adamant about Flora having the opportunities college will offer and she knows Flora needs to learn how to make friends her own age. There's no arguing with Rosemary, education always comes first.

"Knowledge is Power," I always say.

The family business is growing but they are taking it slow. At some point Michael will need a COO, unless he decides to quit teaching his Sculpting Masterclass – not likely if you ask me.

Working on the business plan for Flora Fare will be a positive experience for her next year, and she's taking some business classes along with music. As Tera's some-day-in-the-future apprentice, Flora's getting really excited about marketing. Go figure.

Quinn finished building the Westwoods Music Studio and Keely's already generating money—another great business decision for Michael and Rosemary. This past year has been every girl's dream. Flora's in seventh heaven but handling it well so far, thanks to the guidance of her doting parents.

"Wow, the original copy of <u>Flora's Story</u>," June exclaims, gleeful. "I thought I gave this to Rosemary right after the adoption was finalized."

Resisting the urge to page through it, she gets a little lump in her throat as she recalls how they worked on it together.

While browsing, June reflects on this case. It seems like she worked on it for a long time but, really, it was just a blip in a person's lifetime. It was an important case, though, mostly because she felt like she did it all RIGHT for once. There were problems, she knew, but they got worked out. The kid ended up with the best parents around and her future prospects are fantastic. The new parents were healed from their previous loss and are now tickled pink. Even Sarge and Hal got to flex their professional muscles on this one, and it seems like all the 'guys in the white hats' won, for a change.

After so many professional compromises over the years, and some cases that seemed to yield more harm than good, this one gave June and the whole gang renewed hope in the system. She can feel the warmth of success, in a business where the best one can usually hope for is, well... a little less pain for everyone.

June finds a photo of Flora and Keely singing their duet at the first family visit. She sets that on the 'save' pile. The Tribune column from the Open Mike Fiasco in Chicago goes in the 'save' pile, too. June can't help but smile.

That Keely is sure an operator. Lucky for Flora!

A spiral notebook peeks out from under a bunch of papers, dark blue, scratched, and tattered. Inside the front cover is Flora's name and a description: "English II", the teacher's name, and the date, Spring Semester.

"This was before I met you, Kiddo," she smiles to herself.

Flipping through the assignments, she reflects on how childish Flora's handwriting looks compared to today. It's only about half full, sort of like her life was at that juncture.

"Oops!" The notebook slips from her fingers. Reaching out and catching it by the back cover, the paper pages flop forward to expose the last page. Watercolor shades of gel pen, pink and green and blue, in scribbled doodles. June smiles again and takes a closer look, memories of girlish insecurity washing through her head. Little curlicues and hearts, flowers and suns and moons, "Cute...what's this?":

Flora Jacobie
Mrs. Flora Jacobie
Mrs. Brendan Jacobie
Brendan and Flora Jacobie
Brendan ♥ Flora

Flora ♥ Brendan
Flora + Brendan 4EVER!

Pulse racing, June thinks back and tries to understand what she's seeing. This was long before she met Flora. During the whole sexual abuse investigation, Brendan referred to her infatuation, his year-long struggle with Flora's growing obsession with him. His allegation was seemingly vengeful, that she made up the abuse to get back at him.

"Oh, no…" June thinks back to her conversations with Flora, the school nurse, and her counselor. None of them knew of any infatuation. Flora denied it completely.

She recalls a disturbing remark Sarge made during that time, wondering if the abuse really happened and whether or not we were wrong about Flora, wrong about Brendan. Even the therapists at Fallon Clinic indicated that Flora was not capable of such manipulation or deceit, and Brendan certainly demonstrated many of the indicators of a sexual perpetrator.

"I admit it," June thinks, "I believed Flora absolutely." In the end, everyone did.

"It wouldn't matter if the kid had a crush on him," June reminds herself. If the boy molested her, it was still abuse.

This could have been written one afternoon, one day in her life, and never revisited again. A girl at middle school might have said something like, "Your brother is so handsome – I'd marry him!", or something equally silly. Every young girl thinks of romance with a movie star, rock star, an athlete, or someone equally out of reach. It's a normal part of development.

Isn't it?

June feels guilty for her doubts as she thinks about Anita Hill, Dr. Ford, and all women who have been ignorantly judged when a man took liberties he shouldn't have. She remembers what people said during those very public trials:

She encouraged him.
She should have known better.
She flirted.
She drank.
She led him on.
What was she doing alone with him anyway?

It turns out, after all this time, women still take the blame for being vulnerable, trusting, and expecting to be respected. Male entitlement and abuse of women in our culture is a sticky wicket, he-said, she-said. But, in the case of children, we have to be careful to listen closely and protect them from the deceits of the powerful adults around them.

Brendan was not harmed by the process and has moved on, gone away to enjoy all that college life has to offer. His record is clean, no tell-tale signs of trouble from that last year of high school. Even his scholarship remained intact. June got that information from Russ Monty and remembers feeling a little angry at the distinct lack of repercussions for Brendan.

"Oh, well," she philosophized at the time, "I can't save everybody." In her heart, she knows Brendan is an angry, disturbed young man, and hopes he gets help before he really acts out.

Flora has moved on, too, obviously.

Min once pissed June off when she said the research shows many abused and neglected kids grow up to do great things, and some schools of thought directly relate it to their victimization early in life.

June argued with her that the end does not justify the means. "After all," she ranted, "even Hitler did some good things for Germany, but that doesn't make him a hero!"

Min sat on her until she calmed down, explaining her belief that it's all in how the kid is taught to cope, the same as in any adversity—builds character, and all that.

I'll never know if Justice was served. I'll just have to trust myself.

Flipping through the notebook, June finds no other

notes of a personal nature. It could have been written on the day Flora moved in to the Jacobie house, for all she knows. Her hands shake a bit as she rips out that last page. She reaches over next to her desk, and does what she thinks any self-respecting caseworker would do under the circumstances: feeds it to her shredder.

She picks up the piles of papers and crap off the floor and dumps it all back into the cardboard box. She puts the lid on it and pushes the box into a corner, stacking a bunch of professional journals on top of it like a coffee table. Pretty soon it will be as dusty as the rest of the stuff in this old office.

§

Later, at home in her chair by the wood stove, June gazes out at the night sky with the lights out. No fire tonight, the weather is balmy.

She sits, watching evening turn to darkness and the moon rising behind the trees. She can't really make it out clearly, but it's a quarter moon, a crescent. She can see the sharp grey edge that completes the circle, nearly invisible unless you look for the shadow out of the corner of your eye. If you look directly at it, the light of the crescent blinds you to the whole picture.

Truth is like that, she thinks. Sometimes the dark is obscured, hard to see. Does it only matter if you get burned? Or if someone else does?

Shifting her eyes to the wineglass in her hand, June evaluates her move over to Donna's office, as the new Services Coordinator. She has certainly taught those folks a thing or two about dealing with foster kids and adoptees, but does she enjoy it?

Yes, she does, and the substantial raise that came with it. When she misses working in the trenches, she can sink her teeth into a case at Fallon. Drew saves the dicey ones for her. "Inspiring" is what Drew calls her. She's inclined to believe it's because she's older and more driven than most of the bright young folks who work for him. By comparison, who wouldn't look good?

The first draft of the book is completed and an editor at a university publishing company is looking to get it published. June suggested Drew's name be first on the cover because he did most of the work. In turn, he wrote an acknowledgement describing her genius idea and inspiration for the program. Still a mutual admiration society.

She hears Sarge growling in her ear, "You never know your impact, Hunter. Someday, somewhere, people may just surprise you."

Got that right, Sarge. What happens if the person that surprises you the most is YOU?

I wonder if I will ever sleep like a child again, releasing the lessons of the day and slipping into a world outside of my control? Will I always wrestle my demons in the dark, alone in that secret spot inside my mind? I think for a moment about all the other people who are right this minute sitting up, unable to sleep until they solve their moral conflicts. For just a moment I feel honored to be a member of their club, better company than those who don't give a shit.

June drains her wineglass, silently toasting the moon's progress across the sky.

ABOUT THE AUTHOR

Kathleen Tresemer was born and raised in Chicagoland; she now lives in the rural Midwest near the Illinois/Wisconsin border. She's earned degrees from NIU and Nova Southeastern University, enjoying careers in both social services and professional writing.

Tresemer was co-founder of In Print Professional Writers Organization, while earning awards for her fiction and leading workshops for new writers.

Kathleen loves to write about different kinds of families. *A Case of Peaches* is first in a series "from the files of June Hunter." Her debut novel, *Time in a Bottle* was published in 2016.

Photo by William Swick